DOUBLE SHOT

also by RAYMOND BENSON

THE JAMES BOND BEDSIDE COMPANION

ZERO MINUS TEN

TOMORROW NEVER DIES

(based upon the screenplay by Bruce Feirstein)

THE FACTS OF DEATH

HIGH TIME TO KILL

THE WORLD IS NOT ENOUGH

(based upon the screenplay by Neal Purvis & Robert Wade and Bruce Feirstein)

Ian Fleming's JAMES BOND 007 in

DOUBLE SHOT

G. P. PUTNAM'S SONS • NEW YORK

RAYMOND BENSON

Ben

This book is a work of fiction. Names, characters, places, and incidents are either the product of the author's imagination or are used fictitiously, and any resemblance to actual persons, living or dead, business establishments, events, or locales is entirely coincidental.

G. P. PUTNAM'S SONS
Publishers Since 1838
a member of
Penguin Putnam Inc.
375 Hudson Street
New York, New York 10014

Library of Congress Cataloging-in-Publication Data

Benson, Raymond, date.
Ian Fleming's James Bond 007 in doubleshot / by Raymond Benson.
p. cm.
ISBN 0-399-14614-8
1. Bond, James (Fictitious character)—Fiction.
2. Secret service—Great Britain—Fiction.
I. Title: Doubleshot. II. Title.

PS3552.E547666 I23 2000 00-023224
813'.54—dc21

PRINTED IN THE UNITED STATES OF AMERICA

This book is printed on acid-free paper. ♾

10 9 8 7 6 5 4 3 2 1

Book design by Gretchen Achilles

ACKNOWLEDGMENTS

The author and publishers wish to thank the following individuals and organizations for their assistance in the writing of this book—

IN GIBRALTAR

Andrew Bonfante; His Excellency the Governor, Sir Richard Luce and Lady Luce; Gail Francis—Gibraltar Tourist Board; Pepe Rosado

IN LONDON

Carolyn Caughey; Peter Janson-Smith; Corinne B. Turner; Zoë Watkins; The Heirs of Ian Lancaster Fleming

IN MOROCCO

Said Arif, Bazid LaHoussine; Philippe Seigle and Reto Grass—Le Royal Mansour Meridien Hotel (Casablanca); Khalil Tass—Magic Carpet Adventures S. A. (Tangier); Rizki Mohamed Zouhir

IN SPAIN

Victoriano Borrego Aguayo; Javier Conde; Felipe Paramio Alonso, Francisco Amorós Bernabéu, Agustin Lomeña, and Diana Serop—Costa del Sol Patronato de Turismo (Torremolinos); Pepillo de Málaga—El Ranchito Equestrian School (Torremolinos); Iwan and Margareta Morelius; Antonio Carlos Muñoz ("El Cuqui"); Francisco Rivera Ordoñez and Maria Eugenia, Duquesa de Montoro; José Antonio Guerrero Pedraza, and D. Alberto Urzaiz—Plaza de Toros (Ronda); Peña Juan Breva (Málaga); Restaurante El Chinitas (Málaga); Javier Rosenberg and Frederick A. Parody, Marbella Club Hotel (Marbella); José Navio Serrano—Parador de Ronda Hotel (Ronda)

IN THE U.S.

Paul Baack; Tom Colgan; Paul F. Dantuono, EC Tours; Sandy Groark—Bannockburn Travel (Chicago); James McMahon; Moana Re Robertson; Gary Rosenfeld; Dr. Michael Sergeant; Patricia Winn—Tourist Office of Spain (Chicago)

FOR RANDI

CONTENTS

DOUBLE SHOT

PROLOGUE

PASEO

ONE

DRAMATIS PERSONAE

The Convent's Security Officer gasped when he saw what came up on the computer screen. Domingo Espada's British bodyguard had given his name as "Peter Woodward," but he was positively identified as James Bond, agent 007 of SIS.

"Better have a look at this, sir," he said to the aide-de-camp, a tall young captain from the Gibraltar Regiment.

The captain looked over the officer's shoulder at the monitor and recognized the face—it was indeed the man who had walked into the Governor's Residence that morning with Espada and the rest of his Spanish entourage. He was now upstairs with the other delegates, politicians, and their aides.

"I'd say he has a lot of nerve coming here like this," the captain said. "He knows we can't arrest him because he's here with diplomatic immunity. I had better get on to London and let them know about it. You're sure he passed through the metal detectors all right?"

"Yes, sir."

The aide-de-camp frowned. "I don't like it. The man's a menace. 'Peter Woodward' indeed. How long before the Governor and the PM arrive?"

Another officer was just hanging up a telephone. "The PM's plane just landed. I would say half an hour."

The Convent, the Governor of Gibraltar's official residence on Main Street for over 250 years, was a hive of activity. As they were under a "Red" security alert, it was crawling with extra men from the Gibraltar Regiment. VIPs from several neighboring countries were upstairs, awaiting an important summit meeting between Britain's Prime Minister, Spain's Prime Minister, and others who had an interest in the Gibraltar conflict.

Another security officer rushed to the captain with a piece of paper. "This urgent fax just came in, sir."

The captain read it. It was from the Ministry of Defence headquarters in London.

"My God" was all he could manage to say after he had absorbed the message.

Upstairs, Nadir Yassasin looked across the long table in the Banqueting Hall at the man the aide-de-camp was worried about. The man *was* the British secret agent, wanted by his own people, suspected of having turned terrorist, and one of the most dangerous men on the planet. There was no mistaking the face—from the three-inch scar showing whitely down the sunburned skin of his right cheek to the black hair, parted on the left and carelessly brushed so that a thick comma fell down over the right eyebrow. The gray-blue eyes were set wide and level under straight, rather long black brows. His jaw was firm and strong. His mouth was wide and finely drawn; Espada's aide, Margareta Piel, had been correct in describing it as "somewhat cruel."

Yassasin took a deep breath and congratulated himself for having finally arrived at this fateful moment. It had not been easy, but the project would surely go down as his finest hour. Everything had fallen into place, and he was confident that his new assassin would come through and perform his final task without hesitation. The man was already a cold-blooded killer. After undergoing the necessary "remodeling" and reconditioning, the Brit was now under Yassasin's total control. The fool would do anything for him.

Yassasin almost allowed himself a smile. It was all going to happen in a few minutes, and agent 007 would take the blame. History would be made today, and Nadir Yassasin, the Union's most accomplished strategist, would have a part in it. Yet, if all went according to plan, no one would ever know that he had even been in the room. Today, he was "Said Arif," a Moroccan representative from a United States agency. He would leave the Rock under the same alias. It was sad, Yassasin thought, not to be remembered as he deserved for his role in the day that Gibraltar was besieged.

Never mind, he thought. His reward was that he had planned the entire operation, and that it was going to succeed.

Jimmy Powers glanced for the fifth time at the *Gibraltar Chronicle* sitting on the table beside him. The headline screamed, "PM TO MEET ESPADA TODAY," beneath which was a picture of the Spaniard, standing at a podium with a painting of Franco behind him. His fist was raised and he was shouting to the throngs of people who would do anything he ordered. He certainly had something of Franco in him—not to mention the deadly charisma of a Hitler or a Mussolini. Another story on the front page announced, "Spanish Mob Gather at Border—UN to Mediate."

"Gather" . . . that was funny, Powers thought. "Ready to erupt" would be more accurate. There were a couple of thousand men, armed and dangerous, waiting for the signal to storm across the border between Spain and Gibraltar. The Gibraltar Regiment and the Gibraltar Services Police had lined up a battery of weapons and were more than willing and ready to take them on—but this was a question of numbers, not strength. With the reinforcements from the U.K. delayed, the "Rock" didn't have a chance. They had underestimated the power that Domingo Espada held over his people. More important, they also had no idea that the Union was behind the brilliant plan that would topple the British colony and make them look foolish. This was one time that history would not repeat itself. The most impenetrable fortress in the world was about to be assailed—from the *inside*.

Powers moved his right hand surreptitiously to his waistband and felt the Browning 9mm, waiting for the fateful moment when it would be called into play. According to the plan, he was not supposed to do anything unless something went wrong. If all went according to plan, then he would walk out of the Convent alive. If not, well . . . he would die killing as many people in the room as he could.

No one could detect the Spanish 9mm Super Star inside Margareta Piel's jacket pocket, for she was unusually adept at moving with grace and poise. After all, she was one of the most accomplished equestrians in Spain.

Margareta took stock of the room and what was about to happen in it. She was beginning to have doubts about the Union's choice of an assassin. If her suspicions were correct, then the entire operation was blown. She would have to do what she could to save her own skin and get out of the room alive.

Margareta scanned the others' faces and carefully considered who might be a threat when the shooting began. The Spanish Prime Minister and the other politicians from the U.K., America, Gibraltar, and other U.N. representatives posed no danger. The only additional woman in the room was an Arab, dressed traditionally in a caftan and a veil, which hid her face entirely except for a shadowy slit for her eyes. Margareta was confident that she wouldn't be any trouble either.

Margareta had to admire Espada, who at sixty-two looked more like fifty. He had made a fortune and won the hearts of the people during a three-decade bullfighting career. Now a businessman and politician, Espada was a staunch supporter of those who repeatedly called for Gibraltar, that "pebble in Spain's shoe," to be ceded back to his country. He hated the British. He had used his considerable power and influence in the Costa del Sol region of Andalucía to bring about what history would someday call a revolution. The government in Madrid didn't like it, but there was not much they could do because of his popularity.

Many of his followers called him *El Padrino*—"Godfather." This was appropriate, for Domingo Espada was perhaps the most efficacious racketeer in the Mediterranean area.

Margareta turned her attention once again to the killer next to her. Her lover. The incongruous Brit, sitting among the group of Spaniards at the table. He certainly *had* become a different man in the last three months. She studied his features, the broad shoulders, and his unbelievably relaxed demeanor. . . . The name "James Bond" fitted him nicely. It was blunt and masculine, just as he was.

But things were not as they seemed. What should she do? She *had* to speak to the assassin.

The gun was warm in the pocket near her breast. She squeezed her legs tightly, forcing waves of pleasure to jolt up through her spine and into her brain. The sudden stimulation brought her focus back to the task at hand.

She patted the warm metal in her pocket once more for inspiration, then prepared to make her move.

For his part, Domingo Espada looked upon the day's political meeting as a formality that must be suffered before the day's real business could begin.

So far everything had gone smoothly. The British PM and Governor were on the way. This would be a day long remembered in Spain's history. Screw the politicians in Madrid, he thought. Espada was satisfied that they were, quite simply, afraid of him. He had single-handedly amassed more support and power from the lower and middle classes than any other Spaniard in the twentieth century except Franco. It was only fitting that the millennium launch a new era of Spanish dominance in the Mediterranean.

Domingo Espada was quite prepared to die for his cause. Even if the plan failed, he would be happy to go down in history as the instigator of the Great Siege of the Millennium.

Today, Gibraltar. Tomorrow . . . ?

The man who had been identified by the Convent's security apparatus as James Bond was ready for the assignment at hand. He mentally checked his body to make sure that the Walther PPK was in place in his waistband. He was now itching to get the act over and done with.

For the hundredth time, the hired Union assassin went over the details of the plan. When the PM entered the room, the killer was first to take out the Double-O agent serving as the PM's bodyguard and then the Governor's bodyguard. The next target was the PM himself, who would die with a single bullet to the head. Before anyone else had time to react, the Governor of Gibraltar would be shot. By then, Espada, Agustin, and the woman would have sprung into action. They would draw their own weapons, kill any guards who might be in the room, and then hold the rest of the delegates hostage. The Spanish prime minister would be executed if he didn't agree to Espada's demands. Yassasin and Powers were to use their weapons only if something went wrong. Otherwise they would maintain their covers as diplomats, become "hostages," and eventually be released. Espada would declare himself the new Governor of Gibraltar, and the signal would go out for his men to storm the border and take over the colony.

It seemed easy enough. He knew he could handle it.

Finally, the door opened and the aide-de-camp stepped into the room. "The car has just arrived," he announced. "The prime minister and His Excellency are just entering the Convent now. They should be here any moment."

It was time. The Union members in the room shared a quick knowing glance as the captain stepped out and closed the door.

The man identified as James Bond gripped the gun at his waist and waited for the door to open again.

ACT ONE

TERCIO DE VARAS

TWO

SUICIDE MISSION

As the sun had risen over North Africa two weeks earlier, the plaintive morning call to prayer had floated out over the rooftops of Casablanca. Mixing verses from the Koran and a traditional beckoning for religious Muslims to offer the first of five obligatory prayers to be performed each day, the melancholy voice was one of the few things that the people of Morocco's largest city could count on. While the new king and the government did their best to keep the population content, the country was suffering from vast unemployment and, as a result, crime. This was especially true in the larger cities such as Casablanca, Rabat, and Tangier. Casablanca, far from being the exotic and romantic locale for the famed Humphrey Bogart film, exhibited an odd conflict of traditional Moroccan culture with the trappings of a modern, metropolitan business center. The latter was winning, even though the city's poor and needy were evident on every corner. Wherever there was money to be made in the face of outright poverty, a criminal element naturally gestated.

Even so, the awe-inspiring Hassan II Mosque, towering over the city like a benevolent sentinel, served to remind the people that Morocco was well ahead of its Muslim neighbors in terms of economic stability and that all was right with the world. In a way, the mosque represented a blending of the modern Muslim world's idealism and its desire to exist on an equal basis alongside the West.

The ambitious leader of an organization that held its meetings not far away from the great monument shared this view.

As the religious faithful hurried to mosques and those who held honest jobs commuted to their places of employment before the early morning rush of business, the worst of Casablanca's criminal element were also preparing for the new day. Several very different businessmen and women gathered to begin their day's work in a high-tech conference room decorated in reflective sheet metal. It was not an ordinary meeting room in that it was located two hundred feet below street level, beneath the old Central Market, which ran the length of a city block along Rue Allal ben Abdallah. The room was part of an immense, private, underground complex that extended northwest nearly a mile from the Market to the old *medina,* the centuries-old section of town that consisted of narrow, winding passageways where shopkeepers sold produce, arts and crafts, clothing, and souvenirs.

The complex had been built in the mid-nineties by a consortium represented by a powerful Arabic law firm. As most of the construction was below ground, very few Casablancans knew of its existence. In fact, the only two entrances to the complex were well hidden behind seemingly innocent stalls in the market and *medina.* A loading lift was also located in the market behind what appeared to be a rubbish skip. Much of the vast structure was empty. Workers inhabited perhaps a fifth of it, while supplies and weapons occupied another fifth.

The consortium that owned the property was made up of three banking firms—one located in Morocco, another in Switzerland, and one in Monaco. An offshore oil corporation with assets all over the Mediterranean and in North Africa was also a major shareholder in the property. Silent partners based in the Middle East and France were involved. Mostly, though, the funding came from a private individual who was now calling a meeting to order in the darkened, chilly steel chamber that was the conference room for the international criminal organization known as the Union.

"Are we all here?" *Le Gérant* asked.

The others casually spoke in the affirmative. As usual, *Le Gérant* was sitting in shadow, wearing dark glasses. Today he wore an Armani suit that fitted snugly over his rather large frame. This meant that today's meeting would be strictly business. *Le Gérant* would stick to a memorized agenda, keep things moving along briskly, and discuss the all-important money issues.

Sometimes he wore a traditional *jellaba*, a gownlike garment with a hood. Although no one could pinpoint exactly why, the meetings were always different when *Le Gérant* dressed in Moroccan clothing. His considerable charismatic powers were somehow more intense when he embraced his mother's ancestral Berber culture. Those in his presence felt an elusive aura of self-confidence and enlightenment, and this had a significant effect on his powers of persuasion and leadership. Meetings became lessons in philosophy or Union ideology, and money was never discussed. One *commandant* had said that *Le Gérant* became more "mystical" when he wore the *jellaba.*

Le Gérant never used or took notes. Everything was in his head. Always. He pulled sophisticated facts and figures from the air. He never needed to be reminded of anything. Anyone who had the privilege of meeting him always came away impressed by his profound intellect.

He was usually fair and generous with the Union's profits. The other people in the room, the *cercle fermé,* were all millionaires thanks to their work for the Union. Each man or woman was a *commandant* responsible for a geographical area somewhere in the world, and employed anywhere from fifty to several hundred people, depending on the needs of the district. It took a lot of money to keep several hundred people happy and the Union was able to provide stability. That kept the *commandants* loyal.

Fear was also a major factor in keeping the *cercle fermé* faithful to *Le Gérant.* If for any reason he believed that someone had cheated him or attempted to do something behind his back, he became furious. He could extract a confession easily and punishment was, as a matter of course, swift and merciless. *Commandant* Jimmy Powers had seen a man's throat cut in this very room.

The twenty-six *commandants* were required to take notes and be prepared with any documentation *Le Gérant* might require. Their leader was very strict, even compulsive, about the appearance of everything. He insisted on cleanliness and order. He dictated what kind of pens and paper would be used in the conference room, and what coffee was served and in which cups. He liked everything to be in its place. A desk light was essential at every station at the table, because *Le Gérant* kept the room so dark. The *commandants*, although they were used to them, never liked these policies and wished *Le Gérant* would change them. Why should they matter to him?

After all, *Le Gérant* was blind.

A servant entered the room with a tray full of tall glasses filled with hot mint tea. A Moroccan tradition, the tea was served with mint leaves floating in the narrow glass, and each person had the option of adding sugar or not. It was yet another part of the ritual *Le Gérant* insisted upon.

Jimmy Powers disliked mint tea intensely. It was something he put up with, though, for he had to admit that the Union had brought him more wealth and interesting things to do than the founding Union boss, Taylor Harris, could ever have hoped to offer. He had been wise to stick with *Le Gérant* after Harris was killed in Oregon. The original Union broke up after that, but *Le Gérant*'s reformed Union rose from the ashes. While the original Union made a show of being an organization of mercenaries willing to perform any paramilitary task for the right price, *Le Gérant* transformed the group into something far more serious. Once *Le Gérant* had outlined what the new Union could do for him, Jimmy Powers turned coat as well and left America for Morocco. He had been there for three years, acting as one of *Le Gérant*'s most trusted *commandants.*

Julius Wilcox, the other American charter member, was the ugliest and meanest-looking *commandant* at the table. He had a particularly gruesome scar above his right eye, a hawk nose, and greasy, slicked-back gray hair. He was, perhaps, the Union's most accomplished executioner. He, too, was happy that he was working for *Le Gérant* rather than the temperamental Taylor Harris.

Powers scanned the faces of the other *commandants.* He had never made a point of getting to know any of them personally—it was against the rules. He did, however, know who each of them was and which districts each controlled.

One of the men who intrigued him was Nadir Yassasin, a black Muslim from Morocco . . . or perhaps Mauritania . . . he wasn't sure. Yassasin was known as the Union's "strategist." If anyone could be called *Le Gérant*'s right-hand man, it was he. Powers had been promised that he and Yassasin would work together very soon.

The other *commandants* were from other areas of the globe—Great Britain, France, Spain, Belgium, Germany, Russia, Israel, Argentina, Taiwan, Japan, Australia, Sudan, Lebanon, Syria, Egypt, Libya, Algeria, and the United States. Collectively, they controlled thousands of Union members worldwide. In the six short years of its existence, the Union had grown into a powerful, deadly force that kept Interpol, the CIA and FBI, MI5 and MI6, Mossad, and other law enforcement agencies on alert for any information pertaining to the capture of Union leaders. The organization's accomplishments were impressive. The Union were responsible for several audacious terrorist attacks, political upheavals, high-profile blackmail and extortion cases, murders-for-hire, drug smuggling, prostitution, and arms dealing. The only major failure had occurred within the last two months: the one involving the disastrous Skin 17 project. Powers knew that this had been a thorn in *Le Gérant*'s side since that fateful day in the Himalayas.

As green and black olives were served with the tea, *Le Gérant* decided it was time to begin. He spoke in English, with a French accent.

"I am happy to report that several of our latest ventures have been successful. Thanks to people working day and night in our communications department, we have penetrated nearly every intelligence agency in the world. If we are not already inside them, then they are not worth bothering with."

The group applauded politely.

"Mr. Wilcox, could you please inform everyone of our financial status?"

Wilcox sat up and cleared his throat. "Yes, sir, here we are," he said, thumbing through his notes. "Total income for the last fiscal year was twelve billion dollars in U.S. funds."

The group applauded once more, this time a little more enthusiastically.

"The distribution of the money will occur by the end of this month," Wilcox continued. "You are all aware of your percentage. If you have any problems, see me."

"And recruitment?" *Le Gérant* asked.

"Up fifteen percent," Wilcox replied. "The payroll indicates that we now employ over ten thousand people worldwide. Like McDonald's, we'll soon have a Union franchise in every major city."

Some of the *commandants* laughed.

"Very good," *Le Gérant* said, obviously pleased. It couldn't be said that he didn't have a sense of humor. "I believe our efforts to escalate the war in the former Yugoslavia were what put us back on track after the failure of the Skin 17 project. We have our strategist, Mr. Yassasin, to thank for that."

Again, there was applause. Yassasin merely nodded. He was always given the most "impossible" jobs and always managed to pull them off with finesse. Besides being an expert in computers, electronics, physics, and disguise, Yassasin was a master planner. Like a chess champion, he could predict every possible move and countermove in any job he undertook.

"Which brings us to new business," *Le Gérant* said, shifting the tone of his voice to something more akin to that of a disapproving parent. "The Skin 17 failure cost us much more than the money we invested in it and the lives of the operatives we lost. We had promised to sell the formula to the Chinese. Not making good on that promise left us with bad credit in the Far East. All of the markets in Asia have dried up, and we're having difficulties keeping up our operations there. This is seriously affecting our business, not only in the Far East, but everywhere. When the word got out that the Union slipped up on a major job, it made our clients less enthusiastic about working with us. It damaged our image and reputation. We must work on repairing that damage."

Le Gérant finished his mint tea, then paused to light a cigarette. He never once moved his head as he performed these simple tasks with his hands. His sense of touch was highly amplified to compensate for his lack of sight. Some *commandants* believed that all of his other senses overcompensated for his disability. It was said that *Le Gérant* could hear a mouse flitting about in a room on the other side of the complex and that he could *smell* whether a person was telling the truth or not.

"As you no doubt know, a famous ex-matador in Spain is stirring up trouble with the British. Has everyone seen the latest news? Domingo Espada is very busy with his little revolution that he's organising just north of us. Now, I'll be quite open here, and I trust that nothing I say will leave this room. Domingo Espada, the head of a considerably successful Spanish mafia, refused to join the Union when we first invited him. He has considerable influence in areas we would like to penetrate, such as South America. Ladies and gentlemen, Señor Espada has come back to the Union and offered us an intriguing project for which he will pay a considerable amount of money. Aside from the monetary considerations, Espada has agreed to help the Union access those areas in which we have no influence. His personal organization controls them now.

"Of even more interest to us is the fact that Great Britain is the target of Señor Espada's proposal. Espada has had long-standing issues with the U.K. for political reasons. As you all know, the failure of the Skin 17 project was largely due to the interference by Britain's MI6. Their SIS and Ministry of Defence made fools of us, and I do not take kindly to that."

Jimmy Powers shot a glance at the *commandant* for the district that included Great Britain. The man shifted uncomfortably in his seat.

"One agent in particular," *Le Gérant* continued, "a Double-O, was the man most responsible for the project's failure. Therefore, Espada's proposal is of great interest to me because it may give us the perfect opportunity to exact revenge for Britain's unforgivable meddling in our business. I would like to see this British agent suffer the tortures of the damned for as long as possible, then die a humiliating death that will make world headlines."

Le Gérant paused, taking a couple of drags from his cigarette before extinguishing it in the ashtray in front of him. He knew exactly where it was sitting without feeling for it.

"Espada's plan is really quite insane. It's a suicide mission. When I first heard about it, I told him quite frankly that no one would walk away from it alive. He said that he was willing to die for the cause. But, if we can pull off his proposal, the Union will be the most powerful criminal network in the world. We will be able to demand any price from any country for the merest threat. The name 'the Union' will be so feared that we will have more influence on the world's economy than the New York Stock Exchange. Therefore, I have decided that Señor Espada's suicidal project is worth attempting. And *we,* my friends, *will* walk away from it alive.

"What I would like to do," *Le Gérant* continued, "is to kill two birds with one stone. We will agree to help Espada, for the money, of course, but at the same time, we will exact revenge on Great Britain. When it is revealed that the Union was behind the catastrophe that Espada wants to instigate, the entire world will bow to us. It will solidify our place in history."

"How do you plan to do this?" Powers asked.

Le Gérant smiled and said, "I detect excitement in your voice, Mr. Powers. Is this something you'd like to work on?"

"I'll do whatever you want, *Gérant.*"

"Fine. I've asked our strategist to come up with a plan. And I'd like you to serve as his eyes and ears, since you're so good at that sort of thing."

A chance to work with Yassasin! Powers was pleased.

Le Gérant turned to Yassasin. "Would you like to tell us about it, Nadir?"

Yassasin leaned forward so that the desk lamp cast an eerie light on his face.

"The plan is already in progress," he said. "In fact, it began shortly after the collapse of the Skin 17 project."

The others sat up, alert, waiting to hear what the strategist had to say. Everyone was thrilled that they were about to participate in another Nadir Yassasin project. He was the most respected man in the room, other than *Le Gérant.*

"One of Domingo Espada's closest colleagues and confidantes is a woman named Margareta Piel. We need her help, so we have offered her membership in the Union. She works for Domingo Espada in many capacities and lives at his private ranch in Spain. She is well known in Spain as an equestrian instructor and performer, but she has quite a dark side. She's a vicious homicidal maniac. Her skills at stealth, theft, breaking and entering, seduction, and murder are top quality," Yassasin continued. "Her nickname is *Mantis Religiosa,* or 'Praying Mantis,' because it is rumored that she disposes of her lovers after she has had her way with them."

"My kind of gal," Julius Wilcox said. There were some chuckles, but *Le Gérant* abruptly snapped, "Silence!"

After a pause, Yassasin continued. "She will be an integral part of the plan. Whether or not she turns against Espada remains to be seen, but I think she is enticed by the financial possibilities of being a member of the Union.

"I have also enlisted one of our top mercenaries; he had been working for us in Africa. He's Welsh, a man by the name of Peredur Glyn. He was a former football hooligan who was convicted of murder a few years ago. The Union helped him escape from prison in the U.K. and he has lived underground ever since, working for us. He's in excellent physical shape and he's a formidable killer. Most important, he possesses the necessary physical attributes that will suit our plan perfectly."

"Has he agreed to the fee?" *Le Gérant* asked.

"He has agreed to the payment of a half-million U.S. dollars," Yassasin confirmed. "Besides, he feels that he owes us a service for helping him get out of prison."

"Good. Tell us about the remodeling and reconditioning."

"Glyn went through the remodeling well over a month ago, and it was more successful than I had hoped it would be. He is now currently undergoing reconditioning and training." Yassasin smiled. "We won't have a problem with him. He is a very gullible man. Very susceptible to our techniques. Not very bright, but eager to please. In two weeks' time, Glyn will be ready. Everything is in place for the plan to proceed. We will be on a very strict schedule."

"Very well," *Le Gérant* said. He looked at the *commandant* for Great Britain. "What is the latest on attempts to replant an operative inside SIS? It was unfortunate what happened to that girl at MI6 . . . what was her name?"

"Marksbury," the man answered. "Forget her, she was insignificant. We are still working on replacing her. These things take time."

"Perhaps you need to step up your efforts," *Le Gérant* suggested with the slightest hint of menace in his voice.

The *commandant* swallowed hard and continued. "But, *Gérant,* with all due respect, you are aware that our primary operative in the U.K. has been in place for two years and continues to provide us with valuable information on MI6 personnel."

Yassasin spoke up. "And this operative will continue to play a part in our plan," he said, cutting through the tension with equanimity. "As you know, the information that was furnished to us was the catalyst for the scheme. When we learned that our target was on an extended medical leave since the events in the Himalayas, we felt that the opportunity was too good to pass up. He is still currently off duty and therefore extremely vulnerable."

Le Gérant nodded. "Will the *commandants* in charge of the British, Spanish, and North African districts meet me in precisely one hour in my office. We must commend Mister Yassasin, for he has come up with a truly ingenious and highly imaginative plan, albeit a risky one, to exact revenge on Great Britain, as well as eliminate the Union's number-one enemy—James Bond of Her Majesty's Secret Service."

THREE

FORTUNE COOKIE

Meeting your double means certain death.

James Bond blinked and read the fortune again.

Odd, he thought. He had never seen such a downbeat fortune cookie in a commercial Chinese restaurant before. That, on top of the havoc raised by the crying toddler who had just been in the restaurant with his rude and demanding father, had brought back Bond's headache.

"Harvey!" he called. The fat Chinese man wearing a messy apron stuck his head out of the swing door that led to the kitchen.

"What now? You not full yet?" he asked in his unintentionally belligerent way. Bond had known Harvey Lo long enough to know that he was never *really* perturbed by his customers. It just seemed that way.

"Come here," Bond said, motioning him over. Harvey looked over his shoulder. "Read this."

"It fortune."

"I know it's a fortune. Read it."

Harvey took the little piece of paper and squinted, reading and whispering to himself. He furrowed his brow. "This not our fortune," he said.

"What do you mean?"

"I never see this fortune before. I know all the fortunes. There are twenty-five fortunes, all the same, all mixed up in cookies. This not one of them."

Bond retrieved the slip of paper. "I think I'll keep it as a souvenir, Harvey," he said. "Maybe it's a lucky fortune."

"Does not sound lucky to me. Sorry about that, Mr. Bond."

"Not a problem." Bond dug into his trousers and found a ten-pound note. "Keep the change."

"Thank you, thank you." Harvey beamed. The only time he smiled was when he was paid. "How was food? You like?"

"Same as always, Harvey. Not quite spicy enough." Bond had ordered shrimp and cashews, Szechuan style, with a bowl of hot and sour soup. "When I say I want it so hot I can't eat it, I mean it."

Harvey laughed boisterously. "Aw, you not serious, Mr. Bond. Remember that time I made it so hot? You really could not eat it!"

"That was because it was burnt, not spicy. You overcooked the vegetables and they came out black!"

"Okay, next time, I make it good and spicy. I make tears in your eyes, you will like."

Before leaving, Bond took a small pill case out of his pocket and swallowed two of the white tablets that Sir James Molony's colleague had prescribed for him. The headache was becoming worse, and he was damned if the pills had any effect.

Bond got up and left the cozy neighborhood place tucked away in an alley off the King's Road, just down a flight of stairs. The Ho Ho Lo Restaurant was marked on the street only by a posted menu. It mostly did a takeaway business, but Harvey provided three tables for eat-in customers. As it was a ten-minute walk from his flat, Bond had become a regular over the years when he was home alone during the week. But he had never seen a fortune like the one he had just received.

Bond got to the street and glanced at his Rolex. It was just after 1:00. Should he take a walk farther into Chelsea and browse through a sports shop he knew, or should he go back to the flat and start the day's drinking?

Damn it all, he thought. He was bored to death. He hated being between assignments, and he especially despised medical leave. It was particularly frustrating because he hadn't had a decent mission since the Skin 17 affair two months ago. M had ordered him off the duty list for a minimum of three months because of the injuries he had sustained in the Himalayas. Bond believed that she was actually using that as an excuse to punish him for the indiscretion with his personal assistant, Helena Marksbury.

Although he had initially suppressed his feelings for Helena, her death had begun to weigh heavily on his mind. He desperately wanted to track down the Union members who were responsible for blackmailing and terrorizing her.

Naturally, he blamed himself—mostly for not recognizing the warning signs.

M had sent him away for two weeks' holiday, so he had gone to his winter home in Jamaica, the house he called Shamelady. There, he had gone on a binge, drinking himself into a solitary oblivion, brooding and staring at the calm, blue Caribbean. Things grew worse. By the time he got back to London, he was a mess. He felt terrible, had no energy, and was still physically sore from the ordeal in Nepal. That was when he went to see Sir James, the neurologist who acted as a consultant to SIS, to ask about the incessant headaches that he had been experiencing since the end of his last mission.

Bond began to walk up the King's Road, thinking back to M's admonishment after she had seen the way he looked.

"You're in no condition to take this matter into your own hands, Double-O Seven," she had said. "I wouldn't allow it even if you were. You're too emotionally involved in the case. Scotland Yard is handling it as a murder, and until they find the culprits, then there's not a lot that SIS can do about it. Our own antiterrorist teams are working on locating the Union members and their headquarters."

Bond had protested, arguing that he owed it to Helena to find her killers. He wanted to go after the Union himself. M wouldn't hear any more and ordered him off duty "until further notice."

"Besides," she had added, almost as an afterthought, "I expect my people to be in top physical shape. And you're nowhere near that."

Now he was doubly anxious to get back into action. It was the only thing that could shake him out of the malaise . . . the depression . . . that he felt himself drowning in. It happened to him every once in a great while. Bond had seriously slipped off the deep end once, after the murder of his wife, Tracy. The previous M had been forced to send his top agent for psychiatric evaluation and then off to Japan on a mission in the hopes that Bond would pull himself out of the well of despair he had fallen into.

If only he *felt* better. The damned headache had crept up on him and was now excruciating. The events in the Himalayas had certainly taken their toll on him. Besides the fatigue, which never seemed to improve, he suffered from various aches and pains. Worst of all were the frequent headaches, which tended to begin midday and continue well into the night. His sleep patterns were disturbed, he had fitful dreams, felt bouts of inexplicable anxiety, and had taken to drinking more. He also felt unusually paranoid for the first time in his life. Ever since returning from Nepal, Bond had sensed that he was being watched, although he had used every trick in the book to determine if that was true. So far he hadn't been able to substantiate his suspicion and he was afraid he was imagining things.

The most alarming event was the blackout incident that had occurred while he had been recuperating in Jamaica. He had been about to take a leisurely swim in the private cove behind Shamelady, when he suddenly felt disoriented. His heart had begun to pound mercilessly and a blanket of dread enveloped him. For a moment he thought he was having a heart attack. He had stumbled back to the shore and had collapsed onto the sand. The next thing he knew, Ramsey, his Jamaican housekeeper and cook, was shaking him.

At that point, Bond had known there was something seriously wrong with him. He had immediately made arrangements to return to London and see Sir James.

Bond approached Royal Avenue and sat heavily on a bench, staring at the street, watching the buses, taxis, and people go by. Bond felt removed from the scene, almost as if he were floating out-of-body. It was an unfamiliar, disconcerting sensation.

Should he go back to the doctor? Sir James was still away on some kind of tour, so he would have to see Sir James's colleague, Dr. Feare, again.

Bond remembered the appointment with the neurologist a month ago. When he had arrived at Molony's office on Harley Street, he was surprised to find that Molony was on an extended, worldwide lecture tour as a guest neurologist. Miss Reilly, the unpleasant, middle-aged woman who served as the clinic's nurse, informed Bond that he would have to see Molony's relatively new assistant, who had introduced herself as Dr. Kimberley Feare. Bond was taken aback, for Dr. Feare was petite, blond, and extremely attractive.

"How long have you worked for Dr. Molony?" he had asked.

"Not long. I was lucky to get the job. Sir James is probably the best neurologist in the world. He's in India at the moment, and he's working his way west toward Africa," she said in a girlish, playful voice. Bond liked her immediately. "Now, what can I do for you, Mr. Bond? I understand your file is classified. You're with SIS, am I right?"

"That's right."

"Then the only other person outside this office who shall see my report will be your chief," she said, making a note in the folder. "As you know, we're very careful about confidentiality with government civil servants."

Bond went through the examination, X rays, an EEG, and returned a day later for a CAT scan. After he had described his various Himalayan injuries to Dr. Feare, she suspected that he might have some damage to his skull. At one point during the expedition up the third tallest mountain in the world, Bond had been hit on the head and knocked unconscious. Exacerbated by the oxygen deprivation at high altitude, the injury could be the cause of the headaches; there might be a blood clot, a crack in the skull, or any number of ailments associated with a blow to the head. The tests came back with somewhat alarming news. The EEG had picked up a lesion on the temporal lobe of Bond's brain. Dr. Feare was of the opinion that it wasn't terribly serious, but the blackout in Jamaica was probably a result of "post-traumatic epilepsy." Although it was a rare condition, it wasn't extraordinary. It was possible, however, that it could occur again without warning.

"With this kind of thing, we could perform a little surgery and remove the lesion with a laser," she had said. "But that's a last resort. I think we should first try to get rid of it with medication and rest. Pure and simple."

Dr. Feare gave Bond an additional diagnosis of "too much stress," and recommended to M that he take it easy—for at least three months. She had prescribed carbamazepine and painkillers and told him to take two tablets at lunchtime and two before bedtime. Dr. Feare warned him that if things hadn't improved in three months, surgery might be the next step. The worst thing about it was that he was forbidden to drive. He wasn't supposed to drink alcohol, either, but Bond ignored that directive.

Unfortunately, the pills didn't work at all. Bond had been struggling with the intense pain in the back of his head for months now, and it was driving him mad. There was only one thing to do—go back to see Dr. Feare.

Bond stood and continued the stroll toward the square lined with plane trees, where for many years he had owned a comfortable flat on the ground floor of a converted Regency house.

He was convinced that a mission was the only thing that could bring him back on track. It had always worked in the past. The only way he could put the demons to rest was to go after the Union and, if possible, destroy the entire organization. If M wouldn't put him on the assignment, then by God he would just have to do it himself. It wouldn't be the first time he had deliberately disobeyed orders. It would be for the good of SIS and Britain. The Union was the most evil menace to threaten international law and order since his old enemies, SPECTRE. Its members had to be smoked out and exterminated like pests.

But Bond knew that he was not in good shape, and it made him irate. He was well aware that the Union was out there, waiting for the right moment. Bond was probably the number-one man on their hit list after what he did to their organization in the Himalayas. He should be prepared for a surprise attack, and he wasn't. It could occur at any time. Bond knew that if he didn't do something about his vulnerability soon, he just might be spending his next holiday in the morgue.

Lost in thought, Bond ambled up the street, closer to his home, when he suddenly noticed a familiar woman walking toward him. She had shoulder-length golden hair, blue eyes, and shocking-pink lips. The woman looked past him and kept walking, but Bond was paralyzed with shock.

It was his dead wife, Tracy!

Bond closed his eyes tightly and opened them. He turned to watch her walk away from him, and then realized that it wasn't her after all. Of course it wasn't. How could it be?

Shaken by the experience, Bond continued his walk, but he felt his heart pounding. He was perspiring heavily, and it was not a warm day. What the hell was wrong? he asked himself.

He had imagined it. That was the only explanation. He chalked the hallucination up to his fatigue, stress, and the headaches. He had been thinking a lot about Helena, and that was probably the catalyst. Sure, that was it.

Best to get home and have a nap.

Bond increased his pace until he was a block away from his street. He was stopped at the intersection by a traffic light. He glanced at his wristwatch again: 1:33. He had taken twenty minutes to walk what normally took him five. He had better snap out of it!

While waiting for the light to change, Bond casually looked across King's Road to the other side of the street. A man was standing on the corner, staring right at him. He was tall, had dark hair, and . . . NO!

Bond suddenly felt dizzy and disoriented. His heart felt as if it was going to push itself through his chest. His mouth grew dry and he had trouble swallowing.

The man across the street was himself, or at least he looked like himself. He wasn't moving; he just stood staring right at Bond!

A bus passed by, momentarily blocking Bond's view of the opposite side of the street. When the bus had gone, Bond saw that there was now no one on the corner. Bond ran across the street, dodging traffic, and began to look for the man, but he didn't see anyone remotely resembling him.

His head was throbbing in pain and he felt sick.

Bond's mind flashed briefly on the fortune cookie from the Chinese restaurant.

Meeting your double means certain death.

His eyes were playing tricks on him, he told himself.

Bond stumbled as he attempted to cross back to his side of the street. A taxi almost hit him and the horn blared loudly. A very unpleasant, suffocating feeling of anxiety rushed over him and locked around his chest cavity. He gasped for breath, felt a sharp pain in the back of his head, and reached out for a phone box for support.

Instead, he crashed to the pavement.

When Bond opened his eyes, he was in his favorite armchair in the sitting room of his flat. The old-fashioned white and gold Cole wallpaper and deep red curtains gave him a feeling of serenity at first, but then he bolted upright in fright.

How the hell did I get here?

His hands were shaking now. He carefully stood and tested his balance. Nothing wrong there. The dizziness he had felt earlier was gone. He looked at his watch.

It was 2:47.

My God! He had lost over an hour!

Had he walked home and let himself in without remembering any of it? He had heard of people having these extended blackouts and not recalling anything that happened during the period of time they were "out of it." In actuality, these people carried on mechanically, often finding themselves in a different location from where they were when the blackout first occurred.

Bond immediately went to the cupboard, removed a bottle of Scotch, dropped two ice cubes into a glass, and filled it. He took a long, burning draught, then sat back in the armchair.

Now he knew something was really wrong with him. He had just had a second blackout and didn't have a clue what had happened in the interim.

FOUR

CHASING CLUES

Bond recalled his appointments with Dr. Feare. He had answered all her questions negatively, including "Have you had any other fainting spells or perhaps hallucinations since the incident in Jamaica?"

At the time, his answers had been the truth. But now? He had experienced both in one day!

And what about the man he had seen on the street? Had the man really looked like him? Had he been a hallucination, like the woman who had resembled Tracy?

Bond was aware of the supernatural concepts of doubles, or *doppelgängers,* and that supposedly they were apparitions of living persons. Popular occult theory held that a double was a projection of an astral body. English and Irish folklore called the phenomenon a "fetch," and, as the fortune cookie warned, seeing one's fetch indeed meant that one was going to die. Legend had it that Shelley saw his double before his death by drowning.

But Bond never bothered with superstitions. There had to be another explanation.

Dr. Feare had told him to come back and see her if there were any change, especially if he began to have new symptoms or if the headaches got worse. Bond had to admit that both of these conditions were true.

Bond was very concerned, playing possible scenarios in his head. His mind raced frantically as he considered every alternative for the future and simultaneously attempted to calm down. But what if it was all in his mind and he was finally going mad after all these years of living on the edge?

Bond threw the glass of whiskey across the room. The glass shattered against the wall.

To hell with it! All he needed was an attitude adjustment.

He decided to go to the office and dig into Helena's case and track down the Union members who had recruited her in London. That should keep his mind focused. First, though, he would call Dr. Feare.

He paused a moment as he considered a positive aspect in having to go to the doctor again. Dr. Feare—Kimberley—was a gorgeous woman. Perhaps all he needed was some female companionship for a night. Since Helena's death, Bond had been celibate. Two months is a long time. His close friend in America, Felix Leiter, would have simply advised, "James, my boy, all you really need is to get laid."

He looked up her number and picked up the phone. When Miss Reilly answered, Bond asked to speak with the doctor personally.

"Dr. Feare is in surgery. You'll have to leave a message," the nurse snapped.

"Will she get it today?"

"I should think so."

"Fine. This is James Bond. I saw her a little over a month ago. I would like to see her again. It's rather urgent."

"Would you like to make an appointment? If so, I'll have to call you back."

"Please. As soon as possible." He left the phone number for his answering service.

Adhering to the no-driving rule, Bond took a taxi to SIS headquarters on the Thames and arrived at 3:30 in the afternoon. When he walked past the security officer and through the X ray, Bond suddenly realized that he must look terrible. He hadn't bothered to shave that morning, and his casual clothes—a Sea Island cotton shirt, navy trousers, and a light-gray jacket—were a bit wrinkled.

Bond ignored the guard's stare and went straight to the lift. He strode onto his floor and was grateful that no one was about. It was fortunate that the offices were rarely occupied, as Double-O agents were usually abroad, and the secretarial pool was very small.

Bond slipped into his small, uncluttered office, and sat at the desk. Two folders from Records were sitting on top of his "IN" tray. Bond took them and saw that they were an update on the investigation into Helena's murder and the latest file on the Union. The former hadn't been sealed, but it was hardly helpful. Everything had been turned over to the Metropolitan Police, who were in charge of the case. Bond noted the contact name at New Scotland Yard and picked up the phone.

"Howard," the man answered.

"Detective Inspector Howard?" Bond asked.

"Yes, who's calling?"

"This is James Bond at SIS."

"Oh yes, Commander Bond, how are you?" Detective Inspector Howard had met Bond while investigating the murder of M's friend, Alfred Hutchinson, a while back.

"Fine, thanks. I'd like to have a word with you. It's rather urgent. Are you free this afternoon?"

Howard paused to check his diary. "I could see you at five o'clock, but I'll only have fifteen minutes or so. Will that do?"

"That's fine, I'll see you then. Thank you."

Bond hung up and felt somewhat gratified that at least someone capable was on the case. Stuart Howard was a good man.

He turned his attention to the other folder, which was actually a thick binder containing a hard-copy collection of information, images, and the latest intelligence from SIS's Visual Library file on the Union.

There hadn't been much progress in unveiling the Union's mysteries since Bond first became involved in their cases. The report reiterated what he already knew: Taylor Michael Harris, an American militant in Portland, Oregon, created the Union circa 1993–1995. A self-professed white supremacist, Harris was arrested in 1993 for disturbing the peace during a rally that became violent and was run out of the state. He returned six months later with a large amount of capital, and with this money he founded the Union. Harris had apparently gone into business with unknown partners from the Middle East and North Africa.

He used specialist magazines to advertise for "mercenaries" to carry out dangerous jobs in Third World countries. Surprisingly, a great deal of men applied, looking for work as soldiers of fortune. After a six-month advertising campaign, it was estimated that nearly a thousand men had joined the organization. They trained at the Oregon facility, but no jobs were carried out before the FBI raided the place in December 1996 for illegal arms possession and distribution. Taylor Harris had been gunned down, gangland-style, in a Portland restaurant a month earlier, believed to be murdered by his own lieutenants. These three men, Samuel Anderson, James Powers, and Julius Wilcox, fled the country, and at least one of them was a suspect in the murder. The killer had paused in the restaurant long enough to slit Harris's throat from ear to ear: an act that became the Union trademark.

Harris's organization, however, lived on. Whether or not the three lieutenants were responsible for keeping it going, no one was certain.

It became a more sinister organization after publicly taking responsibility for several serious terrorist acts committed between 1997 and 1999. No longer merely a band of "soldiers of fortune," the Union became an international network of spies, killers, and militants. They were particularly adept at infiltrating intelligence organizations. The Union quickly became one of the most dangerous organized crime syndicates in the world, on a par with the Italian and Russian mafias, Chinese Triads, and SPECTRE. SIS had experienced a serious encounter with the Union within the last year, and Bond could attest to their loyalty, tenacity, and dangerousness.

Discovering the location of their headquarters was a top priority for SIS, the CIA, and other intelligence organizations. Recent reports from America indicated that the Union was probably located in North Africa, perhaps in Morocco or Algeria.

Bond did find something new in the folder. Interrogation of a Union member who had been arrested in France after a nasty bank bombing revealed that the Union's leader was someone they called *Le Gérant.* The prisoner claimed that no one knew whom he really was, not even the "commanders" who made up the "inner circle" of underlings. The Union was structured much like a mafia, with an executive boss, a number of immediate subordinates—the *cercle fermé*—and branches of groups and leaders extending from there. It was valuable information, but before any further interrogation could be performed, the prisoner had managed to hang himself in his cell.

Bond had a thought and picked up the phone. He quickly consulted his Rolodex and found Felix Leiter's number in the States. His longtime friend, formerly with the CIA, Pinkerton's, and the DEA, was now working as a freelance intelligence agent out of his home in Austin, Texas.

A woman with a lovely Spanish accent answered the phone. "Hello?"

"Manuela?" Manuela Montemayor was Leiter's live-in companion and a formidable FBI agent.

"Yes?"

"James Bond calling from London."

"James! How are you?"

"I'd be better if you were standing in front of me, but I'm fine. How are you and Felix?"

"We're great. It's so nice to hear your voice! Wait a second, I'll put Felix on." Bond heard their Dalmatian barking in the background and Manuela shushing him. After a moment, Bond recognized the easy drawl that he knew so well.

"James! How the hell are ya, my friend?"

"Hello, Felix. I'm fine. And you?"

"We're happier than pigs in slop. Hey, I increased the horsepower in my wheelchair so that it now goes seventeen miles an hour!" Leiter was referring to the Action Arrow power chair he had been using for the past couple of years since the deterioration of his leg muscles.

"That's impressive, Felix, but I hear the Texas highway patrol just loves to give speeding tickets."

Leiter laughed. "What's up? You coming to the States?"

"No, but this *is* a business call, I'm afraid. I need some information."

"Sure, how can I help?"

"The Union. I need everything you have on them."

Leiter whistled. "You and everyone else. Those guys are just gettin' to be too damned popular, you know what I mean? Why, are you havin' more trouble with 'em?"

"Something like that. I'd like to see if your government has any updated information about them—the suspected location of their HQ, leadership, the organization . . . and I'd be interested in any leads you can track down in the Portland area, where Taylor Harris was killed. Are there any Union members left there? Where did his three lieutenants go? What became of them?"

"Hold on, Manuela is just handing me a file," Leiter said. "You know about their leader? He has a French name. . . ."

"*Le Gérant.* I've just read about him."

Bond heard him turning pages. "The lieutenants. You talkin' about Samuel Anderson, James Powers, and Julius Wilcox?"

"Yes."

"Right. According to the file we have here, those three guys left the U.S.A. in 1996 and haven't been heard from since. But I'll see what I can do. I have a contact in Portland. I'll get the latest from Washington, too."

"Great, Felix. It's always a little slow-going for other intelligence agencies to share information. You know how it is."

"You bet I do. When do you need this stuff?"

"The sooner the better. Can you fax whatever you find to my office?"

"Sure thing. Give me two or three hours, is that all right?"

"That's better than all right. Thanks, Felix."

"Take care, James."

Bond hung up the phone and rubbed the back of his head. The headache was manageable now, but it was still a nuisance.

A blinking red light on the auxiliary telephone caught his attention. This was the line he used for incoming messages, usually filtered through a number of security checkpoints. He picked up the receiver, punched in the code, and listened.

"Hello, Commander Bond, this is Deborah Reilly at Dr. Feare's office." Bond detected a distinct, punctilious *sniff.* "I've had a chat with the doctor. I'm afraid she can't see you today. She will be tied up for the rest of the day in surgery. This evening she will be attending a meeting at the hospital and will be having dinner at The Ivy with some colleagues at around eight o'clock. She asked me to tell you that if this is an emergency, I can page her, of course. Otherwise you can expect a call from her in the morning."

Snooty bitch, Bond thought, as he erased the message and set down the receiver. She must have thought that mentioning the doctor's plans to dine at a fashionable restaurant would elevate her feeling of self-importance.

Glancing at his "IN" tray again, he noticed the corner of a brown padded envelope beneath several sheets of interoffice memorandums. He pulled it out and saw that it was addressed to him, marked "Personal," and had been sent through the post. SIS had stamped it "Cleared by X Ray."

He tore it open, found a paperback book inside, and was shocked and puzzled by its title: *Helena's House of Pain.* It was a pornographic book, with a cover illustration showing a dominatrix spanking an "innocent" schoolgirl on the bare bottom. Inside the book was a sales receipt for £5.99 from a shop called "Adult News," with an address in Soho.

Scrawled in ink on the back were the words "She had it coming."

What kind of sick joke was this? Who would send this to him?

Once again, the all-too-familiar waves of nausea and dizziness enveloped him. Was he about to black out again? He felt a rush of warmth to his face and perspiration under his arms. He thought he was about to be sick. . . .

Bond gripped the side of his desk, shut his eyes, and willed the uncomfortable sensations away. Again, his heart was pounding in his chest and he felt suffocated by a blanket of anxiety.

"Are you all right, James?"

Bond opened his eyes and saw Bill Tanner, M's Chief-of-Staff, standing in the doorway. He was holding a stack of files and looked concerned.

Bond nodded grimly. "Just feeling a bit under the weather," he managed to say.

"Well, you look bloody awful," Tanner said, coming into the office. "Should you go to the infirmary?"

Bond shook his head. "I'll be all right in a minute. Just something . . . I ate, I think."

Tanner sat down in the chair on the other side of Bond's desk. "You're supposed to be on leave anyway, James. What are you doing here?"

"I can't stay away, Bill. If M isn't going to put me on the case, I'm doing it myself."

"I didn't hear you say that."

"The bloody Union is still out there, Helena's murder isn't solved, and I'm a bloody sitting duck here in London. I should be out there looking for them, Bill! I'm no good doing nothing. You know that. Isn't there anything you can say to M?"

"Actually, I've tried, James," Tanner said. "She's quite adamant about you staying away for a while. For one thing, you're on medical leave. You have to be cleared for duty. And she also feels that, and I'm afraid I agree with her, you wouldn't treat the case objectively. You're too close to it, James."

"But that's what makes me the best man for the job!" Bond spat, slamming his fist on the desk. "I'm beginning to know these people—the Union. You have to get close to them to understand them. Damn it, they want *me* as much as I want them! One has to be emotionally involved!"

"James," Tanner said gently. "Don't turn this into an obsession. You know the Union is a very high priority, but right now we have our hands full with the Gibraltar situation. You've heard what happened this morning?"

"No."

"Domingo Espada's supporters threw rocks and bottles at the Immigration officials at the La Linea border. There was gunfire. We don't know if anyone was hurt yet. It's becoming ugly. Espada's a menace."

Bond vaguely remembered reading the memorandum on Espada. He was a Spanish millionaire, a businessman with a political agenda. He had recently made a loud noise in southern Spain with renewed calls for the U.K. to give back Gibraltar. He was even at odds with the government in Madrid but apparently had an enormous amount of influence in the country.

"Go home," Tanner said. "You look terrible and obviously need some rest. Don't let M see you like this. Please. Do yourself a favor."

Bond shut his eyes again and took a deep breath, forcing the headache to subside a little. Finally, he nodded.

"Good," Tanner said. He got up. "Call if you need anything."

After the Chief-of-Staff had left the room, Bond slipped the Adult News receipt into his pocket, threw the book into a desk drawer, and made his way to the lift.

Bond rarely had a reason to visit New Scotland Yard, the imposing and unsightly twenty-story structure that seemed to be made of nothing but windows. Since MI6 dealt with cases outside the U.K., the Metropolitan Police at Scotland Yard or the people at MI5 usually handled crimes that were committed within the boundaries of Great Britain. Most of the time this jurisdiction was strictly enforced. Nevertheless, Bond had never paid much attention to protocol. If he needed information from one of SIS's sister organizations, he wasn't afraid to go and get it.

Bond took a taxi to 10 Broadway, not far from Westminster Abbey, and gave his credentials to the guard at reception.

"Detective Inspector Howard will see you now," the man said after calling upstairs.

Bond took the lift and was met at the floor by Stuart Howard, a medium-built man in his forties with a mass of curly brown and gray hair.

"Commander Bond," he said, offering his hand. He squinted when he saw 007's unkempt appearance.

"Hello, Inspector. Please excuse the way I look; I've been working round the clock."

"I hate it when that happens," Howard said, chuckling. "Come on down to my office."

They walked past a dozen secretaries, both male and female, and into a private office that was cluttered with files, papers, photographs, and faxes.

"It may look like a mess, but I assure you I know where everything is," Howard said. "Do sit down. Would you like some coffee?"

"That would be fine," Bond said. "Black, please."

"Right. Be back in a sec . . ."

Bond sat and rubbed his temples, glancing around the room for anything pertaining to Helena's case, but the only things that stood out were various unrelated gruesome crime scene photos tacked to the bulletin board.

Howard returned with the coffee and sat behind his desk. Bond took a sip and said, "You fellows must use the same coffee vendor as SIS."

"Well, it's not the gourmet stuff," Howard said, smiling. "Now, what can I do for you?"

"Helena Marksbury. I'd like you to tell me how the investigation is progressing."

Howard frowned.

"Please."

"Commander Bond, this is slightly irregular, wouldn't you say?"

Bond leaned forward. "Inspector Howard. Helena was my personal assistant. I had a nasty scrape with the Union a few weeks ago, as you know. I just want information. I'd like the peace of mind of knowing what is happening with the case. That's all."

Howard studied the disheveled man in front of him and, against his better judgment, said, "All right. I don't suppose there can be any harm in telling you what we know. It's confidential, of course."

"Of course."

Howard dug into a pile of folders on his desk and found the appropriate one. He opened it and scanned two or three pages quickly.

"I'm afraid we haven't got very far," he said. "Whoever killed her at that hotel in Brighton left no traces. No fingerprints. Nothing. The blue van that was seen outside the hotel was abandoned at Heathrow. It had been stolen."

"I suppose you've investigated her background?" Bond asked. "She had family in America."

"Yes, with the help of the FBI in California, we were able to locate them. No leads there, but we've arranged for their protection. We conducted interviews with Miss Marksbury's neighbors, people listed in her address book, and her landlord. No clues there either. . .."

Bond held out his hand. "May I?"

Howard shrugged and handed the file to him. Bond scanned the typed pages of interviews. There were two or three girlfriends who all stated that Helena never mentioned anything unpleasant, and several neighbors and a building maintenance man who reported that they barely knew or rarely saw her. Bond stopped at the interview with the owner of her building in West Kensington. His name was Michael Clayton.

"You won't find anything there," Howard said. "The landlord seemed clean enough. He claimed he had never met his tenant. A superintendent looks after the building and an estate agent handled the lease."

"English?"

"I beg your pardon?"

"This Michael Clayton. Is he English?"

"Yes. Owns a number of residential buildings, a pub, and some bookshops in Soho."

This news shook Bond. "Bookshops?"

"Yes, what does he say down there near the bottom? About his business partner?"

Bond read further and found the passage Howard was referring to. Michael Clayton had a partner named Walter van Breeschooten. They owned the various properties jointly.

"His partner is Dutch?" Bond asked.

"That's right. Kind of a sleazy character, but we did a background check and he came up spotless. The bookshops are the adult variety. They sell pornography, you know, videos, magazines, books. . . ."

Bond did his best to keep the excitement of this discovery to himself. Helena had told him before she died that the two men from the Union whom she had "dealt with" were English and Dutch. She had always spoken to one of them on the phone and had never met them until that fateful day in Brighton.

Bond closed the folder and gave it back to Howard.

"I'm sorry there isn't anything else, Commander Bond," Howard said. "We're doing our best."

"I understand. I am sorry to have troubled you."

"No trouble."

"Do me a favor, please, and keep me informed, would you?" Bond asked.

Howard nodded. "Certainly."

Bond got up, shook the inspector's hand, and left the building. Rather than going back to Chelsea, however, Bond grabbed a taxi and told the driver to take him to Soho.

FIVE

ESPADA

The woman whistled sharply so that her gloriously white Percheron stallion performed a neat *elevada,* a trick in which the horse rose high on its back legs. She gave him a gentle kick with her boots, and the horse leaped into the air, executing a flawless *cabriola,* one of the most impressive stunts the animal could do in front of an audience. The horse literally jumped up and kicked out with all four legs, suspended in midair for a moment. Its beautiful, sleek rider completed the picture by holding her hat high above her coal-black hair that was tied neatly in a bun.

When the horse was safely back on his hooves, Domingo Espada applauded from the other side of the bullring.

"Bravo," he called. "You got him to do it!"

Margareta Piel reached around and stroked the horse's neck. "I knew you could do it, my darling." She pulled the reins and the horse trotted back to the bullring entrance, where Espada was standing.

"You have your new star," she said. "I think he's ready for an audience."

"I think you're right," Espada said. He opened the large wooden door that led to the *pasillo,* the area beneath the seats that encircled the bullring. He then turned and watched with interest as Margareta, who had been riding sidesaddle, slid to the soft ground. Her tight-fitting pants with a slit at the bottom, worn by female equestrians, were especially flattering of her firm, rounded buttocks and muscular legs. She wasn't a tall woman, but she had a body that most men would die for. Ironically, this was often the case. He had heard stories that claimed she could be a cruel mistress in bed, although he had never had the pleasure of finding out. Domingo Espada knew better than to make love to the *Mantis Religiosa.*

Margareta flicked her wide-brimmed hat, which sailed neatly, like a discus, onto the fence post. She then undid the bun, shook her head, and let her long, straight hair fall around her shoulders.

"Has our guest arrived?" she asked.

"Not yet. I expect him soon. We should get back to the house."

"Let me take care of Sandro," she said, leading the horse toward the second set of doors beneath the stands, to the stable in the expansive building that was part of Espada's estate. Besides having room for a dozen horses, the annex, as it was called, also had facilities to stage a modern bullfight. There was the regulation-size bullfighter's practice ring, which, oddly, Espada had covered with a roof after he had retired from professional bullfighting, a bullpen, facilities for bullfighters and their teams, including a chapel and infirmary, and, in a more remote section, a slaughterhouse.

Not far from the annex was a smaller house that was referred to as the "compound." It was off-limits to anyone except Margareta and a few other select employees, and trusted guests.

They left the annex and walked out into the bright Andalucían sun. Domingo Espada's estate was ten miles north of Marbella, the Costa del Sol's smartest, most expensive resort. Espada had built the property in the hills just beyond Conch Mountain, which overlooked the city and faced the Mediterranean. The rich and famous all came to Marbella for holidays. Wealthy organized crime moved in as well. A "Spanish Miami Beach" of sorts, Marbella became the crossroads for smuggling in the Mediterranean area. Far too many drug and arms dealers had been caught in Marbella, simply because they couldn't resist the urge to flash their money.

Domingo Espada had never needed to do that, for everyone in Spain knew who he was. He could probably get a free meal in any restaurant he walked into. Everyone knew the face of the bullfighter who had simply gone by the name "Espada" in the bullring. His portrait was usually featured on the walls of tapas bars and restaurants along with the photographs of Spain's other legendary matadors. He, too, was a national hero. But in Marbella they affectionately called him *El Padrino*, paying tribute to the efforts he had made to boost the area's economy. With the fortune he had earned as a matador for twenty years, Espada had invested wisely in several ventures, including tourism (in the form of casinos, hotels, and clubs) and had helped bring Marbella back from the decline in popularity it had suffered in the 1980s. He also owned and managed three bull-breeding ranches, acted as manager of several successful matadors, and had considerable influence in the world of bullfighting. The fact that he was often linked to organized crime did not lessen Domingo Espada's popularity.

Although he had aged considerably since his bullfighting days, Domingo Espada still cut a commanding figure. At exactly six feet, he exuded an authority and self-confidence that demanded attention. At sixty-two, he remained devilishly handsome, with dark wavy hair, now streaked with gray, and a bushy mustache that covered a sullen mouth. His chin was adorned with a short, pointed salt-and-pepper beard. Women virtually swooned when he stared at them with his piercing brown eyes that seemed to be both hot and cold at the same time. The twenty-two-year-old scar that extended from the outside edge of his left eyebrow to just over the cheekbone also served to give him a sinister, Mephistophelean appearance.

His boots made crunching sounds on the tiny gravel as Espada and Margareta walked up the path to the magnificent ranch house he had built on the property. It overlooked a small artificial lake stocked with fish. Typically Spanish in its design, the house took additional elements from some of the more modern structures in Marbella, such as the palace built by the financier and arms broker Adnan Khashoggi. The main building consisted of a single level, but a unique guard tower rose four stories high so that sentries could spot approaching vehicles from miles away. The entire estate was over six hundred hectares in size, was surrounded by a high stone wall, and was protected by state-of-the-art security equipment.

The grounds contained an Olympic-sized swimming pool, a tennis court, a garage for several vehicles, and a putting green. Beyond the annex and the compound was an enclosed field, where dozens of *Bos Taurus Ibericus* roamed free. The beautiful black bulls, the special lineage that were bred for one purpose—to die in a *corrida*—lived a luxurious life eating the best food and mating with the best cows until the fateful day when they were chosen to meet their destiny. Sometimes Espada enjoyed walking in the field amongst the animals, admiring their power and pride. The bulls usually left him alone unless he came too close to the calves or made sudden moves. From birth, they attacked instinctively when they felt cornered or threatened, but in an open field they turned and walked away.

Espada and Margareta stepped onto the open patio, where a young female servant met them and asked what they wanted to drink. Espada looked at her and snapped harshly, "Where is Maria?"

The girl jumped at his bark and shyly said, "I don't know, sir. They asked me to fill in for her today."

"Is she ill?"

"I don't know, sir."

"Very well." He asked for a bottle of Barbadillo Solear, a sherrylike wine made in Sanlucar de Barrameda. The girl gave a subservient bow and went inside.

Agustin, Espada's loyal *mozo de espadas,* the title of a matador's dresser and keeper of the swords, now Espada's most trusted right-hand man, came out of the house to deliver a message.

"Where is Maria?" Espada asked him.

"She is gone, Domingo," Agustin said with a stern face. "She has escaped."

"Escaped?" Espada nearly choked with surprise. He looked at Margareta. She stared at Agustin and asked, "How could that be possible?"

"When we sent for her this afternoon, we learned that she had left with a man. One of the other girls told me."

"Who?"

"She didn't know him."

"Where is . . . who was guarding them? Where is Carlos?"

"Carlos was on guard all day. Would you like to speak with him?"

"Yes! Go and fetch him." Espada was trembling.

"Yes, sir," Agustin said. "By the way, your visitor has arrived," he said. "They're parking his car. Shall I bring him outside, sir?"

"Keep him waiting until after I talk to Carlos."

Agustin nodded and went inside.

Margareta had never seen Espada so upset over the disappearance of one of his girls. He refused to admit that several had escaped with his guests in the past, despite efforts to keep them in the compound. Margareta had been lobbying for tighter security measures. She had worked for Espada for a few years; her job was to train and look after his secret harem residing in the compound. She knew that he often obtained the girls from poor families in Spain and Morocco. After they spent some time learning their "trade," the girls were sent out to points abroad that were managed by Espada's organization. If they were lucky, they became high-class call girls and earned a lot of money. If not, some of them simply disappeared.

"She must have been a favorite," Margareta observed. "Was she particularly good at something?"

"Shut up," Espada said. "Maria was the freshest, most beautiful girl I've ever found. She was the best. So pure, so . . . tight . . . I cannot believe she would leave!"

"Why not? You *do* keep them prisoners. . . ."

"But they have a great life here . . . it's paradise . . . all the food and sun and . . ."

". . . *sex*, whether they want it or not," Margareta continued.

"Part of this is your fault!" Espada said.

"Oh, please, Domingo," she said. "I train them and patch them up after you get too rough with them, but I don't guard them."

Carlos, a large man in his late twenties, came out onto the patio. He appeared nervous, fingering the Beretta M92 that hung on his belt.

"You wanted to see me, sir?" he asked.

"Did you see Maria today?" Espada spat.

"No, sir."

"What time did you come on duty?"

"Eight o'clock this morning."

"And the girls were in their quarters all day and night?"

"Except for those with chores, sir. Maria wasn't scheduled to work until this afternoon," Carlos explained.

"You must have seen something."

"No, sir, I swear," Carlos said, shaking his head.

Espada looked at him hard. Agustin stood behind the guard, waiting for a signal from his boss. Espada glanced at his lieutenant and gave him the slightest of nods.

"Very well," Espada said to Carlos. "You may go."

"Thank you, sir," Carlos replied, then went inside.

"Agustin," Espada said. The lieutenant stopped. "Have him interrogated. In the meantime show our guest outside. I'd like you to join us, too."

"Yes, sir."

"Oh, Agustin?"

"Yes?"

"What are the enrollment figures for today?"

Agustin cleared his throat. "I've just checked on that. We're up to about one thousand four hundred."

"Only fourteen hundred men? We must do better than that!" Espada turned abruptly, holding his arms up in frustration.

"If we had a little more to spend on recruitment . . ." Agustin suggested.

Espada rubbed his chin a moment, then turned back to his friend and confidant. "All right. Call the accountant and tell him to release another three million *pesetas.* We have to reach our goal of two thousand five hundred men quickly."

"Yes, sir." Agustin went back inside as Espada and Margareta sat in comfortable lounge chairs with a view of the green, manicured lawn and the pool twenty meters away.

The servant girl brought the wine and poured glasses for the couple. Margareta looked her up and down, admiring the girl's youth and wholesomeness. She was probably no more than fifteen. After she had left, Margareta said, "You sure know how to pick them, Domingo."

Espada held up his glass and said, "*Salud.* Yes, I certainly do. I've been picking them all my life. That one, she's from Granada. My men found her in a particularly poverty-stricken area. Her parents were quite happy to accept the money that was offered for her."

"And how has she worked out in the bedroom?" Margareta asked with a wicked smile.

"I haven't had the opportunity to try her out yet. I was still breaking in Maria," Espada said, twisting his mustache. "You're a fine teacher. So are the other girls. They all do whatever I want. Damn, that upsets me about Maria."

"Tell me, Domingo. What would the police say if they knew you were keeping sex slaves against their will?"

"Nonsense. I give these poor girls a wonderful life. They are treated like queens. They eat the best food, live in a nice home, and have access to the outside world through the miracle of television and video. A far better life than they had before."

"They also have to submit to you anytime you want."

Espada laughed and said, "You're jealous! You would like your own harem of young men, I think!"

"And tell me, Domingo. What do the police say when a body is washed up on the shore near Marbella? It happens, what, every other year or so?"

"You don't know what you're talking about."

"Oh, I don't, Domingo? Young girls, most of them unidentifiable, runaways, street kids . . . There's a steady stream of them being found up and down the Costa del Sol."

"You're imagining things. Besides, the local police turn a blind eye when they see me coming. I have them all in my pocket."

"There *is* a high turnover rate of your girls, Domingo."

"That's because they get jobs within my organization—as expensive call girls. There is no better training ground than here. They travel to exotic locations like South America or Mexico to work."

Margareta looked sideways at Espada. "Not all of them. Come on, Domingo. What do those girls have to do to incur so much wrath that you dispose of them in so . . . ignoble . . . a fashion?"

"Look who's talking." Espada wagged an accusatory finger at her, then shrugged. "That only happens when one of them disobeys me. It's not often."

Agustin returned with a tall, dark man in a suit and fez and said, "Señor Nadir Yassasin, sir."

Espada didn't get up, but instead motioned to the chair next to him. "Welcome, Nadir, sit down. Did you have a pleasant journey?"

Yassasin gave a slight bow and replied, "Yes, thank you, Señor Espada. It's a pleasure to be here."

"How are things in Casablanca?"

"The same. As you know, the *cercle fermé* met last week."

The servant girl returned and poured the wine for Yassasin, then left. The Arab pulled a thin cigar from his jacket. "Mind if I smoke?"

"Go ahead." Agustin leaned over with a lighter and lit the Arab's cigar. Yassasin held it pretentiously, close to his face with his hand bent, palm upward. Margareta thought this enhanced his stereotypical image as a mysterious North African spy. Agustin sat down and pulled his chair closer.

"Now," Yassasin said. "*Le Gérant* has given me instructions to thank you for your generous and impressive offer of five million dollars to the Union. The territories you control are profitable."

"It's my pleasure," Espada said. "However, I do hope that *Le Gérant* realizes the tremendous risks I take to keep operations going. South

America and Mexico are still quite new and require a lot of payoffs. Law enforcement is particularly strong when one gets near America. The drugs are doing well, but I've lost several men. Some were arrested, others killed by the police. It's becoming more difficult."

"We can all appreciate that," Yassasin said. "It's time to discuss your proposal."

Espada brightened. "So *Le Gérant* has agreed to help me? Is he committing Union resources to my cause? I thought he said it was a 'suicide mission.' "

"He still believes that, but . . . that's where I come in."

"Oh?"

"*Le Gérant* has taken into consideration your generous offer, your enthusiasm, and the opportunity for the Union to even the score with an enemy. So, yes, the Union will become involved in the Gibraltar project."

"That's very good news." Espada lifted his glass and finished the wine.

"There are some conditions."

"What are they?"

"*Le Gérant* will supply the necessary manpower to accomplish your goals. The North African district will be employed, under my supervision. You will be in charge of the Spanish district, but you must follow a plan that I have formulated."

"You? What plan?"

"These are *Le Gérant*'s specific instructions. We will go into the details after dinner. Suffice it to say that my plan will accomplish much more than the siege of Gibraltar. You want to be the first Spanish governor of Gibraltar in over two hundred years? The only way you will see that happen is if you follow my orders to the letter."

Espada's eyes narrowed. No one ever talked to him in this manner.

"Why should I?" he asked. "I could still do this without the Union."

"Domingo," Margareta said gently, putting a hand on his arm.

"That wouldn't be advisable," Yassasin said. "Turning your back on the Union after we've offered to help is not very . . . sporting. You should know that."

Espada grumbled, calming down. "I don't like taking orders from someone else. No offense, Nadir. I know you're supposed to be a brilliant planner, but I've always gone my own way."

"This is *Le Gérant*'s condition. Take it or leave it. Why don't you hold off on your answer until you hear what the plan is. It is . . . risky . . . but very clever, if I do say so myself."

"All right. But before we eat, give me a hint. What happens? How does it end? I like to know the result before the setup."

Yassasin smiled and said, "When the operation is completed, Gibraltar will be the property of Spain. You will be the new governor. The British governor will be dead, along with the British Prime Minister."

"The Prime Minister? We're going to kill him?"

"That's part of *Le Gérant*'s revenge against the United Kingdom for their interference in our previous major project."

"Sounds dangerous . . ." Espada rubbed his chin and looked at Yassasin with doubt in his eyes. Then he grinned broadly. "I love it already! Yes! Let me hear what you have to say after dinner."

"Very well. The important thing now is for you to build up your group to intimidating proportions. One of our concerns is how the government in Madrid will react to your revolution. They may strike you down."

"They wouldn't dare. They may be putting up a good face with Britain over Gibraltar, but they want it back as much as I do. I think they'll let me get away with it."

"And if Great Britain declares war on Spain?"

Espada rubbed his hands with glee. "What could be more exciting? Two NATO powers going at it, *mano a mano!* What a way to start the new millennium!"

"You could be killed, Domingo," Margareta said.

Espada shrugged. "I have been prepared for that for a long time. I'm sixty-two years old. If I can make a difference in the history books . . . if I can take Gibraltar for just *one day* . . . then I will die fulfilled."

"I take it, then, you agree to the plan? I have full control?" Yassasin asked.

"Yes."

"Then I'm happy to tell you that the plan has already been put into effect, and in less than a week it will all be over. I am here to set up command central at your home, for it will all culminate here. My lieutenant is in Britain as we speak, keeping watch on things as they progress. His name is Jimmy Powers, an American."

"Command Central? Here? What the hell? What if I had said no?" Espada asked, incredulous.

"You don't want to ask that, Señor Espada."

Espada was silent a moment, then eyed Yassasin and said, "If I did not know you and have respect for your reputation, Nadir, I would have killed you just now. But I know enough about you to trust that you know what you're doing. *Le Gérant* must have a good deal of faith in this thing as well. All right, I agree. Let's hear your brilliant plan."

"After dinner," Margareta said, pulling on Espada's arm.

Much later, after a luxurious dinner and a tense two-hour meeting, Yassasin was put up in a guest room and Espada retired to his study. Espada liked time alone in this room, which also served as a library of sorts and a place in which he could display the many trophies, posters, and photographs from his bullfighting days. He also enjoyed putting on a costume, red-and-black traditional matador garb, the *traje de luces,* or "suit of lights"; although it wasn't the same one he had worn when he was younger. This one had been made especially for a man who had gained a bit of weight since that time, even though he was physically fit and in good shape. Agustin had laid the clothes on a long wooden table, each item in placed in the requisite order.

There was a knock at the door.

"Come in."

Agustin entered the room and saw that his boss was back in the past once again. He had pledged undying loyalty to Domingo Espada, but he did think that his benefactor lost touch with reality every now and then. Once a *torero* retired from the bullring, he was never supposed to put on the costume again. Not *Espada* . . . he could not let go of his past and still longed for the cries of *"Olé!"* and the exhilarating feeling of being carried out of the ring on the shoulders of his friends and relatives after a successful *corrida.*

Some nights, Agustin would find Espada alone in the study, dressed in the costume, standing and staring at the stuffed bull heads that were mounted on the walls as trophies. They were all missing at least one ear, signifying the reward Espada had received after the fight. One ear was cut off for a good fight, two ears for a better one, and both ears and the tail were for the best. Espada had collected more ears and tails than he could count. He had kept some of them, but most of the time he had thrown the trophies to fans in the audience—usually beautiful *señoritas* who he knew would accompany him to his hotel or villa for the night.

This evening, Espada stood in the center of the room, holding the *estoque,* the thin sword used to thrust into the bull's withers and through the vital organs for, hopefully, a quick kill. Espada extended the sword at one of the bull heads, his arm straight, concentrating, as if he were readying himself for the moment of truth.

"Domingo," Agustin said.

"Yes?"

"We got Carlos to confess. Roberto Rojo paid him five hundred thousand *pesetas* to help him free Maria. She has run off with Roberto."

"*Roberto?*" Espada cried. "How could he do this to me? That ungrateful . . . !"

"We will catch up with Roberto," Agustin said.

"Roberto is one of my star matadors! He and his brother have glorious futures ahead of them. Why would Roberto choose to ruin it by stealing this girl from me?"

"Carlos said that Roberto was in love with her."

"Damn him! He shall pay for this," Espada said, pacing the room.

"What about Carlos?"

"He must answer for his betrayal."

"In that case, the prisoner is ready."

"I'll be there in a minute."

Agustin nodded and left his friend and master alone with his memories . . . and his madness.

Domingo Espada entered the practice bullring and raised his hat to the throngs of people sitting in the stands. He could hear the tumultuous applause and cheers, he could see them saluting him, standing for him. . . .

None of them were really there, of course. But to Domingo Espada, it was all real. The empty stands projected the same amount of noise and excitement as if they had been packed full of spectators.

Agustin and two other men stood inside the 1.2-meter-high *barrera,* the fence that enclosed the working area of the ring, near the *burladero,* the "trick" shields built slightly out in front of the openings in the fence. Bullfighters stood behind these to escape the charging beast. Agustin approached Espada and handed him the brightly colored *capote,* the cape that was red on one side and yellow on the other—traditionally used in the first two acts of a bullfight.

Once Espada was ready, Agustin gave the signal to the man at the *puerta del toril,* the door out of which the bull would charge. It swung open, and for a moment there was silence. Espada waited patiently, the excitement and anticipation just as powerful as it had been in the old days.

Then the object of the *corrida* came out into the ring. He stumbled on two legs and appeared to be lost. Carlos, badly bruised from beatings, was wearing a dirty white shirt and black pants. In his hands was a pair of bull's horns, the kind used in training bullfighting beginners. Another person would "act" as the bull, charging the student so that he could practice with his cape.

Agustin announced loudly, as if he were projecting his voice so that the people in the very top seats could hear him, "Carlos Rodriguez, you have been found guilty of the crime of betraying your employer. Therefore, you must fight for your life in the bullring against the supreme matador, *Espada!*"

Carlos looked at Espada standing there in all his glory. The cape twirled with a flourish. Espada called to him as if he were a bull.

"*El toro!* Come!"

When Carlos realized what was about to happen to him, he turned to run back through the open doors, but they slammed shut in his face. He turned to face Espada, his eyes wide with fear. He backed up against the wooden doors, dropped the bull's horns on the ground, then fell to his knees.

"Please, Señor Espada, have mercy!" Carlos cried. "I beg you! I'm sorry!"

Espada ignored the man's pleas and simply waved the cape. "Come!"

After a minute, Espada saw that Carlos wasn't going to "play." He nodded to Agustin, who picked up a picador's lance, and walked toward the helpless man. As Carlos cowered on his knees, kissing the dirt, Agustin brutally thrust the lance into the man's back and withdrew it. The sharp point had been shortened so that it would not mortally wound the man, but merely cause him pain.

Carlos yelped in pain, then rolled over. Agustin spoke to him calmly, telling him that his fate would be far worse if he didn't get up and fight.

"Who knows," Agustin said. "If you show great courage and spirit, the matador may grant you an *indulto.*" This meant that the bull's life would be spared. "Now get up and charge!"

Carlos finally realized that he had no other choice. He got up, gave a frightening war cry, and ran at Espada. The matador performed a neat *verónica* with the cape, sidestepping the man. But, unlike a bull, the human could not be fooled. He swung at Espada with his fists, ready to jump on his opponent and beat him to a pulp if he had to. Espada, though, was prepared for the attack. Using the cape to protect himself, he managed to keep the bleeding, angry man from connecting his punches.

The "fight" went on like this for several minutes. Carlos was obviously becoming tired as his lunges at Espada grew less inspired. Not one of his blows had connected. Espada eventually walked away from the man, who collapsed in the middle of the ring, out of breath. Blood soaked his clothes.

Espada took two *banderillas,* short spikes used in the second act of a bullfight to further weaken and enrage a bull, and calmly walked back toward his victim.

Carlos saw what Espada had in his hands and knew that he could do only one thing. He pulled himself to his feet and started to run away, toward the edge of the ring. But before he could make it behind a shield, one of Agustin's assistants pulled a switch located behind the fence.

All of the shields in the ring mechanically moved in a few feet until they were flush against the fence, blocking off any possible escape for the prisoner. All of the regular doors were shut tight.

The prisoner gathered every last bit of strength that he could muster, then charged at Espada, screaming.

Espada deftly thrust the two spikes neatly into Carlos's back as he sidestepped the charging prisoner. The man screamed and fell to the dirt. The spikes hung grotesquely out of his back. He reached around and managed to pull one out.

Espada walked away from him, approached Agustin, and took the *estoque* and *muleta,* the sword and smaller red cape used in the final act of a bullfight. He approached the cowering, wounded man.

"*El toro!* Come!"

He waved the cape, the deadly sword positioned behind it.

Carlos picked up the spike he had pulled out of his back and held it like a spear. He slowly got up and faced the matador. Then, cursing, he charged, the spike out in front ready to plunge into Espada's chest.

Like a dancer, the matador executed a smooth *pase de trinchera,* a low pass performed with the right hand. Carlos missed Espada entirely, falling to the dirt again.

Espada moved around to the man's front, then held the sword at arm's length.

Carlos, further enraged and desperate for the ordeal to be over, got to his feet and charged at Espada with the spike one last time.

The sword pierced Carlos's chest and went cleanly through his heart.

Domingo Espada had at least one more ear to add to his collection.

SIX

LIVE GIRLS, ETC.

Lodged between the busy theater district to the south and the shops of Oxford Circus to the north, Soho was unusually quiet for a late weekday afternoon. The commuters had left and the theater crowds had not yet arrived. The streets were only moderately crowded with tourists and curiosity-seekers who were gawking at the sex shops, the "modeling studios," and the "Live Girls!" dives that pervaded the area. While it tended to come alive at night, in daylight Soho was undeniably seedy.

James Bond found the Adult News shop on Berwick Street and stood across the road to observe the building for a few minutes. Men of various types went in and out—mostly white middle-class businessmen in suits and ties—and Bond saw nothing unusual. It was a small, ground-floor establishment with a neon sign proclaiming that the shop sold "XXX Videos, Magazines, Books."

Bond perked up when a middle-aged woman in a business suit emerged from the shop and began to walk north toward Oxford Circus. He did a double take, for he could swear he knew her. Tall, rather severe. Not the type one would expect to see in an adult bookshop. Who *was* she? Damn! The headaches had clouded his normally photographic memory. Bond rubbed his eyes and looked again, but the figure had disappeared into the crowd.

He crossed the street going north in an attempt to catch sight of her again, but she was gone. She had slipped into a side street or got into a taxi. Had his eyes been playing tricks on him again?

Bond walked back to his position across from the bookshop and decided to make his move. He crossed the street and entered through the strings of beads hanging in the doorway. The shop was devoid of customers at the moment, and there was a large, obese man with greasy, stringy hair sitting behind the counter and watching a portable television. Bond pretended to browse at the skin magazines for a moment, then approached the counter.

"Excuse me, but is Mr. van Breeschooten here? He's the manager, isn't he?" he asked.

The big man eyed Bond without moving his head.

"Yes, he's the manager, and, no, he's not here."

"Can you tell me when he might be available?"

The man turned his head to look Bond up and down. Not many people asked for the manager.

"Are you a cop?"

"Of course not. I'm a salesman. I wanted to talk to him about a new line of videos my company is selling. Amateur stuff. Hard-core, of course. Very high quality."

"He's at the office. You'll find him there."

"Ah. Thank you. Might I have the address?"

"Down near Brewer Street." The man rattled off a number.

"Right," Bond said. "Many thanks." He turned to leave, then hesitated, as if he wanted to ask the man something but was too shy.

"Is there anything else?" the man asked.

"Uhm, yes, I couldn't help but notice that pretty woman who came out of here a few minutes ago. Does she come here often?"

Now the man really thought Bond was some kind of pervert. "I don't know who you're talking about. Lots of women come in here. Men with their wives, couples, lesbians, you name it . . ."

"Right," Bond said sheepishly. "Well, thanks." This time Bond hurried out of the place.

He walked south and found the office on the ground floor of a seedy-looking building. The upper floors presumably contained residential flats. A plaque on the door read: "Clayton Enterprises." Next to it was the residents' entrance to the building. An intercom and listing of the tenants with buzzer numbers was attached to the alcove. He scanned the list and found a "van Breeschooten" in number 302.

Bond knocked on the office door, but there was no answer. He tried the knob—it was unlocked. He went inside and found a cluttered room that smelled of stale coffee and cigarette smoke, but there was no one there. It contained a desk, computer, telephone, coffeemaker, and stacks of papers all over the place. The ashtray overflowed with cigarette butts. Behind the desk was another door that was ajar. Bond peered inside and saw that the rest of the ground floor had been gutted to make a storeroom for the boxes of products carried by van Breeschooten's shops. Two men were inside, packing videos into padded envelopes for posting. They both had Cockney accents, were heavily built types, and appeared to be in their thirties. They were probably strong-arms in van Breeschooten and Clayton's organization. He was surprised to see from the bulges at their waists that they were both armed.

". . . But then he said that the money would be bloody good, and it was!" one of them said.

"Last month's check was a nice surprise, I must admit," the other said.

"The company must be doing well. We'll get the details on the new job any day."

"If the money is as good as last time, I'm there!"

"Where is Walter, anyway?"

"Upstairs in the flat. Clayton is with him."

The first man snorted. "Couple of poofters, they are . . ."

Bond left them alone and turned his attention back to the cluttered office. The papers were invoices, packing slips, order forms, and the like. He opened a desk drawer and found an unsealed envelope from a travel agency addressed to Walter van Breeschooten. Bond looked inside and found airline tickets for both Clayton and van Breeschooten to fly from London to Tangier, Morocco, later that night.

Interesting, Bond thought. The Union's headquarters was believed to be in North Africa.

He replaced the tickets and envelope in the desk, gave the other drawers a cursory search, and decided there was nothing else of interest.

Bond slipped out of the office and tried the door to the residential part of the building. It was locked, so he pressed the button marked "Deliveries." After a moment, someone buzzed him in. The building's narrow stairwell smelled of garbage and dirty nappies. He could hear a baby crying in one of the flats above him. Bond quietly crept up to the first floor and listened at the landing. No one was about. He went up two more flights to the third and top floor. He could faintly hear the voices of two men talking behind the door of number 302, which was next to a window that opened out onto the fire escape.

Bond raised his left foot and pried off the heel of his field-issue shoe. Major Boothroyd had recently added an ingenious listening device to the equipment inside the shoes, which included a first-aid kit, escape tools, and other odds and ends that were neatly packed in the hollowed-out spaces. The device was a high-power UHF transceiver the size of a two-penny coin. A suction cup/microphone was attached to the side so that the device could stick to any surface. Bond licked the suction cup and placed it firmly on the door. He then pulled out the earpiece that was attached to a tension wire embedded within the device. With the earpiece lodged firmly in his ear he could hear the voices clearly.

". . . And the process will continue with the distribution of the latest payments. But the new project will bring in a lot of money. I think we'll do very well."

"I've heard that it's very risky."

"It is, what I know about it. They're keeping the details under wraps for now. You know as much as I do."

The first voice was Dutch, all right, so that must be van Breeschooten. The other voice was decidedly English. Michael Clayton.

The Dutchman sighed loudly and said, "I sure don't want to have to go back to Morocco again. I hate it there."

"I'm looking forward to it," the other man said. "It will be nice to get out of London for a change."

Bond waited, hoping that one of them would reveal something that might implicate them as Union members.

"Well, let's just hope that tonight goes as planned," van Breeschooten said. "Your cousin's news was encouraging."

"Yes. Everything is in place. We'll make the bloke wish he'd never been born."

"How come your cousin's always so cross?"

"I don't know," Clayton said. "Been that way forever."

A noise in the stairwell distracted Bond. He heard the front door open downstairs. Someone was on the ground floor and was beginning to ascend. Bond willed whoever it was to stop at one of the lower floors. He was determined to hear as much of the conversation as possible.

A Cockney voice boomed out from the stairwell, "Get your own bloody sandwich. I'm going upstairs. Back in a minute."

Damn! It was one of the storeroom workers. He was coming up here!

Bond listened intently to the two men inside the flat. Come on, he thought, say something about the Union. . . .

"Did I tell you what happened at the meeting three months ago?" van Breeschooten asked.

"A *commandant* was killed?"

The footsteps were growing louder. The man was at the first floor.

"Throat slit, ear to ear. Right in front of us."

"What did he do?"

"Cheated the company. The boss doesn't like that."

The ascending worker was at the second floor. In a few seconds he would appear and Bond would be trapped.

"The boss doesn't like a lot of things, from what I gather."

"He's quite a character," van Breeschooten said. "I admire him a great deal. You know he's given the orders to move the headquarters out of Casablanca."

"Where are they moving?"

"I don't know yet."

The Cockney was a few steps from the landing. Bond was ready to pull the listening device off the door when the Englishman in the flat said, "Do you think I'll really get to meet *Le Gérant* this trip?"

That was all Bond needed. He tugged the device off the door just as the Cockney thug appeared around the corner. He saw Bond and yelled, "You there! What are you doing?"

Not giving Bond time to explain, the man pulled out a .38 Special. Bond immediately went on the offensive and kicked his right leg out and up, sending the handgun flying. Unfortunately, it discharged a round when it hit the floor and the noise reverberated in the stairwell.

The thug swung at Bond, but 007 dodged the punch and delivered one of his own to the man's chin. Bond felt his knuckles burn as the man fell backward and crashed into the wall. The entire building seemed to shake. Bond didn't stop there. He lunged into the man, punching him twice in the stomach, then once more across the face. Blood splattered from the man's nose.

The noise attracted the attention of the tenants, several of whom opened their doors and peered out into the hall. Van Breeschooten and Clayton also looked out to see what was going on. Bond turned in time to catch a glimpse of both men, who were staring at him, wide-eyed and mouths agape. The taller of the two, probably van Breeschooten, was middle-aged, had white hair and blue eyes, and fair skin. Clayton also had a pale complexion, appeared to be a bit older, had brown hair streaked with gray, and brown eyes.

One of the other tenants yelled, "I'm calling the police!" and slammed the door.

The distraction gave the thug the time he needed to recover from Bond's attack. While his head was turned, the muscleman slammed his fist into Bond's face. The impact sent bolts of lightning into Bond's skull, and he fell to the floor but rolled just as the big man tried to kick him in the ribs. Bond managed to grab hold of the man's foot and twist it hard. The man yelped and lost his balance.

Bond jackknifed to his feet, spun on one leg, and kicked with the other, causing the man to fall into van Breeschooten's open doorway, knocking them all down as if they were bowling pins. Bond immediately ran for the stairs as a bullet whizzed past his head. The other man from the storeroom was below him, on the second landing, pointing a revolver at Bond.

"Don't move!" the man shouted.

Bond did the opposite, jumping back out of the line of sight, just in time to meet the first thug head-on. It was then that Bond realized how physically out-of-shape he really was. The man hit him hard, causing the corridor to spin. For a moment, Bond thought he was going to collapse, but he was able to steady himself on the edge of the stair railing. He was truly stunned.

Van Breeschooten shouted, "Don't kill him!"

The big man paid no attention. He lifted Bond by the shoulders and threw the limp body at the fire escape window. Bond crashed through the glass and fell onto the metal platform just outside the building, and he couldn't stop himself from rolling off it. He tumbled down the steel stairs, blindly reaching for the nearest solid object that could prevent him from falling three stories to his death. Luckily, it was the railing around the intermediary landing above the second floor fire escape.

Above him, the first thug leaned out of the broken window and fired his gun. Bond ducked and pressed himself against the glass. Bond drew his Walther PPK and returned fire, shooting through the holes of the third-floor fire escape landing.

He heard police sirens squealing in the distance and they were growing louder. He had to disappear, and quickly. He didn't dare risk going back into the building.

More gunfire zipped around his head and he heard Clayton and the Dutchman both shouting, "Don't shoot him! Let him go!"

Bond heard the men arguing above him but couldn't make out what they were saying. He looked around him and saw that the adjoining building was one story shorter than the one he was in. There was a gap of approximately ten feet. He wouldn't get much of a running start on the little fire escape platform. Nevertheless, Bond holstered his gun, carefully calculated the distance, and leaped.

He landed hard on the edge of the other roof, and it knocked the wind out of him. He held on, gasping for breath until he was able to suck in some air. He swung his legs up and over the side, fell to the roof, and lay there for a few seconds before peering over at the other building.

The men had disappeared from the third-floor fire escape. The police sirens were just moments away.

Bond got up and ran to the other side of the roof. It was another ten-foot gap to the next building. Now that he had more room, Bond performed a broad jump and this time landed on his feet. He kept going, looking for a way down. A metal-rung fire escape ladder extended from the roof to the pavement below.

Bond swung his body over the top of the ladder and began to descend, when he felt a sudden jolt in his chest and a searing pain knifed through his head. For a moment he thought he had been shot.

His heart pounded frantically and the world was spinning. Bond wasn't sure if he was standing up or falling. He thought he was going to die, right then and there.

Fight it! he commanded. Bond continued to descend, but in his state, he lost his footing on a rung. He slipped and attempted to catch the ladder, but instead he missed and slid down, crumpling with a slam onto the ground below.

In pain, Bond rolled over and sat up. His vision was blurred.

The wind was cool on his face. He reached up and rubbed his eyes and pressed the sides of his aching temples. As his eyesight returned, he could see a man and woman staring down at him. They appeared to be Japanese tourists. When they saw that he was stirring, they quickly ran away.

He had fallen into an alley, some twenty feet from a pedestrian-filled street.

After a minute, Bond slowly got to his feet and looked around, disoriented. His head was still pounding, but the awful nausea and dizziness had disappeared. He had a few aches and pains from the fight, and his jaw hurt, but otherwise he was in one piece.

Bond made his way to the street, not far from the Adult News bookshop. He walked south, back to the apartment building where the office was located, and saw a constable patrolling the pavement in front.

Rather than make any more trouble for himself, Bond decided to get away from Soho. He had two hours before he could catch Kimberley Feare, and there were still a few things he needed to take care of.

Of least priority to Bond was his state of mind.

As he hailed a taxi, three men watched him from the third-floor flat in the building overlooking the street. One of them was on the phone.

"That's right, he's fine. He just got in a taxi. Right."

Walter van Breeschooten hung up and said to Clayton, "Come on, let's get going. We have to get to the airport."

The third man waved them on. "Go on, get out of here. I'll keep close tabs on our boy," Jimmy Powers said.

SEVEN

DAZED AND CONFUSED

Bond took the taxi back to SIS. The setting sun shone brightly off the green reflective surfaces of the building, suggesting that it might belong more in the Emerald City of Oz than in London.

He took the lift back to his floor, slipped past the few secretaries, and entered his office. There were no new messages, but there was a fax from Felix Leiter. Bond snatched it from the machine and read it.

Dear James—
Not much luck. Probably things you already know. Taylor Michael Harris left no relatives in Portland. What leads we have on the three lieutenants are sketchy and speculative. One of them, Samuel Anderson, was confirmed dead just two months ago. His body was found in Algeria, riddled with bullets. The other two, James Powers and Julius Wilcox, are thought to be alive and stationed somewhere in North Africa. *Le Gérant* is believed to be an Arab, citizenship unknown, although a Mossad report claims that he might be French. It's possible that *Le Gérant* was the business partner of Taylor Harris when he first solicited financing for the Union. The FBI believe that Julius Wilcox was the man who killed Harris at the restaurant in

Portland. Eyewitnesses identified his mug shot. Wilcox was an ex-Marine and forest ranger before joining the Union. Immigration reports that he made several trips to Morocco before disappearing from the U.S. for good.

Will overnight further information on the Union.

Hope this helps.

—FELIX

Bond picked up the phone and dialed Detective Inspector Howard. He got one of the deputy inspectors, who said that Howard was in a meeting.

"Tell him it's James Bond, and it's urgent."

He waited three minutes, then Howard came to the phone.

"Commander Bond?"

"Inspector Howard," Bond said. "Sorry to interrupt your meeting but I have some information for you."

"Yes?"

"Michael Clayton and Walter van Breeschooten are both Union members."

"How do you know this?"

"I overheard them talking about it just a couple of hours ago."

"You what?"

"I paid a visit to their office in Soho. I overheard them talking about a job that was going to occur tonight . . . and they definitely have ties to *Le Gérant.* I think you need to pick them up."

He heard Howard sigh. "Commander Bond, to be frank, I don't appreciate you taking this matter into your own hands. You spied on them without authorization."

"It needed to be done. You were overlooking them."

"Commander Bond, I have a mind to inform M about this. You're out of order. Now, is there anything else?"

Bond decided against telling him about the plane tickets to Morocco.

"No. But I still suggest that you pay a visit to their office tonight." He gave Howard the address.

"I'll see what I can do. Now let us do our job, Commander."

Howard rang off and left Bond holding the phone. He slammed it down and cursed aloud.

He paced the floor a minute, considering his options. Finally, he picked up the red phone and dialed Miss Moneypenny's line. It was possible she had left for the day, but . . .

"Executive Director's office."

"Moneypenny, it's James."

"James! How are you? You're in the building? At this hour?" Miss Moneypenny had long been an ally of Bond's, through thick and thin. He could depend on her.

"I was just going to say the same thing about you. It's past six."

"This intelligence racket never stops, didn't you know that, James? M's got me looking into this Spaniard's background. You know who I mean?"

"Espada?"

"That's right. He's stirring up trouble in Spain."

"I know. You say M is in the office?"

"She's here, but not for long. Why?"

"I'm coming up." He hung up before Moneypenny could protest.

Five minutes later, he entered the outer office of M's sanctuary. Moneypenny was standing at the filing cabinets, digging through folders. When she turned and saw Bond, her mouth opened.

"My God, James, where have you been?" she asked, concerned.

"Why?" he countered sarcastically.

"You look like you've been up for days. What's wrong? Are you ill?"

"I'm fine. I . . . haven't slept much lately. Didn't shave this morning, that's all."

Bond strode toward M's office.

"Wait, James, I don't think—"

But he was already at the door, opening it. He gave a cursory knock and stuck his head in.

M was behind her desk, wearing reading glasses, intently poring over a tall stack of legal documents.

"Ma'am?"

She looked up and blinked. "Double-O Seven?"

"May I disturb you a minute?"

M gave a brief smile. "You already have. Come on in." The smile dropped and her eyes widened when she got a good look at his appearance. He closed the door and sat down in the comfortable leather chair in front of the desk.

"How's your leave going?" she asked with a slight hesitation in her voice.

"Fine, although I'm quite ready to come back to work," he said.

"You look . . . tired."

"I'm very restless, ma'am," he slapped his hands on the arms of the chair in frustration. "You should know how inactivity is the worst thing for me. I need an assignment. I need to be on the Union case. Please, I'm asking you. I need the work."

M leaned back in her chair. She obviously saw something in her top agent that disturbed her.

"What is it you're not telling me?" she asked.

"I can't keep away from the case," he replied. "I've been doing some digging of my own."

"Double-O Seven, you are not assigned to the—"

"I know, ma'am . . . please, hear me out."

She folded her arms and raised her eyebrows, indicating that he should go on.

"Helena Marksbury's landlord, a man named Michael Clayton, is a Union member and is probably the man who recruited her. He's a partner of a Dutch fellow, Walter van Breeschooten. Together they own some residential buildings, adult bookshops in Soho, and some nightclubs. They're into some shady business, and in fact I think they have something planned for tonight."

"Like what?"

"I have no idea. I think they're planning to kill someone."

"How do you know all this?" M asked. She wasn't particularly impressed with the information, but was perturbed that Bond had knowledge of it.

"I overheard them this afternoon. I . . . happened to be near their office so I did some eavesdropping."

"Double-O Seven, I must say that I don't approve of this. The Metropolitan Police are handling the case. MI5 are involved as well."

"Ma'am, with all due respect, I am quite prepared to pursue this alone, with or without your blessing."

"You're too emotionally involved in it!" she snapped. "I can see that from here." She attempted a softer approach. "You look terrible, Double-O Seven. Are you getting enough rest? How's that head of yours?"

"You're not the first person to tell me that I look terrible today."

"Well, you do. You look ill. What's the matter?"

"I need an assignment!"

The intensity in Bond's voice frightened M for the first time since she had known him. She waited a beat, then leaned forward and looked Bond in the eyes.

"James," she said. "I care about you a great deal. We all do. You're under a great deal of stress. We can all see it. You know what your medical report from June revealed. You've been ordered to get at least three months' rest and this is only the first Tuesday in August. Now . . . I know you're troubled about Miss Marksbury. I understand. I felt a great deal of guilt when Alfred was murdered. I'm sure that what you're feeling is not at all dissimilar. Now I want you to *go home,* and get some rest. I don't want you thinking about this. We have a team working on the Union night and day. MI5 and the Metropolitan Police have Miss Marksbury's case. We must let them do their job."

The sincerity in M's voice calmed him down. Bond looked away from her, feeling ashamed of his behavior.

"All right," he said.

"Good. Why don't you come back in two weeks? Go back to your place in Jamaica for a while."

Bond nodded grimly, stood up, and started to walk out of the office without another word.

"Double-O Seven?"

He stopped and looked back.

"It's for your own good. Surely you know that."

He forced a smile, nodded, and left the room.

Damn her and everyone else!

He paced the floor of his little office as he mulled over what M had said. The events of the day had frightened and infuriated him, but he had no intention of giving up now.

Bond refused to believe that there was anything "wrong" with him. It was just not a possibility, he told himself. The blackouts—stress related, surely. But what about the hallucinations? The stress and headaches probably brought them on. That had to be it. Perhaps Dr. Feare could tell him more. He didn't want to wait another day to see her. Bond thought that the best thing to do would be to track her down at The Ivy that night.

Nevertheless, Bond was convinced that he could beat whatever mental or physical ailment he might have by simply getting back into action. That was the key to clearing his head.

He sat at his desk and turned on the computer. He got into the airline schedules' program and found what he was looking for.

British Airways had one flight a week to Tangier, and Clayton and van Breeschooten were on it. It was also completely booked. Luckily, Royal Air Maroc had two flights a week, and one of them was the next morning.

He glanced at his watch: 6:50. He had an hour to go home, get cleaned up, pack a bag, and try to find Kimberley Feare at the Ivy. Before leaving, though, he wanted to stop by Q Branch.

Major Boothroyd had left for the day, but technicians worked round the clock in the little laboratory in the basement of the building. Located near the gun practice range, Q Branch was accessible only to privileged members of SIS, a group that included Double-O agents. Therefore, Bond had no problem walking in through the security check.

"Can I help you, Double-O Seven?" the man at the front desk asked.

"No, thank you," he replied. "I'm just inquiring about a piece of equipment I left for repair. Be right back."

The official let Bond through the doors, not thinking anything of it.

Bond went to the small-arms cage and said hello to the attendant. There it was, in the glass case with the other semi-automatics. Bond liked the new Walther P99 in .40 caliber S&W, but he hadn't yet talked Q Branch into issuing him one. Certainly more powerful than the standard 9mm, it looked the same, was designed the same, but used more potent ammunition. This resulted in a slow round, due to its added weight and size, but packed a stronger punch at the other end. With laser sight and flashlight accessories, the new P99 was a powerful handgun, but not ideal for hiding under a jacket. Bond had used the earlier model P99 and preferred to keep it in his luggage or automobile as backup. When he did wear it, Bond used an ISP-3 slotted-belt attachment holster, custom-made for the P99 by Del Fatti Leather.

When the attendant wasn't looking, Bond took the gun from the case and put it in his waistband. He then grabbed the holster and thrust it into his pocket, turned and said, "See you later," to the attendant, and left the building.

He hailed a taxi and directed the driver to a travel agency. There, he booked a one-way trip in economy on the Royal Air Maroc flight to Tangier. He paid with cash and gave his name as John Cork. The Cork identity, one of several aliases he used, was one that even SIS didn't know about.

Bond felt better as he entered his flat minutes later. He showered, shaved, and put on a clean white shirt, a navy jacket, red and blue tie, and dark trousers. Underneath the jacket was the Bianchi X15 leather shoulder holster and Walther PPK, still his choice of weapon for concealment. He had loaded the magazine with prefragmented ammunition. He chose Glaser Silvers for better penetration.

Bond packed a bag for the trip to Morocco and left instructions for May, his housekeeper.

At 7:45, he left the flat and took another taxi back to the theater district.

EIGHT

THE HEAT OF THE MOMENT

The Ivy is a chic, old established restaurant frequented by the theater community, and by professionals in television, film, publishing, advertising, and journalism. In many ways, it is a modern, living Poets' Corner. Located at the junction of West and Litchfield streets in London's busy theater district, the Ivy's history dates back to 1917, when it was a modest café that quickly gained a reputation among the theater society.

But it was not James Bond's kind of place. While he appreciated the food at the Ivy, which was always excellent, the idea of going to a restaurant to see and be seen was not his style. He preferred anonymity and quiet. The Ivy can be a noisy place when it was crowded, which it usually is. Tables have to be booked weeks, if not months, in advance.

When he entered the Ivy shortly after 8:15, the maître d' asked, "May I help you, sir?"

Bond peered past him. "I'm meeting someone. May I take a look and see if they're already here?"

"What is the name?"

"I'm not sure whose name the reservation was under. They're doctors."

The maître d' shrugged and gestured toward the dining room as if to say, "Be my guest." Bond nodded and walked past him. He entered the crowded dining room that was buzzing with noise and excitement. London's favorites were out in force, all deeply animated in conversation and luxuriating in culinary delights. At least a half-dozen people were on their feet talking and laughing with diners.

He finally spotted her at a large table conversing with two other women and two men. Bond guessed that they were all physicians.

Dr. Feare was the youngest and most attractive in the group. She had bright blue eyes, a long but pretty nose, thin lips that seemed to be always on the verge of a sexy smile, and shoulder-length blond hair. Bond had found her to be good-looking, but the clinical atmosphere of a physician's office tends to neutralize any thoughts of sex. Here, in the restaurant's golden illumination, Kimberley Feare looked marvelous.

Bond turned and slipped out of the room. As he passed the maître d' he said, "Wrong restaurant. Sorry."

He went outside and quickly crossed the street. Luckily, the light was fading; loitering in the shadows would be less noticeable. Bond took a position under an awning, leaned against the building, and waited.

The pounding in his head seemed to mark the seconds. . . .

At one point, Bond felt that he was being watched. He scanned the street and buildings around him, but he couldn't see anything out of the ordinary. His nerves were acting up again, he told himself.

It was nearly an hour later, long after the sun had vanished, when Dr. Feare emerged from the restaurant. The others were with her. They noisily said good-bye to one another, shaking hands and hugging, then all went their separate ways. Dr. Feare got into a waiting taxi.

Another taxi pulled around the corner. A stroke of luck! Bond hailed it and got inside.

"Follow that taxi, please," Bond said.

The driver accepted this as a challenge and said, "Right."

After a brief uneventful drive, Dr. Feare's taxi pulled up in front of her building on Harley Street. It was the same building in which Sir James Molony kept his office, as well as his own flat. A battery of doctors who all had private offices in the building shared the ground-floor waiting room. A few of them lived there as well.

Bond instructed his driver to stop fifty feet behind it. He got out, paid, and approached the doctor just as she was completing the transaction with her own driver.

"Dr. Feare?" Bond asked.

She looked up, startled, but then she relaxed when she recognized a familiar face. "Yes?"

"James Bond. I saw you a few weeks ago. . . ."

"Right! My nurse told me that you had called. Mr. Bond, how are you?" She smiled.

"I was hoping that you could tell *me*," Bond said. "Please excuse the invasion of your privacy, but I simply had to see you."

The cab drove away and left them standing in front of the building. The porter was just inside the glass windows, watching them.

Her expression changed to one of concern. "Oh dear, what's wrong?"

"I'm leaving the country tomorrow morning on classified business. There wasn't time to make a proper appointment."

Dr. Feare frowned. "I thought that you were off-duty. Medical leave."

"Never mind that," Bond said. "Please, is there somewhere we can talk?"

She looked at him closely, noting the amount of stress his face revealed. "You're right, you don't look well, Mr. Bond. You have dark circles under your eyes."

"Sleep deprivation," Bond said. "It's the bloody headaches. They're becoming worse, and I don't think those pills you prescribed are doing anything for me. And . . . well, I seem to have experienced another episode of blacking out."

"What do you mean?"

He didn't want to mention seeing the double just yet. "I got a feeling of overwhelming anxiety—almost like I was having a heart attack—as well as a pounding in the head. Suddenly, I passed out. I woke up an hour or so later, and I couldn't remember what had happened. The odd thing is that I'd moved. I wasn't in the same place I was when I blacked out."

"Mr. Bond, you should have called me immediately," she said. "How long has this been going on?"

"Just today."

"I see. Perhaps you should come upstairs. Let me have a look at you."

He followed her into the building. She greeted the porter and led the way through the luxurious marble-floored lobby area. The clinic's waiting room was to the left, now closed and locked, of course. He followed her straight ahead into a lift, where she pressed button number 5.

Dr. Feare's flat was a modest one-bedroom with a living room, kitchen, bathroom, and a dining alcove. It was tastefully decorated in green and white, but it was also decidedly feminine, and very comfortable. A large rug covered the living room floor. A glass-top coffee table was the focus, and a green leather couch and two chairs surrounded it. A television and stereo system stood in the corner, near the window.

She took off her jacket and flung it over a chair. "Have a seat in the living room, Mr. Bond. Make yourself comfortable. I'm going to make some coffee. Would you like some?"

"That would be lovely," he answered.

She went into the kitchen. Bond removed the jacket, followed by the shoulder holster, and draped them over a chair. He then stood idly in the living room, glancing at the various knickknacks and pieces of art on the walls. Dr. Feare evidently liked to collect miniature elephants, as she had at least two dozen of them on a silver tray. All of them were posed so that they had their heads raised, trunks in the air. The elephants were made of various substances: glass, silver, wood, onyx, even gold.

"When the trunks are raised like that, it means good luck," she said, bringing out a small tray with cups and a bottle of mineral water. She placed it on the coffee table and approached him.

"First of all, do you have your medication with you by any chance?" she asked.

"Yes," Bond said, sitting on the sofa. "And please call me James. I haven't taken this evening's dose yet. I thought I should talk to you first."

"Let me see your pills."

He took the small container out of his pocket and handed it to her. She opened it, poured a few into her palm, nodded, then replaced them. She handed the container back to him. "Just checking to see that you had the right pills. Go ahead. Take four tablets instead of two."

"Now?"

"Yes, James."

Bond swallowed four pills with the water.

"Good," she said. "I'll be right back."

He watched her move back to the kitchen, admiring the shape of her hips. She was a lovely woman. Despite her youth, there was something comforting about her. Bond found her very attractive.

A few minutes later, she brought in a coffeepot and they sat on the couch together.

"Black, please," he said. She added a little cream to hers, but no sugar.

"Is the headache worse before these episodes?" she asked.

"Yes. I've had only one other blackout, if you recall. Three months ago. What could have caused it?"

"It could be a number of things," she said. "We don't call it a blackout; we call it poriomania, a condition in which the patient suffers a loss of cognizance, yet his body continues to function normally. It's uncommon, but it happens, especially with raging alcoholics and people who might have post-traumatic epilepsy, which we considered before. Normally it occurs six months or later after an injury, but in your case it was much sooner."

Bond didn't like the sound of that.

"James, I suggest that we run some more tests. I'd like to do another EEG. That lesion in your head may not be shrinking like we hoped. Must you leave the country tomorrow?"

"Yes. It will have to wait until I return."

"But James, you have a dangerous condition. You might never know when you'll have another episode of poriomania."

"I promise not to drive. Last time you told me that my symptoms could be stress-related. I'd like to believe that. I'm convinced that if I get out of this bloody rut I'm in and get back on the active duty list, I'll be fine."

He realized that he inadvertently gave away the fact that he was indeed still on medical leave.

"I see," she said. "Then you *don't* have to leave tomorrow."

"It's personal," he replied. "I need to go."

"I'm not sure that's what you need, James. You must take this seriously," she said, placing her hand on top of his. She hadn't meant for it to be an intimate gesture, yet neither of them could deny the electricity they felt. Encouraged by the look in her eyes, Bond raised the charm a notch by turning his hand and squeezing hers.

"Or perhaps I need a different kind of diversion," he suggested. He gave her a smile that penetrated her defenses.

Whether or not it was due to the wine she had consumed earlier, or perhaps to the immense amount of charisma that he had, Kimberley Feare suddenly felt vulnerable. She tried to tell herself that he was, after all, a patient, but his overwhelming masculinity instantly crushed that delineation. He was one of the most attractive men she had ever met, and she was alone with him in her flat.

Bond knew enough about women to recognize when the barriers were down. The seduction of a woman had everything to do with attitude, not looks or wit. Bond reflected—just for a moment—how unprofessional it might be for her to sleep with him. Most women in her position would have resisted going this far. Bond chalked it up to her youth and enthusiasm, and, giving himself a small boost to his ego, to his experience with the opposite sex.

He turned to her and put his arms around her. She looked up at him, her mouth parted. Her lower lip trembled a bit, and he could feel her shaking.

Bond brought his mouth down on hers and roughly held her against him. She submitted with a soft moan, then opened her mouth to receive his tongue. They kissed passionately until she finally, gently, pushed him away.

"Mr. B—James, please," she said, breathlessly. She took a sip of coffee, then said, "Uhm, tell me more about your, uhm, condition. You said you haven't been sleeping well?"

"That's right," he said, lightly brushing a strand of blond hair from her face.

"Any hallucinations?"

Bond hesitated.

"Seen anything unusual? Things that shouldn't have been there?" she asked.

"I'm not sure," he replied truthfully.

She reached up and rubbed his eyebrow slowly with her thumb, as if to brush away something caught there.

"Feelings of paranoia?"

Bond closed his eyes as she continued to massage his forehead with both thumbs. "Mmm hmm," he answered.

"James, we have to do another EEG."

She rubbed his temples with care for another thirty seconds, then stopped. She was unsure how to handle the situation or her desire.

After a few sips of coffee in silence, she looked at him and tried to smile. He took this as an invitation and leaned in to kiss her again. She nearly spilled her cup setting it on the saucer, then pulled him down on the couch on top of her. Her hands ran through his hair, pulling it, clawing the back of his neck with her fingernails. With his mouth firmly on hers, he brought his right hand up the side of her left leg, pushing the skirt up until it was above the tops of her nylon stockings.

They rolled off the couch, crashing into the coffee table and spilling the coffee. They didn't notice, though—such was the unexpected passion that had overtaken them.

They lay naked on the carpet next to the overturned coffee table. Bond had lit a cigarette and was using a saucer as an ashtray. The sex had been intense, as if neither of them could get enough of each other. The world outside could have been on the brink of disaster, but they would not have known it. The first time had been rushed and anxious, almost a selfish race to pleasure themselves rather than climax together. The second time was more relaxed and slower, but just as fierce. There was more give-and-take, and they had focused their energies on each other. They were by now exhausted.

Now she snuggled next to him, her firm breasts pressed up against his rib cage. She was still attempting to catch her breath and said, "Just so you know, I don't do this with all my patients."

"I'm so glad to hear that," he said. The throbbing in his head had just returned, and he rubbed his brow.

"I think it was your brooding angst that was so dreadfully attractive," she said with a laugh. "What's wrong? Head again?"

He nodded.

"I tell you what." She sat up. "I'm going to the loo. When I get back, I'll give you a proper massage. We'll see if I can work out some of that tension."

He closed his eyes as the warmth of her body disappeared. When he heard the bathroom door shut, he tried to sit up, but found that he couldn't. The room was spinning again, just like when he had been on that rooftop earlier in the day.

So he lay there for a few minutes with his eyes closed. When he thought that he heard something at her front door, but wasn't positive, he tried to sit up again.

Bond cursed aloud and reached for one of the leather chairs nearby. He managed to pull himself up to his knees, but now the pain in his head increased tenfold. This was accompanied by the dreaded anxiety that flooded his senses. Once again, his heart began to pound, bringing on that horrible feeling that he was about to die.

"Kimberley . . ." he tried to call, but his voice came out in a whisper. Exerting every bit of strength in his body, he pulled himself up against the chair and got to his feet.

The room went dark as he lost his balance and fell over the glass coffee table.

He was aware of a cold sensation on his right cheek. It was hard and wet.

A tile floor. Shards of broken mirror.

He opened his eyes and saw a toilet. But something was wrong. The normally white appliance was streaked in red.

Blood.

Bond felt a burst of adrenaline as life poured back into his body. He groaned and rolled over.

He was lying in Kimberley Feare's bathroom, naked. He coughed and put his hand to his face so that he could rub the haze from his vision. He got a jolt when he saw that his hand was covered in blood.

He sat up quickly, alarmed.

There was blood all over the bathroom and on his body. The mirror had been shattered. He examined himself and found several cuts on his arms, legs, and torso. He vaguely remembered falling into the glass coffee table.

He gingerly got to his feet and looked in the broken glass around him.

My God.

Dozens of ghosts stared back at him.

His skin was pale, frosty white. Streaks of blood went from his face and down his chest. Looking around the bathroom, he saw that the door was closed and noticed that his hand and footprints were all over the place in blood. On the floor by the door was a large bloody kitchen knife. He already knew that his prints probably covered it.

"Kimberley?" he called.

Dreading the worst, he opened the door and looked out.

The living room was a shambles. The glass coffee table had been broken. The cups, saucers, and coffeepot were on the rug. Their clothes lay in heaps on the floor, some of them torn. The collection of elephants had been scattered, some broken.

The green-and-white design scheme of the flat had been smeared with red.

"Kimberley!"

Bond stumbled to the open door of the bedroom and gaped in horror at the gruesome tableau before him.

Kimberley Feare was lying on the bed, naked, covered in blood. Her throat had been slashed, ear to ear, and she had been stabbed several times.

NINE

SUNRISE IN THREE COUNTRIES

James Bond rarely panicked, but he was on the verge of doing so now.

Did he kill this woman? What the hell was going on?

Trembling, he stepped into the bedroom to take a closer look. The multiple stab wounds suggested rage on the part of the killer. The blood trails on the carpet indicated that the body had been dragged from the living room and placed on the bed. She had probably been killed in the other room. Bond suspected that the throat-cutting had probably been done in here, postmortem.

But who could have done it? Not he! He might be a professional killer in the line of duty, but he was incapable of doing this to a person.

Or was he?

Bond backed out of the room, frantically going over everything that had happened in the last few hours. He looked at the clock in the living room: it was 2:48 in the morning. He had been unconscious for a long time.

He moved to the front door and saw that it was still locked.

My God, what the hell happened here? Was he losing his mind?

Shaken by the turn of events and the uncertainty of his mental condition, Bond began to act irrationally. He rushed into the bathroom, grabbed some towels, and started wiping up the blood. He mopped up the hand and footprints, cleaned off the knife, and scrubbed down the walls and broken mirror. After ten minutes, the towels were soaked in blood, and the place was still a mess.

What the hell am I doing? he thought. *I DID NOT DO THIS!*

He sat on the toilet seat.

Think . . . think . . . Calm down . . .

Wait a minute . . . he thought. The throat slashing . . . that was the *Union*'s way of killing! The Union murdered Kimberley Feare! It was the only possible explanation. But how did they get in? And why kill Kimberley? If the Union were inside the flat that night, why didn't they kill him, too?

Were they trying to frame him? His prints were everywhere. He had been seen with her that night. How could he prove that he didn't kill her? Perhaps that was it. They wanted to pin a murder on him.

Bond buried his face in his hands and took a deep breath.

Right. Let's get cleaned up, he decided.

He found some clean towels in the linen cupboard and got into the shower. He washed himself thoroughly, rinsing the blood down the drain. The wounds on his arms and legs were superficial, but one on his arm was still bleeding. He probably needed a stitch or two, but he wasn't about to bother with it.

He stepped out of the shower and looked inside the medicine cabinet. He found some adhesive bandages and put one on the cut. He then gingerly stepped out of the bathroom, avoiding the broken glass and blood spots, and picked up his clothes. He dressed quickly, even though a couple of buttons were missing off his shirt. He thought he should get on his hands and knees and search for them, but the carpet was such a mess that he would probably have made a bigger one had he done so.

The shoulder holster was still on the chair where he had left it. He put it on and surveyed the scene.

The flat looked like the devil's workshop.

He glanced at the telephone and considered calling the police.

Not a good idea at this point.

He needed to find out who had done this terrible thing and make sure he could clear his name.

Bond refused to believe that he had done it.

He put on his jacket, opened the door to the flat, and looked into the corridor. All clear. He turned back to the flat and whispered, "I'm sorry, Kimberley," then shut the door.

As he left the building, the porter watched him suspiciously.

The thought kept nagging at Bond: *What if he* had *done it?*

He walked the streets in a daze.

For a moment he thought that someone was following him. He turned quickly, but didn't see anyone.

Get hold of yourself! He was jumping at shadows.

The obvious thing to do would be to contact Bill Tanner. Bond should tell him everything—about the blackouts, the hallucinations, and Kimberley. On the other hand, if he did that, he would be detained and questioned by the police. He would be in the middle of an inquiry, and would end up being the prime suspect. M would suspend him from duty indefinitely, and he would *never* get to the bottom of this.

No, even if it was totally imprudent, Bond knew that he had to keep quiet.

Bond was unsure of where to go and what to do. He flagged down a taxi on a main street and decided that his flat was the safest place to go. In the cab, he kept telling himself what he wanted to believe. *The Union was responsible.*

He had to get closer to them. It was the only way. If he could track down Helena Marksbury's killers, he would probably also find Kimberley's murderers. If he could face his enemy, he would come to grips with what was happening to him. It just *couldn't* be anything physical. He hadn't much faith in psychiatry, either, so he was loathe to seek out additional help.

Bond made a vow to beat this himself. The only way to do it was to go after the Union with guns blazing. Leave no stone unturned. Flush them out and smash them like insects.

When he got to his flat, it was nearly dawn. His flight to Africa was looming.

He double-checked the bag he had packed and looked at the message he had left for May. He had written that he would be out of the country for a while. Bond scribbled an additional sentence—that he didn't know when he'd be back. That was good enough.

He caught another taxi outside and went straight to Heathrow. Using his alias "John Cork," he went swiftly through Immigration and boarded the Royal Air Maroc flight to Tangier.

As the sun rose on the southern coast of Spain, Royal Gibraltar Police border control officer Captain Brian Berley eyed the group of protestors with understandable apprehension. This was the largest group he had ever seen, and he had been stationed on the border between Spain and Gibraltar for nearly fifteen years. The mob had appeared the previous night in the sleepy town of La Linea, just north of the border. They had arrived in buses and cars, and on bicycles . . . and had stayed in hotels or camped out in their vehicles. As soon as the sun rose, they were out in force.

Berley picked up the phone and made a call.

"Commissioner, I think the situation down here looks extremely bad. They're becoming quite noisy, and if they decide to storm the border, we're outnumbered twenty to one. We need MACA immediately." MACA stood for Military Assistance to the Civil Authorities.

He was assured that military police were on the way, but that the border should be closed until further notice. Berley issued the instructions to the Immigration officials, who lowered the barriers and told pedestrians and people in cars that there would be no entry into Gibraltar. Besides, the mob had all but blocked the road in and out of the colony.

The hundred or more protestors were bunching up as close as

possible to the gates. Many of them were carrying signs that read, in Spanish and English, "Gibraltar Is Spanish, Not British!" Some signs proclaimed, "Espada—Governor of Gibraltar!" While the inhabitants of the British colony were accustomed to protests and demonstrations, having dealt with this kind of thing for centuries, the recent turn of events had them a little worried. The U.K. had been slow in sending reinforcements and, in fact, the decision to do so was being held up for political reasons.

Berley had read the newspaper reports with cynicism. The U.K. Prime Minister was attempting to find a peaceful settlement with Spain. The Madrid government's official line was that they "disapproved" of Domingo Espada's actions, but they were making no attempts to curb him. Berley thought that this was merely a public relations ploy and that they were in fact rubbing their hands with glee. If an upstart like Espada could take back Gibraltar without the "approval" of Spain, then the Spanish government wouldn't be blamed. Seemed pretty simple.

A truck carrying twenty Gibraltar Services Military Police officers drove across the Gibraltar airfield's runway, which was inconveniently located just south of the border (people entering or leaving the colony had to cross it!), and stopped at the Immigration building. The men, carrying SA-80 5.56mm assault rifles, leaped out of the truck and formed a line at the border. This prompted more shouting and abuse from the protestors, who had by now pushed themselves up as far as they could get to the border.

When the rocks started flying, Berley made another call to his superiors. The Royal Gibraltar Regiment was being dispatched as well.

The security alert at the Governor's Residence went from "black" to "amber." The Governor made an urgent call to London, again requesting assistance. Unfortunately he was told that rock-throwing did not constitute a threat of "serious violence" and that NATO's European Rapid Reaction Force, which was drawn from Allied Command Europe Mobile Force Land (ACE), would not be dispatched. NATO were discussing the situation in Brussels, but these things took time. However, the U.K. was sending the 1st Battalion of the Parachute Regiment based in Aldershot. They were expected to arrive by midday.

The Governor gave the order to secure the airport and allow only the reinforcements from Britain to land. All other traffic in and out of Gibraltar was to cease.

Captain Berley was told to keep calm and stand his ground. Help was on the way, but it wouldn't arrive until midafternoon.

The mob was becoming ugly. The shouting and insults were increasing by the minute. The police were doing their best to keep cool and not retaliate in kind. The situation was a powder keg, ready to ignite. Rocks broke one of the windows in the Immigration office. Berley wondered if he should employ tear gas in an attempt to disperse the crowd.

Suddenly, a deafening explosion rocked the Immigration building. A fireball engulfed the surrounding area. Chaos erupted as some of the Spanish crowd cheered, while others screamed and ran. Several soldiers had been caught by the blast and were now lying on the pavement, dead or seriously wounded.

Berley ran out of the smoking building and ordered the men to fire warning shots to disperse the crowd. As the guns went off, the Spanish mob thought they were being fired upon.

Several Spaniards pulled their own guns and began to fire at the police.

Berley was horrified. He dropped to the ground, avoiding the gunfire, and crawled for cover just as a second bomb detonated at the gate.

This one created a huge explosion, killing several people on both sides.

Berley cursed aloud. He was now in the middle of a shooting war.

The events that morning at the Gibraltar border prompted a major panic in the governments of Britain and Spain. By noon, fingers were being pointed, tempers had flared, and both sides were blaming each other for the catastrophe.

The morning sun had also brought life to the streets of Casablanca. As the merchants and shopkeepers and bankers and beggars went to their respective places of business, the Union subordinates had already been working round the clock, packing various files, pieces of equipment, weaponry . . . it wouldn't be long before they had finished.

Le Gérant rose from his magnificent Louis XIV four-poster bed. He reached for and felt the silk robe hanging on the hook by the bed. Putting it over his naked body, he wrapped the sash snugly around his thick waist. *Le Gérant* wasn't fat, but he was what is often referred to as "stocky."

Knowing the exact path to the bathroom, he walked in his bare feet across the tiled floor. Even if something unexpected had been placed in the way, *Le Gérant* would have sensed the obstacle's presence and moved around it. He had been able to do it since he was very young. He possessed some kind of sixth sense that allowed him to "see" when he couldn't do so physically. His mother had noticed that he had a gift, and she believed that he was a messenger from Allah. A Berber woman with a strong tribal heritage, she came from a group of Riffians in the eastern part of Morocco, near the Algerian border. He had lived with her as a child until he was ten years old, when she unexpectedly died. His Corsican father fetched him out of Morocco and brought him to Paris so that he could be educated in the Western ways. There was also hope that a cure could be found for his blindness.

Le Gérant returned to his mother's people in the Rif Mountains for a brief period of time as an adult. Even though he had adopted the ways of the West, he was accepted warmly, for many people remembered him.

From the moment he returned, the other Riffians regarded *Le Gérant* as some kind of divine being. They were amazed that he could navigate his surroundings so easily. Some wondered if he were truly blind. When he was able to call them by name before they said a word, the people were so impressed with "the Western Berber" that they became his loyal followers.

Le Gérant was a man from two countries and two cultures.

In the bathroom, *Le Gérant* splashed water on his face. He would miss the Union quarters here in Casablanca, but it was time to move on. Discovery of the base was imminent, and it was too costly to maintain the complex. By the end of the day, the Union would be gone. Vanished, without a trace.

Le Gérant had thought long and hard about where to move the central headquarters to. He thought that the authorities would temporarily ignore Marrakesh. That was where they would go for the time being. He thought that perhaps he should move the operations to Europe. But where to? France? He would have to think about it some more. Marrakesh would do for now.

He heard the buzz of the telephone. He walked back through the bedroom to the study. He sat in a large cushioned chair and picked up the phone.

"Yes?"

"*Gérant,* it's Nadir, I hope it's not too early."

"I've been expecting your call. I trust you are on a secure line."

"Most secure, sir."

"Very well. What have you to report?"

Yassasin said, "Everything has worked as planned. James Bond is behaving exactly as we had hoped. He is on his way to Morocco now."

"That's excellent news. What about the *commandant* from London?"

"Mr. van Breeschooten and his colleague Clayton will also arrive this morning, sir. They have instructions to go to the training camp in the mountains, as you wished."

"And you're sure Mr. Bond will find them?"

"If he picks up the clues we left for him, he will. He's smart enough to find them."

"And Clayton's cousin?"

"Still in place and under cover. An excellent operative, I must say."

Le Gérant was pleased. "How is Señor Espada feeling this morning? He must be fairly happy."

Yassasin allowed himself to smile. "He is thrilled that the confrontation at the border is going as well as it is. Just enough people have died to make the various politicians sit up and take notice. After tomorrow's events, he is certain that his proposal to the governments of Britain,

Spain, and Gibraltar will be accepted. The Governor of Gibraltar has already expressed an interest in hosting the summit meeting."

"Perfect. Nadir, you continue to amaze me."

"It is my pleasure to serve you, *Gérant.*"

"Tell me, Nadir, does Espada suspect anything?" *Le Gérant* asked.

"I don't think so. He isn't aware of anything but his own selfish dreams. He is becoming careless."

"I'm not so sure that will matter much in a few days."

"Oh?"

"I've decided that when he becomes the Governor of Gibraltar, his tenure shouldn't last very long. When we gain control of his operations, it would be best if he wasn't in the picture."

"I understand. I have already built that option into the plan. His tenure will last . . . say . . . a minute?"

Le Gérant smiled. "You are a genius, my friend."

"No, sir," Yassasin said. "You inspire me to do my best. How is the moving going?"

"Smoothly. The next time you see me, we'll be in Marrakesh."

"*Ma' as-salaama,* then," Yassasin said.

"*Ma' as-salaama* as well."

Le Gérant hung up the phone. He felt very pleased with himself. Before long, the Union would be as powerful as any country on the face of the earth, and he was its rightful leader. It was *he, Le Gérant,* who had made the Union what it was today. He had the business sense of a metropolitan Westerner, but the spirituality and tenacity of a Berber tribesman.

As the first phase of the plan came to a close, everything was in its place. Domingo Espada believed that he had employed the Union to do his bidding, when, in fact, he was but another chess piece in the grand game that Yassasin and *Le Gérant* had concocted.

The best moves were yet to come.

ACT TWO

TERCIO DE BANDERILLAS

TEN

ON THE RUN

At noon, the Royal Air Maroc flight touched down at Tangier's tiny Boukhalef airport, fifteen kilometers southeast from the town center. James Bond disembarked and immediately felt the cultural shock of being on another continent. North Africa was indeed a completely different world from Europe. Sights, sounds, art, food, and religion all contributed to making the way of life in the Muslim world distinctly unique. In many ways, English-speaking Westerners were the least at home in *al-Maghreb al-Aqsa,* the "land of the setting sun." They were treated with a certain degree of suspicion, although this was less so in Morocco than in some other Muslim countries.

Signs printed only in Arabic and French pointed the way to baggage claim and the exit. Porters descended upon Bond before he'd cleared Immigration. He waved them away, nearly barking at one persistent one, and made his way outside to the taxi stand. He carried a small holdall containing necessities and a box wrapped in brown paper. Its label was addressed to "Mr. Latif Reggab" at an address in Tangier, and a Customs label claimed that it contained machine parts. The official who had cleared it spoke to Bond in French, saying, "Oh, you're friends with Mr. Reggab? He's always importing or exporting something." In fact, the box contained Bond's two firearms, carefully masked by X ray–proof material perfected by Q Branch.

Bond negotiated a price of two hundred dirhams for the taxi driver to take him to Tangier. It was a twenty-minute ride, and the landscape was atypical for what one might expect from a port city like Tangier. The countryside was hilly and green, dotted with the occasional shepherd in the distance. There was surprisingly little development out this way, but the city was suddenly upon them. Bond felt the change in the atmosphere, for Tangier was famous for its unique, decaying character of the post-Interzone days.

People from all over the world have inhabited the port for over 2,500 years. During the days when resident diplomatic agents of a number of countries controlled Tangier, it was known as an "international zone." Then, every kind of dubious activity developed in the port, including money laundering, smuggling, currency speculation, arms dealing, prostitution, and slave trading. It was also a fashionable resort haven for artists, writers, refugees, exiles, and bankers. When Tangier was reunited with the rest of Morocco in 1956, this notoriety fell by the wayside, but the legends lived on.

Bond had been to Tangier a number of times and he was always put off by the amount of hustling that went on. The trick, Bond had learned, was not to act or look like a tourist. Because Bond had black hair and a relatively tanned complexion, it wasn't immediately obvious that he was British. A glare from his cold, steely eyes also worked to dissuade faux guides from offering to "show him the medina."

The driver let him off in the Grand Socco, a poor imitation of the famed Djemaa el-Fna in Marrakesh, where snake charmers, musicians, storytellers, makeshift shops, and food stalls filled the air with smells, noise, and spectacle. Outside the chemist's was a group of tattoo-faced Berber women dressed in traditional *izars* or *haïks,* hoping to secure a housecleaning job. A Moorish horseshoe arch led from the Grand Socco into the medina, the city's oldest quarter. Navigation by foot, bicycle, motorcycle, or donkey cart were the only options in this labyrinth of narrow passages and winding paths.

Bond walked into the medina, shaking his head at a man who wanted to "show you something special, my friend," and moved past the numerous shop fronts where anything and everything was sold. The small streets were full of donkeys and cats, beggars and children, hawkers and tourists. It was the smell of the place, in particular, that seemed to be a common trait with all of the medinas in Morocco. The fresh fish, meats, and spices combined with the surrounding humanity to create a confusion of odors that, to Bond, smelled of rotten eggs mixed with incense and urine.

Bond made his way deep into the medina to the busy little square known as the Petit Socco. Children were kicking a ball back and forth between the constant movement of carts and wagons, women dressed in caftans and veils who were buying the day's produce, and "students" looking for tourists to befriend. He passed the Pension Fuentes, which had been one of Tangier's luxury hotels at the end of the nineteenth century. At that time, the medina was the sole center of activity and the city's administration was established there. Important international offices had once resided in the medina, such as the old American Legation, which was now a museum. This all came to an end when the ville nouvelle was built at the beginning of the new century.

At first Bond thought he might have taken a wrong turn, but then he recognized some landmarks and continued on his way up Rue de Almohades to a three-story Berber house. Built around a courtyard, the square structure had high ramparts and corner towers. Magnificent, colorful, handmade carpets hung on the outside, and the ground floor was covered with arts and crafts, from textiles to pottery and ceramics. Brass and copperware were abundant, and jewelry, woodwork, and basketware dominated the premises. Everything was of very high quality.

A teenage boy approached Bond, saying in English, "Come in, sir, come in. *Español?* American? We have best prices in Tangier. You like carpets? Please, we give you free demonstration."

"No, thank you," Bond said. "I'm here to see Latif Reggab. Is he here?"

"Yes, sir, he is always here. Please, come in and look around. I will find him for you."

The walls and floor of the room were decorated in the intricate and exquisite tile work that was prevalent in Moroccan architecture. The smell of incense was stronger inside, covering the foul odors of the medina. A few American tourists were haggling with a shopkeeper over the price of a black leather jacket. Some Spaniards were admiring the precious stones that were protected in a glass case.

"*As-salaam 'alaykum,* may I help you?" said a familiar voice behind Bond.

He turned to see a rather short man in his fifties. He was dressed in the traditional white *jellaba,* wore glasses, had dark, curly hair flecked with gray, and large brown eyes with an unusual bluish tint. His skin color was light, as was common among indigenous Berber people. When the man saw who it was standing in his shop, he beamed.

"Well, Allah be praised. I don't believe it!"

"Hello, Latif," Bond said. "It's been a long time."

"James Bond, as I live and breathe. Welcome!" Latif Reggab laughed heartily and embraced Bond warmly, planting kisses on both cheeks. "Why didn't you let me know you were coming?"

"I couldn't, for security reasons," Bond said, quietly, as he glanced around to make sure no one was listening. "Latif, I need your help. I need a place to stay while I'm here, and no one must know about it."

"Of course, of course! No problems. You are always welcome here. Consider this your own personal *funduq.*" Latif was referring to the smelly "motels" used by caravans.

"And," Bond added, "I would also appreciate it if London didn't know I was here as well."

Latif grinned conspiratorially and said, "Oh, are we up to some kind of international intrigue? Are you in pursuit of dangerous terrorists? Has the spy network returned to Tangier?"

Bond laughed. "Not quite. Let's just say that I'm on a personal mission. So, tell me, Latif, how are things in T Branch of Station NA? How is your family?"

"Come upstairs, James, please, and I'll tell you." He led Bond up the flights of stairs, past the carpet and rug gallery on the first floor, upward beyond the living quarters, and onto the flat roof, where several carpets had been hung or laid out to dry in the sun. On the way, Latif had barked an order in Arabic to a young man on the second floor.

They could see the entire medina from this height. It looked much as it did hundreds of years ago, with the crowded clusters of flat rooftops, hanging laundry, and the occasional minaret. The only difference was that now most of the rooftops were sprinkled with television aerials or satellite dishes.

"My family is wonderful," Latif answered. "My wife is still beautiful and my children are almost all grown. My eldest has already made me a grandfather. You met my youngest son earlier. That was Hussein."

"My lord, the last time I saw him, he was—" Bond held his hand at his waist to indicate the boy's height.

"Yes, they grow like wildflowers, these kids."

"Grandpa, eh?"

"Yes, it's a blessing," Latif said, smiling broadly, revealing large, yellow teeth. "Anyway, they're all fine, and the branch is fine, too. To tell the truth, I am very bored with intelligence work. Most of the time these days I simply run my shop and sell beautiful carpets to tourists. There is hardly anything for me to do anymore. Most of the North Africa station's activity is concentrated in Egypt now; we never have any excitement in Morocco. I'm hoping you have some excitement up your sleeve and that you will allow me to have some of it."

The second boy appeared, carrying a tray with two glasses of hot mint tea.

"Please, James, have some tea," Latif said.

Bond wasn't a big admirer of tea in any form, but he knew that it was customary to accept the offer of mint tea in Moroccan households. It was way too sweet for his tastes, but he made a show of drinking it.

They sat in two wooden chairs overlooking the medina. Just to the north, they could see the coastline. A European cruise ship had just put in to the port, which they could plainly see to the northeast.

"We're getting all the cruise ships that were supposed to stop in Gibraltar," Latif said. "Sticky situation there, eh? Anyway, so tell me what this secret mission of yours is."

"I need to locate two men who flew here from London last night on the British Airways flight. An Englishman named Michael Clayton, and a Dutchman named Walter van Breeschooten. Can you get on to your contacts at Immigration?"

"Sure, no problems. They can tell us if they passed through Immigration all right. But they could be anywhere in the country by now, you know."

"It's essential that I find them."

"Perhaps they wrote their Moroccan address on their Immigration card," Latif said facetiously.

"That would be the headquarters of the Union."

Latif raised his bushy eyebrows. "I see. That's what this is about, then."

"What can you tell me about them? Do you have any idea where the Union keeps its main base?"

"As you know, we have an ongoing directive from London to gather information on the Union. I have a little, not much."

"Then I'd like to get started as soon as possible."

"We'll have some lunch and can talk," Latif said. "Let me show you to your room."

Bond found his room modest but comfortable. It was small, with a single bed, a tiny window, and a dresser. The bathroom was down the hall, and he would be sharing it with Latif's extended family. He didn't plan to stay long.

He went into the bathroom and stared at his hard face. It didn't reveal the torment he was feeling inside. He looked tired, but otherwise seemed fit and alert. In fact, he felt like hell. He was still jittery after the shock of discovering Kimberley Feare's body. He hadn't had a proper night's sleep in days. The headache was stable but persistent.

Bond did what he could to make himself look presentable, put on his shoulder holster and PPK, and covered them with a light sports jacket. He also put on the ISP-3 holster for the P99. The handgun was bulky, but he felt it would be better to keep both guns on him at all times. He rejoined Latif in the family room on the second floor, where a woman in a caftan was setting the dining table.

"You remember my wife, Maliza?" Latif asked, gesturing to her.

"Of course," Bond said. "Thank you for your hospitality," he said to Maliza. She smiled and nodded at him, then scurried out of the room.

"She doesn't speak English," Latif said. "Sit down, my friend. Tell me more about this mysterious mission you're on."

Bond sat down in a wooden chair as Latif offered him an ashtray. He removed the gunmetal case that was as much a fixture on his person as his beloved Walther, removed a cigarette with the three distinctive gold bands made by Tor Importers, and held the case open for Latif. The Ronson lighter appeared and lit both cigarettes.

"The Union killed someone close to me," Bond said flatly. "They almost killed me. They've made it personal. I want them. That's all."

Latif looked at Bond a long time before saying, "My friend. You realize that when they make it personal, it becomes too dangerous. You lose objectivity. That's when you need to step back and let someone else handle the job."

"I hear you, Latif, but I can't do that. That's not all. Last night, I'm pretty sure the Union tried to set me up for murdering a woman in London—a doctor."

Latif's eyes narrowed. "So let me understand this . . . you're on the run?"

"You might say that," Bond said. "I'm looking for answers."

"Do you even know what the questions are?"

"I'm making them up as I go along."

That caused Latif to smile. "My friend, James. Don't worry. You can trust me. I will help you in any way I can."

After a bit of silence, he spoke again. "You know, I read somewhere . . . I think it was on the Internet . . . that if we could shrink the earth's population down to a village of precisely one hundred people, with all the existing human ratios remaining the same, the results are quite extraordinary. I was so struck by the revelations that the numbers are permanently imprinted on my brain. There would be fifty-seven Asians and twenty-one Europeans. There would be only fourteen people from the entire Western Hemisphere, both north and south. There would be eight Africans. Of these hundred people, fifty-two would be female, forty-eight male. Seventy would be nonwhite, thirty white. Seventy would be non-Christian, thirty would be Christian. Eighty-nine would be heterosexual, eleven homosexual. Fifty-nine percent of the village's wealth would be in the hands of only six people, and all six would be Americans. Eighty people would live in substandard housing. Seventy would be unable to read. Fifty would suffer from malnutrition. One would be near death, one would be near birth. Only one person would have a college education, and only one would own a computer."

Reggab let that sink in, then said, "When one considers our world from such a compressed perspective, the need for both acceptance and understanding becomes glaringly apparent."

Maliza brought food to the table and beckoned to the men. They sat down to a meal of chicken curry with rice, served with bottled sparkling water. Bond knew that Latif, purportedly a devout Muslim, didn't keep alcohol in his home. He wasn't adverse, though, to slipping into bars with Bond for the occasional drink.

"I'll tell you what I know about the Union," Latif said. "Everyone is becoming scared of them. They are the number-one priority with Interpol. The Union have gained a lot of power in the past couple of years."

"Yes."

"I think they're in Casablanca. It makes sense. It's the financial center of Morocco. It's a port and has the largest airport."

"Do you think *Le Gérant* is Moroccan?"

"Yes. Partly, anyway. I've been waiting for some more information before I submit my report on the Union to London. I think I know who *Le Gérant* is."

Bond's heart skipped a beat. "Do tell."

Latif shrugged. "I'm not sure yet. You see, I'm a Berber. My people came from the Rif Mountains. I have heard talk of a man, a Westerner, whose mother was Berber. He came to the mountains some years ago and was regarded as some kind of prophet. The word was that he had a French father who had once served in the government here during the Second World War. Anyway, this man, they say, is blind, but he possesses extrasensory powers that normal human beings do not have. He had tremendous influence over some of the tribes in the mountains. He took many people with him and disappeared back into Western civilization."

"Do you know his name?"

"If it's who I think it is, his name is Olivier Cesari."

"A French name? Corsican?"

"Corsican. Although he was born into the Berber tribe, he was raised and educated in France by his father. He probably has a Berber name as well, but I don't know it."

"How did you find this out?"

"Well . . . for one thing . . ." Latif said, smiling devilishly, "I went to university with Olivier in Paris."

"Really?"

Latif nodded. "It's true what they say about him. Tremendously gifted. He was an excellent student, extremely intelligent. He studied law, as I did, but changed to economics. And I remember him walking on campus with a stick, never bumping into anything. Once I came into the classroom and he was the only one in there. I didn't say anything, and after a few seconds, he greeted me by name. Uncanny."

"Why do you think this man is *Le Gérant?*" Bond asked.

"I don't know," Latif said. "As I said, I've heard these stories from the Riffians about this so-called prophet. In fact, that's what they called him in the mountains. *Prophet.* Unfortunately, no one has seen him in fifteen, twenty years."

"We should go ahead and have London investigate him."

"They already have. I put in the request a long time ago. According to official records, Olivier Cesari disappeared from Paris when he was in his twenties."

"Which was . . . what, thirty years ago?" Bond surmised.

"Right. Olivier is my age, roughly, which is fifty."

Reggab's mobile rang. He answered it, speaking in Arabic. After a few short exchanges he hung up and said, "Your two men came through Customs last night, all right. So they're in the country."

"How do we find them?"

"My source at the airport said that they took a taxi toward Tangier. That's all we know. But don't worry. I have eyes and ears all over this country. Let me make some calls this afternoon."

Latif's youngest son came in with an overnight courier envelope. "This came for you, Papa."

"Thank you, son," Latif said. He examined it, his brow wrinkling. "Now what is . . . ?" He opened it and found a large brown envelope inside. "Ah. It's for a case I'm working on. These are the photos I was expecting."

"Anything interesting?"

"In a way. There's a strange campsite in the mountains, between the villages of Chefchaouen and Ketama. It sprung up there about a year ago on some land that's owned by a private company. A bank. Anyway, it's like a compound—they have it surrounded by barbed wire and the dirt road leading to it is guarded off the main highway. It looks like soldiers are in training there, but no one has got close enough to make sure. I've been ordered by London to find out if it's some kind of terrorist training camp."

Latif shared the photos with Bond. They were eight-by-tens in black-and-white and looked as if they had been shot with a camera hidden in someone's clothing. The lighting was bad, as they were obviously night shots and had depended on the little illumination made by a couple of spotlights at the scene.

"These are quite good, considering the location of the camera," Latif said. "We had to put it in Rizki's *tarbouch.* He's one of the men who helps me. I had him stationed on the hill above the entrance to the camp. It's quite a way off the main road. He was to take photographs of everyone going in and out."

The photographs, obviously blown up from a smaller size, showed various figures at a checkpoint gate. Bond could make out tents, lean-tos, and campers within the compound. Among the figures in the shots were men in military fatigues sitting in a jeep, being waved through by two guards dressed in traditional Berber *jellabas.* The guards were carrying automatic weapons, but it was difficult to discern what they were.

Bond flipped through the photographs and stopped at the last one. It showed two Caucasians in business suits getting out of a taxi at the gate.

They were Walter van Breeschooten and Michael Clayton.

"Latif, when were these photos taken?" Bond asked.

"Last night. Rizki got them to me quickly, he's a good—"

Bond slapped the photo. "These are the men I'm looking for!"

"Really?" Latif took it and stared. "That's incredible!"

"How soon can we get to this camp?"

"We'll have to go after dark. Is tonight soon enough?"

For the first time in days, Bond smiled and breathed a sigh of relief.

ELEVEN

SWIFT SETTLEMENT

It was midafternoon when M rang off with the Prime Minister and Miss Moneypenny buzzed.

"Yes?"

"Chief-of-Staff is here and would like a word."

"Send him in."

M was still thinking about the conversation that she had just had when Bill Tanner came into the office and sat down. He was carrying a folder and had an odd expression on his face. M sat up, instinctively sensing that something was wrong.

"I have some disturbing news, ma'am," he began.

"What is it?"

"Have you heard about the murder of the young doctor in Harley Street last night? The police and building superintendent found her body this morning. . . ."

"I heard something on the news. What about it?"

"She was one of ours."

"What?"

"Dr. Kimberley Feare. She was a colleague of Sir James Molony. He's away and Dr. Feare had taken over some of his cases."

"I remember her name on some reports."

"I've just had a look at the police report. Ma'am, it was a particularly brutal murder. There is one detail in particular that concerns me."

"What is that?" M was a bit shaken by this news.

"Her throat had been cut, Union-style."

"My lord, what could they want with a girl like her? She was young and new, wasn't she?"

"Just the type the Union go for. If she was involved with the Union, we could have some security problems again."

M cursed. Bill Tanner rarely heard her do it, but this wasn't the first time and it surely wouldn't be the last.

Tanner shifted in his chair.

"There's something else, isn't there?" M snapped.

"Yes, ma'am," Tanner said. "It's Double-O Seven, ma'am."

"What about him?"

"He may be involved."

"What do you mean?"

"Dr. Feare's nurse reported that Bond had called her office yesterday, insisting on an appointment. Preliminary investigation has shown that he was seen with Dr. Feare last night in front of her building."

"Is that true?"

"Well, we don't know. The porter at the building remembers her coming home in a taxi and being approached by a man on the pavement. He accompanied her inside the building and he matched the description of Double-O Seven."

The expression on M's face indicated that she simply didn't know what to say.

"As you recall, Dr. Feare diagnosed Bond's condition after his return from the Himalayas. That's all we know, except that Double-O Seven doesn't call back when we page him," Tanner said. "We think . . . we think he's missing."

Finally M burst out with, "I don't believe a bloody word of this."

Tanner tapped the folder. "It's all here in the police report. MI5 is being brought in to the case."

"Who alerted the police in the first place?"

"It was an anonymous phone call. Someone called the police and said that a woman had been murdered. They gave Dr. Feare's address and hung up."

"The real murderer, no doubt. Where was Double-O Seven?"

"The porter saw him leave the building after midnight, if that's what you mean. There is one puzzling piece to the porter's statement."

"What is that?"

"He says that after he had seen Dr. Feare and the man enter the building, an hour or two later he saw the same man, alone, coming into the building with a key. The porter thought that he had probably missed seeing him leave the building the first time, perhaps on an errand to fetch a bottle of champagne or something, and that Dr. Feare had given him a key to use upon returning."

"What do you mean?"

"If it *was* Double-O Seven, he was seen going into the building twice. Once with Dr. Feare, and a second time alone and with a key. Doesn't that sound strange?"

"Indeed. The porter was mistaken, I should think. How long has Bond been seeing this woman on a social basis?"

"I have no idea. This is the first I've heard of it. He met her when he visited Sir James's office."

She tapped her fingers on the desk a moment. "Well. There he goes again, mixing business with pleasure. I shall have his hide."

"I'm afraid the government will have more than that if he's charged with murder, ma'am."

She looked at him incredulously. "You're not serious. James Bond is *not* a murderer. Not that kind. Surely you agree that he could *not* have done this?"

Tanner nodded. "Absolutely, ma'am. It's extraordinary."

"They can't possibly realistically suspect Double-O Seven. . . ."

"He's wanted for questioning, ma'am. We have to try and find him." Tanner frowned again and added, "There's something else that disturbs me."

"What?"

"The attendant in the small arms cage down in Q Branch reported a firearm missing this morning. A Walther P99, along with its holster and some Glaser ammunition. The last man seen in the cage yesterday was Double-O Seven."

"Are you implying that Bond stole a gun?"

"I'm afraid that's what it looks like."

M shut her eyes and rubbed her brow, attempting to take it all in. Finally, she pushed her chair back from the desk. "On top of all that, we have to deal with the Gibraltar situation. I was just on the phone with the PM. He has decided to accept the offer to go there for a meeting with this Espada fellow, the Spanish Prime Minister, and the Governor of Gibraltar. We're to send someone to accompany him as an extra bodyguard."

"I'll take care of it," Tanner said. "I think Double-O One is free." He got up to leave, still carrying the police report. M stopped him and held out her hand.

"Oh, right," he said, handing it to her. He, too, was disturbed by what the day had brought.

After he had left the room, M began to study the contents of the folder with trepidation.

Set astride the awesome hundred-meter-deep El Tajo gorge amid the beautiful Serranía de Ronda mountains, the enchanting village of Ronda bathed in the rays of the late afternoon sun. About an hour's drive north of the southern Spanish coastline on a winding, mountainous road that cut through forests of cork and *pinsapo* trees, Ronda is said to be the birthplace of the art of bullfighting. Indeed, the oldest bullring in Spain, Ronda's Plaza de Toros, serves as a monument and symbol of the quaint community. Ernest Hemingway and Orson Welles (whose ashes were spread over Ronda per his wishes) loved the town. One of Spain's most prestigious matadors, Antonio Ordoñez, had his ashes scattered *in* the bullring, in accordance with his desire to give the bulls the pleasure of stepping on his remains after he was dead.

Today, the bullring was filling up with spectators. Even though it was Wednesday and not Sunday, an exciting *corrida* was scheduled for 6:30 P.M., and one of Spain's rising stars had top billing. Everyone in town had turned out for the bullfight and many fans from Marbella and Málaga had made the trip to Ronda.

However, before the bullfight, the audience was subjected to a political speech delivered by Domingo Espada. As promoter and manager of the most influential matadors in the country, he was able to do things that no one else dared to. He had been traveling through the provinces and making impassioned pleas to the people to join his party, demand that Gibraltar be ceded to Spain, and reform the current government. The people didn't mind. To them he was a legend. He was *Espada.*

A surprising number of men always volunteered to join Espada at these political rallies. It helped that Espada pretended that matadors all over Spain gave him their full support.

Just southeast of the bullring stands the magnificent Parador de Ronda Hotel, perched on the edge of the gorge. Just beyond a railing, the cliff plunges down steeply to the valley of the Río Guadalevín far below. The best rooms in the five-star complex featured balconies looking out over the dazzling view. It was the most fashionable place to stay in a town where celebrities often went for a little quiet and beauty.

Margareta Piel walked across the plaza in front of the Parador, where tourists and locals sat at tables having drinks and tapas. A large number of police were positioned there as well, for the matadors staying at the hotel were on a par with rock stars; very often fans could become a nuisance.

All of the men turned their heads to look at Margareta as she walked through. She was dressed in a sleek black bodysuit that showed off her every curve, and was wearing a dark backpack and sunglasses. She knew that people, and the police, would notice her entering the hotel. They always noticed her.

There was still an hour to go before Espada's speech. She would have preferred to perform the business at hand under the cover of darkness, but time did not permit it. She strode into the lobby as if she knew where she was going, past the bellboy, who stopped and stared, and snaked around the lounge to the lifts, got into an empty one and pressed the button for the second floor.

Inside room 214, a deluxe suite built on two levels, like a townhouse, a naked man and woman were finishing a pleasurable primal ritual.

Roberto Rojo rolled off the girl, who had said her name was Maria. The sweat was beaded around her forehead, and she was still breathing heavily, her breasts moving up and down with the heaving of her chest as her heartbeat began to subside. Rojo sighed, "Oh man, oh man," then pulled her closer. She snuggled up to him, wrapping one slinky leg over his torso. Maria had been extremely lucky that Roberto Rojo had taken a liking to her at Domingo Espada's ranch. While leaving her family to "work" for Espada had seemed, at first, like a good idea, it had turned out to be a nightmare. She had become his concubine and he could do whatever he pleased with her. It was horrible and degrading. One day, Roberto Rojo and his brother, Javier, came to visit Espada. They were two of the most popular matadors in the country. At twenty-three, Roberto was fast becoming a superstar. His sultry looks had been plastered all over the covers of the major Spanish magazines, and his private escapades often found their way into the tabloids.

"I'm not letting you go," she said playfully. "Forget the bulls tonight, all right?"

Rojo just laughed. "Are you kidding? I will make a million *pesetas* tonight. Providing I'm not killed, of course."

"Aren't you frightened?"

"Certainly. But not of the bull. I get stage fright. I'm afraid of the people in the audience. I don't like to be booed."

She laughed. "They never boo you. You're a hero to them."

He shrugged, "Yes, well . . . Still, it's more of a challenge to go out there in front of all those people than to face a charging bull."

The phone rang. He groaned and picked it up.

"Sí?"

The voice on the other end was muffled. "Señor Rojo?"

"What is it?"

"You have something that belongs to your manager," the voice said. "Señor Espada asks that you give it back."

Rojo sat up, nearly knocking Maria off of the bed. "You tell that son of a bitch Espada to leave me alone! He's a crook and a liar and a madman. He has single-handedly given the art of bullfighting a bad name. After tonight's *corrida,* I'm through with him. I'm changing managers."

"We beg you to reconsider, Roberto. Your life may depend on it."

"Is that a threat? Are you threatening me?" Rojo was furious. How dare they call him here! "How did you find me, anyway? How did you know what room I was in?"

"That doesn't matter now. So, do we take it that your answer is no?"

"That's right, it's no!" He slammed down the phone. "Bastards," he muttered.

"Who was it?" Maria asked, a little frightened at the show of temper.

"Someone who works for my ex-manager," he said. "Espada knows you're here. I don't know how he found out, but he did. He wants me to give you back."

Her eyes widened with fright.

Roberto kissed her. "Don't worry. I won't." He kissed her again. "Espada is trying to control his matadors in ways that he shouldn't. It's part of his grand plan to get his party elected. I'm supposed to be there in time for his speech and stand up there with him. He thinks that if the matadors are part of his political machine, then the rest of the people will follow him, too. Most of the *toreros* I know can't stand him. He's double-crossed them, cheated them, and disgraced the art."

Rojo got up and slipped on the terry-cloth robe that the hotel supplied. He opened the doors to the balcony and stepped outside. He deeply inhaled the fresh air and used the serenity of the landscape to help calm down.

"Want to take a shower together?" Maria called.

Rojo thought that was an agreeable suggestion. There was still time before he had to get to the bullring.

He went back into the bedroom and gazed at the naked girl on the bed. Perhaps he had time for one more. . . .

"Let's do it again first."

She laughed. "Roberto! You are a machine! No, thank you. You have worn me out. I'm taking a shower."

Maria got up and went into the bathroom. Roberto was about to follow her, but there was a knock on the door downstairs.

"Christ, who could that be?" he muttered. He bounded down the wooden stairs into the living room. Without bothering to look through the peephole, he unlatched and opened the door.

An absolutely stunning woman with long, flowing dark hair stood in the hallway.

"What do—oh, hello," he said.

"Roberto Rojo?" Margareta asked, smiling seductively.

Oh, he thought. She was a fan. She probably wanted his autograph.

"How did you find me?" he asked. "The hotel is supposed to keep autograph seekers like you away." He didn't recognize her, as Margareta had never met him when he had visited Espada's ranch.

"I was very determined to see you," she said.

"Well. Normally I would turn you away, but since you are so beautiful . . ."

He held the door open and gestured for her to enter. She sauntered in, pausing to run her index finger along his chin as she walked by him.

"Oh, I see you're not alone," Margareta said, indicating the sound of the shower upstairs.

"Uhm, no," Rojo replied. "Another fan. You know how it is."

"I sure do," she said. "Now. I want you to sit down in this chair while I take my clothes off for you."

"What?"

"You heard me. Sit in this chair." She pointed to one of the living room chairs facing the television.

"But what about . . . ?" he asked, pointing upstairs.

"We'll ask her to join us," Margareta said. "If she's not interested, then she can leave."

Rojo laughed and practically jumped into the seat. The terry-cloth robe parted, revealing his tight, muscular body. Margareta moved around in front of him and let the backpack slip off to the floor. Then, she slowly pulled down the zipper on the front of the bodysuit, from her neck all the way to her crotch. The suit parted, revealing her shiny, tan skin. She was wearing nothing underneath.

Rojo's eyes bulged as he swallowed loudly.

Margareta stepped out of the suit, kicked it behind her, and then straddled his lap. She ran her hands up and down his chest and leaned in to kiss him.

As he closed his eyes and explored her mouth with his tongue, Margareta guided him into her. Rojo's grunts and moans quickly covered the sound of the shower upstairs as the strange woman rocked back and forth on his lap; leisurely at first, then faster and harder.

Margareta allowed herself a cry of pleasure as she climaxed with him. They remained motionless for a minute, clutching each other.

"What is your name?" he asked breathlessly. His eyes were closed.

She slowly disengaged from his body as the sound of the shower stopped. She reached down to the backpack and unsheathed a knife that was fastened to it. She brought it out and readied it.

"Some men call me *Mantis Religiosa,*" she said.

Rojo opened his eyes. "Why?"

She paused a second, holding his chin up in her left hand. "Because of what those insects do to their mates. Oh, I almost forgot. I'm here to deliver a message from Domingo Espada."

With that, she swiftly drew the knife across Roberto Rojo's throat. Blood shot out in an arc, drenching them both.

Rojo's eyes bulged in horror. His hands grabbed at his neck as he fought for air and made horrible gurgling sounds. Margareta stood back as he slipped off the chair onto the floor, gagging and struggling for life. Margareta placed her foot on the back of his head and kicked it into the floor. That shut him up. He would die in silence.

Then she realized that she had unintentionally killed him the "Union Way." Margareta had heard stories of how the Union would sometimes make a statement by leaving a victim with a cut throat. Would this be interpreted as such? She smiled. It would be a good joke on Espada. Why not? She would soon be a full-fledged member of the Union. She was merely "between jobs."

She had forgotten about Maria until there was a scream on the stairs behind her. Margareta turned to see the wet, naked girl, recoiling in horror at the bloody sight.

Margareta slowly ascended the stairs as Maria fell to her knees on the steps, trembling with fright.

Margareta silenced the girl with one swift slash of the knife.

She then stepped over the body and went into the bathroom. She paused long enough to step into the shower and wash the blood off her body. Back downstairs, she dressed quickly and put on the backpack, then returned to the bedroom and walked through the open balcony doors.

It would not do to stroll back through the hotel lobby and outside in full view of the police.

The valley was one hundred meters below. It was a breathtaking vista.

Margareta reached behind and pulled straps from the backpack, fastened and adjusted them, then stepped up onto the balcony edge. She held herself steady and concentrated on what she was about to do.

BASE-jumping was illegal, but many daredevils liked to attempt it. A BASE rig allowed one to jump from a low altitude, such as a building or a cliff, and use a parachute to land. Margareta's rig was a Precision Dynamics "Super Raven 4" canopy, which was especially well suited for BASE-jumping. The low aspect ratio chute had been free-packed to ensure against "bag spin" or "bag lock" and enhance the odds of a straight-ahead opening. Even so, she had made sure the rig was set with deep and multiple brake settings so that it would fly slowly. That would buy her time to react if the canopy were to open pointing her toward the deadly cliff face. The slider had been removed to give almost instantaneous inflation of the canopy, but to soften that opening jolt, the chute was made of nonzero porosity fabric.

Margareta raised her arms wide, holding the rig's pilot chute in her right hand. She leaped from the balcony as far out as possible and dropped into the abyss. Once she was in midair, she threw the pilot chute out into the air stream. The nine-foot bridle line was long enough to ensure that the pilot chute would easily clear the burble of air. As the bridle line snapped taught, it dragged the canopy out of the pack.

The chute snapped open before Margareta had fallen one hundred feet. The seven-cell, ram-air canopy allowed her to glide like a hawk. She floated down to the valley, where a white Percheron stallion was waiting for her. He was tied to a tree, saddled and ready to go. Margareta flared the chute steeply and lightly touched down in seconds. She stripped off the backpack, and untied the horse. She took a moment to pat his neck and whisper quiet endearments in his ear, then she mounted the beautiful beast.

She looked up at the hotel on the edge of the cliff. Now the sky was a bright orange and blue, as the last rays of the sun streaked across the panorama. It would be ten minutes or so before the bodies were found. By then, she would be long gone. The bellboy and other eyewitnesses might recall seeing a beautiful woman dressed in black come through the hotel lobby . . . but they wouldn't be able to say whether or not they saw her leave.

Margareta jabbed the horse with her heels, and it galloped away into the hills.

TWELVE

THE CAMP

Just before the sun set, Latif Reggab and James Bond drove off in a Land Rover on the main road that led southeast out of Tangier. As they drove toward the Hispanic-Moroccan city of Tetouan, the landscape became more hilly and green. It was a two-lane road populated by numerous slow-moving lorries, and Reggab muttered a prayer under his breath every time he attempted to pass them. After about half an hour the road became steeper and more twisting as they traveled higher into the Rif Mountains. Occasionally the hillsides were spotted with groups of stone houses and clusters of goats or sheep herded by *jellaba*-clad men. Bond noticed that the only landmarks along the road were petrol stations and the occasional checkpoint, where officers in gray uniforms, the *gendarmes,* sometimes stopped vehicles to look for drugs or check identity cards. Taxis were often targets for these random stops, due to regulations that restricted where certain types of them could go.

"Take a good look before it gets dark," Reggab said. "Very beautiful scenery driving into the Rif. Unfortunately, there are all these slow trucks."

Bond noticed that a *gendarme* waved the Land Rover through a checkpoint.

"They all know me," Reggab explained. "It is sad that such beautiful country is the main source for *kif.*"

Kif, Moroccan slang for marijuana, was the region's biggest export.

"Smoking that stuff is an ancient tradition in northern Morocco," Reggab said. "The cultivation is tolerated because it's the only way the people there can make a living. The government is searching for alternative crops, but until then . . ." He shrugged.

They came upon Tetouan an hour after they had left Tangier, but Reggab took the road south, higher into the mountains. Twenty minutes later, Reggab pulled over and stopped at a group of white buildings. The sun had nearly set, but Bond could see some activity behind the structures.

"This is a souq," Reggab said. "It's closing down for the evening, but there's a man here I need to see. It concerns our mission, tonight. We won't be long."

Bond was grateful to get out and stretch his legs. The headache was holding steady, even though he had miraculously caught three hours of sleep that afternoon in Latif's spare bedroom. He had washed and shaved after the nap, then prepared for the evening's excursion by dressing in dark clothing, strapping a Sykes Fairbairn commando knife to his shin, and carrying the P99 in a holster at his waist and the PPK under his arm, plainly visible.

The souq's "parking lot" was filled with mules. The flea market itself was made up of dozens of tents, *berrakas* (canopies supported by four poles), and lean-tos. The Berber tribes had come down from their various mountain homes to sell their wares. Many of them were packing up now, as the business day was finished.

Reggab led Bond through the crowd, shaking his head at the veiled women who were holding and offering live chickens. They came upon a tent where a man in a *burnous* was pouring spices into containers. Reggab and the man spoke Arabic and embraced each other, and then Reggab introduced Bond.

"This is my friend Khalil."

"Hello . . . how . . . are . . . you?" Khalil said in rehearsed English.

Reggab and Khalil continued to speak in Arabic. Reggab reacted to some news with dismay. The conversation continued as Bond wandered a few feet away to gaze upon the extraordinary sights of the souq. Only in countries like this could one see a market that was no different now than the way it was hundreds of years ago. Once one got away from the major cities, Morocco offered such cultural diversity that it would take Bond years to discern between the various tribes and ethnic groups.

Reggab took Bond's arm and said, "Let's go."

When they got back in the Land Rover and drove on, Reggab said, "I just heard some upsetting news. Rizki, my man in the mountains, was found dead this afternoon. They think he was seen taking those photographs last night, and whoever runs that camp was responsible."

"I'm sorry," Bond said. "They killed him for taking the pictures?"

"The strange thing is that he had been dead at least twelve hours. A courier sent that envelope this morning. That means someone other than Rizki took care of sending me the photos."

This revelation sent off alarms in Bond's mind. "You have no other people in the Rif?"

"No. Rizki was the only one."

"Then the enemy must have made sure you got those photos. Why?"

"I don't know. Maybe we'll find out."

A little less than an hour later, they arrived in the quaint village of Chefchaouen, which was known as the "blue city." This was because the walls of the buildings were painted blue four or five times a year. The blue paint supposedly kept the interiors cool in the summer and warm in the winter.

"Chaouen is one of my favorite places in Morocco," Reggab said as he pulled the Land Rover onto a main artery entering the city. "I think I will retire here. We are going to stop a moment, all right? I need to pay respects to Rizki's family."

The blue-washed houses were built up a gentle slope that culminated in a magnificent mountain overlooking the entire village. In the moonlight, they appeared to be ghostly, luminescent structures floating above ground level.

Bond followed Reggab into the medina, which was now sparsely populated and dark. The odors of the day's produce lingered, and Bond wondered if they ever went away. After a couple of twists and turns in the path, they came upon a baker's quarters. Reggab knocked on the door. When it opened, an older man almost said something nasty to the stranger who was disturbing the family's grief, but he recognized Reggab and embraced him warmly.

As is common in Morocco, the door was set into a frame in the wall so that one had to step over a sill to enter the building. A family of six or seven men and women were inside, all mourning the loss of their loved one. Reggab spoke quietly with the older woman, whom Bond presumed to be Rizki's wife. Mint tea was offered, and Reggab and Bond felt obliged to stay for a while. Bond was sorry for the family's loss and that one of Latif's operatives had been murdered, but he was anxious to get to the campsite.

Finally, Reggab made his excuses and stood up to leave. He embraced each family member and led Bond away with a loaf of bread in each hand.

On the way back to the Land Rover, he said, "Rizki's body was found on the side of the road near the camp. His throat had been cut."

The men exchanged glances, knowing full well what that implied.

The journey continued eastward toward Ketama, which was supposedly the hub of *kif* activity in Morocco. At one point, an intimidating black Mercedes appeared from nowhere in front of them, moving slowly. Reggab slowed down and was forced to follow closely behind the Mercedes. The narrow, winding road was treacherous in the dark, and even the most courageous of drivers would think twice before overtaking. Before Reggab could attempt it, the Mercedes stopped abruptly. Reggab slammed on the brakes and turned the wheel to avoid ramming the back of the car. Three rough-looking characters got out of the Mercedes and approached the Land Rover.

Bond was ready to draw his gun. Reggab put his hand on his

friend's arm, indicating that he had it under control. He leaned out the window and spoke quickly to the men in Arabic. Reggab spat words at them, after which they appeared to apologize, bowed, got back into the Mercedes, and drove away.

"What was that all about?" Bond asked.

"They wanted to sell us a kilo of *kif,*" Reggab replied. "If we hadn't agreed to buy it from them, there was a possibility that we would have been forced to do so. They thought I was a guide bringing a tourist into the mountains. When I explained that I was a 'policeman,' they decided to leave us alone. Don't worry; it happens all the time. You just have to know how to handle these characters."

An hour later, the nearly full moon cast a chilling glow over a dark landscape filled with large, ominous black shapes. They were in the very heart of the Rif Mountains.

"We are almost there," Reggab said. He peered through the windscreen, concentrating, as the road was inadequately illuminated by the headlamps. Finally, he pointed and said, "There. That's our landmark."

In the brief moment in which it was visible, Bond had seen a *berraka* built on the side of the road. At least one mule was hitched to the side and there had been a light—a campfire?—just in front of the *berraka.* It had been impossible to see how many human beings might have been there. Bond guessed two.

"They look like a couple of shepherds. The sheep are over there, on the side of that hill, you can barely see them in the moonlight."

Bond said, "I see them."

"They are really some kind of lookout for this camp. The turnoff is up ahead."

"Won't they report having seen you?"

Reggab shook his head. "This is still a major highway. The amount of traffic that comes through would not be worth keeping track of."

"Unless what you're trying to hide is important enough," Bond suggested.

Reggab grunted in agreement and made a sharp right onto a pitch-black dirt road. It wound around a mountain and eventually came to a bridge. Reggab slowed and parked the Land Rover beside the entrance to the bridge.

"The camp is just on the other side of the bridge, about a kilometer away. There's a gate there with at least two guards. Now. We're going to get out here and climb this mountain. Up there you can get a good view of the place. There's no fence on that side of the camp. The mountain serves as the barrier."

"Lead the way," Bond said. Before getting out of the Land Rover, he took four of Dr. Feare's pills. The headache gauge was climbing upward toward the "excruciating" mark.

Without the moonlight, climbing the mountain would have been impossible. They settled on a ledge near the top. The camp was approximately forty meters down the south face of the hill. Several campfires were burning amidst tents, *berrakas,* and some portable buildings. A number of jeeps, four-wheel drives, as well as horses and mules, were set off to one side. Bond could faintly hear Moroccan folk music coming from the largest tent, which was big enough to hold a circus ring.

Reggab handed him a pair of field glasses. Bond put them to his eyes and adjusted the infrared brightness. He could now see men walking about. They were dressed mostly in army fatigues. Many of them looked European or North American. Others were dressed in traditional Arab or Berber clothing. They all carried guns.

"Latif, I think you're right about this being some kind of terrorist training camp," Bond said. "Those men are armed. How do the police let them get away with this?"

"It's private property," Reggab whispered. "Whoever owns it apparently has more influence over these parts than the government. If the Union is behind it, then there is a lot of money to throw around. Morocco is not a wealthy country, so it's very easy to bribe the officials. Look, that big tent is where they feed everyone. It serves as a mess during the day and a bar at night. We know that prostitutes are brought in some nights, and they leave in the mornings. If we could get some hard evidence that they are harboring heavy arms, we could maybe do something. So far, though, all the weapons you see are legal." He pointed to a relatively flat area. "Sometimes helicopters land there in that field. It's used during the day for training; the men are always out there exercising. Some target practice goes on, and we really can't get them for that."

"I'm going down to take a closer look," Bond said, handing back the glasses.

"I can't let you do that, James. It's too dangerous."

"You can't stop me, Latif. Look, meet me back at the Land Rover in thirty minutes. I have to try and find these men. I'll be as discreet as possible."

"If they catch you, you will be on your own. I am sorry."

"I understand. You must protect your cover. Now go on, I'll be all right."

Reggab hesitated, then shook Bond's hand. "Good luck, my friend. I shall see you soon."

Bond didn't wait for Reggab to leave. He moved swiftly down the rocks, darting from one shadow to another. Seven minutes later, he was at the base of the hill, near a dilapidated shack that smelled of excrement. A man in fatigues came out of the shed, buckling his pants. It was obviously the latrine.

Bond stealthily crept behind the shed, then followed the man by scrambling from tent to tent, keeping to the shadows. A laundry line was stretched behind one *berraka.* Bond pulled off a dark *jellaba* and put it on. If they caught him, at least he would look the part. The man ultimately got to the big tent, where the music was much louder. There were at least thirty men out in front with drinks in their hands, and inside the place was packed. Hoots and catcalls could be heard over the live band.

A festive bar atmosphere just might provide the camouflage Bond needed. Determinedly, Bond put the hood on, then walked right through the crowd and into the tent as if he knew exactly what he was doing. The men ignored him as they talked in Arabic and laughed.

A makeshift stage had been erected at one end of the tent. A four-piece band was performing behind a buxom belly dancer who attracted the gaze of every eye in the bar. One man played the *amzhad,* a single-chord violin made of wood and goatskin; two musicians played typical Arab and Berber drums, the *darbuka* and *tebilat.* The fourth man played the Arab lutelike instrument, an *oud.*

Bond wandered through the crowd, scanning the faces for someone familiar. After five minutes, he was about to give up and try somewhere else when a tall blond man came in and went to the bar. It was the Cockney from London—one of the thugs from the adult bookshop's office!

Bond waited until the brute had bought four bottles of beer, then followed him outside. He was almost certainly taking them to his bosses. . . .

The man crossed through the tents toward one of the small portable buildings. Bond took a detour around the latrine and came up behind the building. He was in luck—a window was open. Bond positioned himself at the edge and carefully looked inside.

The man had just delivered the bottles to Walter van Breeschooten and Michael Clayton. They were sitting at a card table playing poker. Wads of dirham notes were piled in front of them.

"Thanks, Rodney," Clayton said. The blond man grunted and left the little building. Bond waited and listened.

"I still don't understand why we couldn't stay in a hotel in the city," the Englishman said.

"This is only for tonight. Will you shut up?" van Breeschooten replied.

"I just don't know what we're doing here!"

"All will be clear tomorrow. We can't leave until . . . you know . . ."

"Until he shows up, I know . . ." Clayton said. "How do we know he will?"

"The strategist is always right," the Dutchman answered. "Now. We'll be splitting up tomorrow. You have the address in Casablanca?"

"Yes, I have it written down. It's in my pocket."

"Don't go to the Central Market. That entrance is closed. You have to go to the medina."

"We've been over this already."

"I just don't want you to get lost. We have to be there at eight in the morning, sharp. Day after tomorrow."

"I know, I know. I have to go and piss."

"Hurry back."

Bond heard Clayton leave the building, then crouched below the sight lines of the windows and moved to the edge of the building. Bond stepped out onto the path, assuming a normal stride behind his prey as he headed for the latrine. When Clayton went in, Bond followed him.

The man went into the smelly stall. Bond reached down and unsheathed the commando knife, which he had previously bound to his shin. He waited until Clayton was finished. When he stepped out of the stall, Bond grabbed hold of him and put the blade to his neck. He shoved him into a dark corner of the latrine.

"Mr. Clayton," Bond said. "Do you know who I am?"

Clayton's eyes were wide with fear. He nodded.

"I want the address of the Union headquarters in Casablanca. Give it to me or I'll carve out your Adam's apple and feed it to the mules."

"It's . . . it's in my pocket," Clayton stammered.

"You get it," Bond said. "No tricks."

The man reached into his trousers and pulled out a slip of notepaper. Bond took it and noted the address.

"Thank you," Bond said. "Now you have to answer for Helena Marksbury."

"Oh, God, please, no!" the man cried. "I didn't do it, I swear! It was Walter. My partner. He's the real Union man. He's one of the *commandants.* I just work for him. I swear. It was all his doing. I just followed orders."

"And did you kill her?"

"No, I swear," Clayton pleaded. "It was Walter. He did it. He does all the dirty work like that. He . . . he *likes* it! Please, don't hurt me!"

"And what about Dr. Feare?"

"Dr. Feare?"

Then Bond remembered. Clayton and van Breeschooten had already left London by the time Kimberley had been killed.

"Do you know who killed her?" Bond applied a little more pressure with the knife. The blade made a small nick in Clayton's neck.

"I don't know anything about Dr. Feare! I swear!"

The man seemed to be telling the truth. He was too frightened not to.

"*Why* was she killed? Was she Union?"

"I don't know! Maybe my cousin does! Please have mercy!"

"Who's your cousin?"

Bond heard voices approaching. At least two men were on their way inside. He had run out of time.

Clayton heard them and started to scream for help. Bond savagely sliced the man's neck, then stabbed him in the heart.

"There's your mercy. I made it quick," Bond spat.

Clayton gasped, his eyes bulging, then fell to the floor. Bond wiped the knife clean on the man's clothes, then walked out of the latrine just as the two men were stepping inside. One of them said something in Arabic and Bond grunted.

As soon as he was outside, Bond began to run. He heard shouts behind him, and the two men ran out of the latrine in pursuit. Bond zigzagged through the groups of tents and headed toward the hill. Shots were fired, and then a siren wailed.

A big man appeared in front of him and shouted, "Hey!" It was Rodney. Bond kicked, swinging his foot in the shape of a crescent moon. There was a discernable *crack* as he connected with Rodney's jaw. The man screamed and fell to the ground. Bond leaped over him and kept running.

Two floodlights snapped on and began to sweep the area. Men were running about in a state of confusion. What's the trouble? What happened? An intruder? Where?

Bond made it to the cliff just as a floodlight beam passed over him. There was more shouting, and two bullets whizzed uncomfortably close and ricocheted off nearby rocks. He didn't stop, praying that he could stay ahead of the light. It found him anyway, and it stayed with him as he ascended.

Bond turned with the Walther in hand to aim at the floodlight, but realized that he was out of range. More bullets chopped up the earth around him. He tried to roll out of the spotlight and keep climbing, but the light followed him to the top. Fortunately, he was up and over before any of the men could stop him.

He ran for the bridge, crossed it, and was never so happy to see a Land Rover waiting for him.

"Are you all right?" Reggab asked.

"Yes, let's get out of here!"

They jumped into the vehicle and fired it up. Reggab spun the wheels and took off. They heard more gunfire behind them. Bond looked back and saw three pairs of headlamps.

"They're right behind us. Step on it!"

"I'm going as fast as I can!" Reggab shouted.

The Land Rover made it to the main highway. Reggab swerved out of the dirt road and skidded on the gravel, straightened, and sped west toward Ketama. As they passed the landmark *berraka,* two men with automatic rifles stepped out into the middle of the road and began firing in their direction. Bullets broke the back window and took out a taillight. The three pursuing vehicles were gaining fast. They appeared to be jeeps, but it was really too dark to tell for certain.

Bond leaned out of the window and fired the Walther at them, but the road had too many bends. He couldn't get a good bead on them.

He sat back in the cab and said, "We're just going to have to outrun them."

"No problem," Reggab said, clutching the steering wheel. "Better fasten your seat belt."

But one of the jeeps had gained ground and was not far behind. More bullets slammed into the back of the Land Rover. There was a loud boom, the recognizable sound of a blowout. The Land Rover swerved and screeched as Reggab struggled to gain control. To avoid sailing off the cliff into a dark abyss, he pulled the wheel toward the mountain. The Land Rover sideswiped a rough patch of rocks, causing it to topple onto its side. The vehicle slid for twenty feet and crashed into the mountainside.

Bond was dazed. The first thing he was aware of was the sound of the Land Rover's blaring horn. Then he smelled the petrol leaking out the back. Bond looked over at Reggab. His friend was slumped forward, his head bent grotesquely. There was a bullet hole at the base of his skull.

Without another thought, Bond kicked at the passenger door above his head. He got it open and struggled to pull himself out. The three jeeps had stopped thirty yards away. Men with guns piled out and stood watching him.

Bond fell to the ground and crawled away from the Land Rover. He fought to get to his feet, but the sudden pain in his head and chest prevented him from doing so. He reached up and felt the sticky, wet blood in his hair. He collapsed on the road just as the Land Rover's petrol tank exploded behind him and the sudden waves of heat rolled over his body.

One of the men in uniform ran to him and dragged him across to the side of the road. Bond was woozy, unable to fight back. He felt his shirtsleeve being unbuttoned and rolled over. There was the prick of a needle, and in a moment he felt nothing.

THIRTEEN

ALL-POINTS ALERT

James Bond opened his eyes.

Three alley cats were eyeing him suspiciously. When they saw that the human was awake, they scurried away.

The smell of urine and rotten eggs was overwhelming.

It was dawn. Bond could hear roosters crowing in the distance. His surrounding were bathed in the dim light of the new day.

He was lying on something scratchy.

Bond rose carefully. His head was spinning wildly, and he had a massive headache. Where the hell was he?

It was a street. A medina. He was lying on a pile of hay used to feed mules. Bond recognized Latif's shop across the little street and down a few doors.

He was back in Tangier! *How did he get here?*

Bond got to his feet and found that he was steadier than he expected. He took stock of his body. To his surprise, the Walther PPK was in the shoulder holster and the knife was in its sheath. His passport was in his pocket.

Hold on . . . the P99. It was gone. The holster on his belt was empty.

There were some cuts and bruises and a crusty wound on his head from the Land Rover wreck, but otherwise he seemed to be in one piece.

Again.

What the hell?

How did he get here? Could the Union have brought him here? If so, *why?* Wouldn't they have left him to die, or better yet, made sure of it?

Then he remembered the needle. He had been drugged.

Bond was convinced more than ever that something extraordinary was going on. Someone wanted him alive. In London, he had distinctly heard Clayton and von Breeschooten order their thugs not to shoot at him. After the Land Rover crash outside the terrorist training camp, he remembered seeing several vehicles and armed men surrounding him before he had succumbed to his injuries. They had put him to sleep and then carted him back to Tangier. It was the only possible explanation.

Bond wearily stumbled to Latif's shop and went inside. Reggab's son Hussein was shocked at Bond's appearance.

"I'm sorry," Bond said. "I have something I need to tell your mother."

The boy knew what the problem was just by looking at Bond's face. He immediately embraced Bond and sobbed. Bond held the boy and stroked his head before going inside to break the news to the rest of the family.

An hour later, Bond was back on the street, dressed respectably, and feeling as refreshed as he possibly could. He walked out of the medina so that he could catch a taxi to the railway station. Once again he examined the piece of paper he had taken from Michael Clayton. The slip said: "14 Ville de Casablanca." The Union headquarters.

As he entered the Grand Socco, he noticed that there was a high concentration of police cars circling the square. There seemed to be excitement in the air. People were rushing about and shouting. Something had happened.

He caught a Westerner and asked in French, "What's going on?"

"Terrorists on a ferry," the man said. "Some men shot a bunch of British tourists last night."

"What?"

"That's all I know. They're looking for the gunman."

Bond went to the nearest newsstand and bought an English newspaper.

He couldn't believe what he saw on the front page. *It was madness! Utter madness!*

The headline read: "TERRORISTS KILL BRITISH TOURISTS!" What was more disconcerting was a police drawing of a suspect who had fled the scene of the crime.

The man in the drawing looked just like Bond.

Bond quickly scanned the article to glean the details. Apparently, the ferry was on its way from Spain to Tangier. Sometime in the late evening hours, three armed men had taken control of the ship. Witnesses described them as "two Spaniards and an Englishman." The men entered the dining room and called for everyone with a British passport to come with them. There were ten in all—six men and four women. The men marched them to the front of the dining room. The British terrorist announced to the crowd, in English, that what they were doing was in the name of Domingo Espada of Spain. The man then called for an immediate surrender of Gibraltar, or war would break out between Spain and Britain. He then said, "This is the first strike." With that, he shot each and every British tourist, one by one. The two Spaniards held the rest of the crowd back with their weapons.

After the murders, the three men ran out of the room and hid somewhere on another deck. When the ferry got to Tangier, the police stormed the boat. Panic ensued as gunfire erupted all over the ship. The two Spaniards were killed, but the Brit slipped away unseen. He might have escaped with the crowd of frightened passengers who rushed the gangway after the incident.

Eyewitnesses described the unidentified Briton and the police were looking for the man shown in the drawing.

Bond dropped the paper in a dustbin and kept walking.

Christ! he thought. This was all becoming too bizarre.

As he couldn't possibly have done that horrible deed, someone was obviously impersonating him. The Union was behind it. That had to be the answer. It was some kind of diabolical plot, and he was a part of it. The only way to uncover this mystery was to go to Casablanca and find the Union headquarters. He would kill everyone in the place if he had to. Walter van Breeschooten would be number one on the hit list.

"*SmeH leeya! Inta!*"

Bond looked up and saw a policeman ten feet away, walking toward him. Without a second's hesitation, Bond turned and ran. The policeman called on him to halt in Arabic and French and the chase began. Bond crossed the square and ran up stone steps that connected to a major avenue, Rue de la Liberté. The traffic was heavy, and Bond used this to his advantage by darting in and out between cars. Horns blared and drivers shouted at him as they slammed on the brakes to avoid hitting him. Bond glanced back and saw that the policeman was still in pursuit. He forged ahead, running down the avenue to the Place de France roundabout, then turned southeast onto Boulevard Pasteur and ran across a bridge overlooking the Grand Socco below. Another set of stone stairs led back down, so he took them three at a time. Bond ran past men selling piles of silver, smelly fish, then slipped into a crowd of veiled women. They screamed as he pushed through and turned a corner, finding himself in a narrow alley. He stopped and pressed himself against a wall, attempting to catch his breath. He waited, hoping he had lost the policeman.

"Put your hands up!" The voice came from the other end of the alley. It was the policeman. He must have known another way around. He held a handgun and was calmly walking toward Bond.

Perhaps the smartest thing he could do at this point was surrender, Bond thought. He should let London handle it. Surely Bill Tanner would believe that Bond had not committed those crimes.

Bond slowly raised his hands. The policeman had a glint in his eye. He had caught the terrorist!

A gunshot rang out, reverberating in the narrow alley. Bond was confused—at first he thought that the policeman had fired his gun. Instead, the officer stumbled and dropped his firearm. A red splotch spread across the man's chest, and he fell to the ground. Bond looked around frantically, trying to pinpoint where the shot had come from. There were some windows in the building overlooking the alley, but they were dark.

He scanned both ends of the alley. They were clear. Rather than ask questions, he decided to keep running. He backed out of the alley and ran back to the square, and then climbed up the stairs to Boulevard Pasteur. He hailed a taxi and told the driver to take him straight to the railway station.

The station was crowded with commuters coming into the city from the outskirts. Bond bought a one-way first-class ticket to Casablanca. His timing was perfect. He could catch a rapid-service train in one hour. Now he only had to stay unnoticed in the waiting area.

At least three policemen were patrolling the station, probably looking for him. Bond went into the gift shop and purchased a pair of cheap sunglasses and an American-style baseball cap with "Morocco!" stitched on the front. It wasn't much of a disguise, but it would have to do for now.

Bond spent the rest of the hour in the small snack bar, where he had a mediocre breakfast of eggs and yogurt. Nevertheless, the food made him feel better, and he thought that perhaps he could get some sleep on the train. If only the damned headache would go away . . . as well as the nagging feeling that he was being watched.

He took his time with the breakfast, then made his way out to the platform, where the ONCF express to Casablanca sat waiting. The trains in Morocco are modern and reliable. They are painted red and yellow with black tops, and the compartment classes are clearly marked on the outside. Bond got into the only first-class carriage and found his compartment. For the moment he was alone, but there were five other seats. He had purposefully asked for a nonsmoking compartment, thinking that it might be less crowded. If he wanted a smoke, he could go out into the corridor or stand on the platform and look out the back of the train.

Before long, the train began to move. The conductor came by and punched his ticket without saying a word. Bond settled into his seat and silently watched the scenery.

He felt more alone than he had ever felt in his life.

"It can't be him," M said, looking at the police sketch of the terrorist suspect.

Tanner shook his head. "I don't believe it, either."

"We need to determine if Double-O Seven really went to Morocco. Still no answer from Station NA?"

"No, ma'am. I've left three messages. If Mr. Reggab is anywhere around, he should have got back to me."

The intercom buzzed. M pushed the button. "What is it?" she snapped.

"An urgent communication came in from Cipher. I'm sending it through on your PC," Moneypenny said.

"All right, thank you," M said.

Tanner looked over M's shoulder as she punched the keyboard and Bond's coded message came up.

LATIF REGGAB, STATION NA, KILLED BY THE UNION.
PLEASE MAKE ARRANGEMENTS FOR HIS WIDOW ASAP.
WILL REPORT WHEN I KNOW MORE.

007

M punched the intercom again.

"Moneypenny, where did this message come from?"

"Somewhere strange," her secretary said. "Wait a second . . . here it is. Thailand."

"Thailand?!"

"Cipher thought that it had been routed through several countries so that we wouldn't know where it originated from."

"Thank you."

Tanner sighed. "Well, I doubt it came from Thailand."

"He's obviously in bloody North Africa!" M said. "You were right. That fax from Felix Leiter indicated as much. Double-O Seven's going against my orders and is off on a mission of personal vendetta."

Tanner sat down in front of the desk. He had found Leiter's fax in Bond's office, as well as the other documents concerning the Union.

"I think you need to look at it from his perspective, ma'am," he said gently.

"I understand his perspective!" she spat. "It doesn't mean that he can compromise SIS and my orders. Have you spoken to Inspector Howard today?"

"No, ma'am. As far as I know, Double-O Seven's still the number one suspect in Dr. Feare's murder."

The red phone rang. M picked it up and said, "Yes?" She listened intently for a moment, then said, "Thank you," and hung up.

Tanner waited for her to speak. She looked at him with concern and said, "A group of Spanish tourists were attacked in London a couple of hours ago. An angry mob surrounded them in Piccadilly. One man was killed."

"My God."

"The PM has asked that the summit meeting in Gibraltar be moved up. We're waiting on the exact date and time, but it will probably be in a day or two. In the meantime, NATO and the U.N. are urging restraint."

The intercom buzzed again. "Now what?" M asked.

"Captain Hodge is here. He says it's urgent," Moneypenny said. Hodge was the head of the antiterrorism section at SIS.

"Well, send him in. I can only imagine . . ."

Captain Hodge, a tall man in his fifties, walked into the room.

"Good morning, ma'am, Chief-of-Staff," he said.

"What do you have for us, captain?" she asked.

"It's not good, I'm afraid." He held up a videocassette. "Something you ought to look at."

M gestured to the VCR and monitor on the cabinet to her left. "Be my guest."

Hodge popped in the cassette and turned on the monitor. The picture was grainy and black-and-white, shot from a security camera. Numerals indicated the date and time of the recording.

"This was recovered from the ferry's camera in the dining area where the shootings occurred. It happened on Deck Seven, also known as the 'boat deck.' "

They could make out a number of people dining at tables. There was a bar in the background.

"The Comarit ferry left Algeciras, Spain, at approximately seven o'clock last night. There were fifty-three passengers and eight staff. Most of them were Spanish or Moroccan citizens. The ten British citizens were businessmen and women in the hotel industry. You can see them sitting together at that table, there." Hodge pointed to a large round table. "Now watch carefully."

Three men came through a passage and entered the dining room. Two of them were strangers, but the third appeared to be James Bond. The trio produced automatic weapons and began to shout. There was no sound on the tape, so M and Tanner had to imagine what was being said. The reactions of the people in the room told all. Many of them ducked down under the tables. Finally, the British citizens stood warily and produced their passports to Bond. He then ushered them to the back of the room. The two Spaniards forced them to stand against the bar, their backs to the room. James Bond then stood behind them and opened fire, killing them in cold blood.

"My God," M muttered.

As soon as the deed was done, Bond turned to the room and said something else. Then he did something strange. The killer placed his handgun on the counter. Hodge froze the frame, pressed a button, and zoomed in on the gun.

It was a Walther P99.

"Is that your missing handgun?"

Tanner squinted. "It's a P99, all right."

"The killer left it there on the counter, its magazine empty. We should have the serial number in an hour or two and we'll know if it's a match," Hodge said. Then he manipulated the frame and zoomed in on the terrorist's face.

Up close, there was no mistaking those features.

"We've positively identified the man as Double-O Seven," Hodge said. "We think that after the shootings the three of them went down two levels, past the saloon deck, to the car deck. They probably hid inside a car or lorry until the ferry docked at Tangier. There were very few personnel aboard the ferry, so there was nothing they could do. Once the boat got to Tangier, the police boarded, but someone started shooting. It's still not clear what happened. The two Spaniards were killed, but Bond was nowhere to be found."

"Damn it, it's got to be a mistake!" M said. "Someone must be impersonating him!"

"Bond wouldn't do this, Captain," Tanner said.

"Nevertheless, I urge you to bring him in," Hodge said.

"Is there anything else?" M asked.

"Yes." Hodge handed a report to Tanner. "These are the police records on the two Spaniards. As you can see, they have a history of terrorist acts. If you'll look at the most recent information on the ugly one, you can see that it's unlikely that these men were working for Domingo Espada."

Tanner and M read it together. One of the men was wanted in Israel for a bombing. The Union had later claimed responsibility for it.

"The Union," M said flatly. "Of course."

"They're trying to stir things up between Britain and Spain," Tanner suggested.

"But why? What's in it for them?"

Tanner shrugged. "Revenge?"

"We need to get this information to the PM and to Spain. It might help alleviate the tension if they know that the Union was behind this attack, not Britain," M said.

"I'll get on the phone right away," Tanner said.

"What about Double-O Seven?" Hodge asked.

M set her jaw. "We have to hope that all of this is a tremendous error, but we also have to assume the worst. We must accept the possibility that Bond has joined the Union. They've been successful in recruiting our people before. I would be remiss in my responsibilities if I didn't issue an all-points alert for the apprehension of Double-O Seven."

FOURTEEN

JOURNEY BY RAIL

The train rolled out of Tangier and headed south along the coastline toward Rabat. Bond stared wearily at the passing scenery, which grew flatter as the journey progressed. For the first time in hours, he had a chance to sit and mull over the events of the past two days. He wished that he could relax, but he was wound up like a coil.

It wasn't long before he craved a cigarette. He got up and left his compartment, made his way through the narrow corridor and stepped out onto the rumbling platform at the back of the train. He removed the gunmetal case, took a cigarette, and lit it.

Had his career finally come to an end? he asked himself. Was it time to give it up? Had he begun to pay the price for living on the edge for so long? He had seen it in other agents. Something in them finally snaps and they have to put in for early retirement. Was this happening to him? Was he absolutely certain that he could beat this thing on his own? What if he really *was* going insane?

Stop it! he commanded himself. Don't be ridiculous. It's some kind of Union plot . . . it's obviously some kind of Union plot. . . .

Bond's thoughts were interrupted when an attractive blonde opened the door and joined him on the platform. She didn't look at him or speak; she dug into a handbag, found her own cigarettes, and attempted to light one.

"Allow me," he said. He produced the Ronson lighter and cupped the flame close to her face.

She got it lit and said, "Thank you."

For a moment, they stood there in the open air, enjoying that exhilarating sensation of watching the tracks rush away from the train.

"I get claustrophobic on trains," she said. "Smoking in the corridor isn't cool even though everyone does it. I'm in a smoking car, but it's just too crowded. I like to smoke but I don't like to live in a cloud of it. I had to get some air."

She had an American accent. She seemed to be in her mid- to late twenties.

"I know what you mean," Bond said. "You're welcome to join me in my compartment. It's nonsmoking, I'm afraid, but there's no one else in there."

She eyed him up and down, then smiled. "That was the quickest pickup line I think I've ever heard."

"Forgive me," Bond said. "I didn't mean it that way. My name's Cork. John Cork."

She looked him up and down again, then smiled once more. "Hello, John Cork. My name is Heidi Taunt."

"It's a pleasure," Bond said. "What brings you to Morocco from the States?"

"How do you know I live in the States?"

"I assumed that you're American."

"I'm a California girl, born and raised, but I don't live there," she said. "We live in Tokyo."

Hell, Bond thought. She was married.

"My sister and I," she added. Heidi looked back through the window into the corridor. "What about you? You sound English."

"I live in London," Bond admitted.

"You don't look English."

"How does one look English?"

"I don't know," she said. "I just meant that you don't look English *here,* in Morocco. You have that 'dark, handsome foreign stranger' quality." She shrugged and smiled.

She was flirting with him!

Heidi Taunt was tall and well built. She was wearing designer jeans, which tightly outlined her long legs without revealing too much and offending the social sensibilities of the Moroccans. She had on a white blouse with the sleeves rolled up. The top two buttons were undone, exposing substantial cleavage.

Her shoulder-length blond hair was fine and straight, parted in the middle. She had dark brown eyes that exhibited intelligence and a sense of humor. Bond found her incredibly sexy.

"So what brings you from Japan to Morocco?" Bond asked.

"My sister and I are travel guide writers. We've done a series of books on various countries. Perhaps you've seen them? The *Small World* books?"

"I can't say that I have. Sorry."

"That's all right," she said. "We've only done four. This is our fifth. We're published in America and Britain."

"That sounds like a fun job."

She finished her cigarette and tossed the butt onto the tracks. "It is. It's more work than you think, though. It's not just traveling to exotic places. The business side of it is overwhelming. But you're right, it's great fun to travel. We hope to visit every country in the world, my sister and I."

"That's quite an ambition."

"I know, it's impossible, but we like to imagine it."

"Where are you going? Rabat?"

"No, to Casablanca. To Marrakesh after two nights. Rabat on the way back. What brings you here?"

"I'm an importer and exporter," Bond replied.

"What do you import and export?"

"Junk, mostly. A whole lot of nothing."

She laughed.

Bond offered the cigarette case to her, but she shook her head. "No, thanks, I'm going back inside. It was nice to meet you, Mr. Cork." She held out her hand. Bond took it.

"Call me John. It was a pleasure, Heidi. Where are you staying in Casablanca?"

Her hand was smooth and cool. She allowed him to hold it.

"The Royal Mansour Meridien."

"What a coincidence!" Bond said. "That's my hotel, too."

"Small world," she said, smiling wickedly.

Actually, Bond hadn't thought about where he would stay, but he knew the hotel. It was one of the best in Casablanca. Staying at a large five-star hotel like that might be what the authorities looking for him would least expect him to do. And if he happened to have a girlfriend . . . ? A perfect cover, one the police weren't looking for . . .

She withdrew her hand, turned and opened the door. "Maybe I'll see you there."

"Heidi," Bond said, stopping her. "Would you care to have dinner with me at the hotel tonight? It has a lovely Moroccan restaurant."

"Why, thank you, John, that sounds terrific. I'll see you later, then."

And she was gone.

Bond congratulated himself. His way with women had not changed. Screw the headache, he thought. There was desire in that girl's eyes!

Bond finished his cigarette and went back inside the train. He made his way back to his compartment, which was still empty, and he collapsed heavily into his seat. He put his feet up on the opposite seat and looked out the window at the passing rows of cacti, which seemed to be more plentiful as the train went farther south. The color of the earth changed, too, as the climate became hotter and more arid.

He shut his eyes and felt merciful waves of drowsiness pull him toward unconsciousness. The movement of the train, combined with physical exhaustion, lulled Bond into a fitful but badly needed sleep.

When he opened his eyes, the train was still rocking and rumbling toward its destination. He felt another presence in the compartment with him.

Heidi was sitting across from him, with a seat between hers and the one where his feet were propped. She was reading a romance novel and had on reading glasses; otherwise she was still dressed in the tight jeans and white blouse.

"Hello there," Bond said, sitting up and straightening his jacket. "I must have dozed off."

She glanced at him and gave a cursory smile and nodded, but kept silent. Her eyes went back to the book.

Odd, Bond thought. What was the matter with her?

"So," he said, "what time are we having dinner?"

The blonde looked up at him over her glasses. "I beg your pardon?"

"Dinner? Tonight? At the hotel? What time?"

Heidi opened her mouth as if she had just been insulted. She closed her book and stood. "I think I'll go back to the compartment I was in before." She opened the door and stepped into the corridor. Her parting words were, "You have some nerve, asshole." Then she walked on.

What the hell? Bond rubbed his eyes. Did he dream that?

He felt foolish and confused.

Dizzy woman, he thought. Well, she had admitted being from California. She had probably grown up on the beach, wearing skimpy bikinis and giving all the teenaged boys inflexible frustration. To hell with her . . .

The train stopped in Rabat, Morocco's capital. There was a half-hour wait before it departed, so Bond took the opportunity to don his sunglasses and baseball cap and stretch his legs. Rabat station is larger and has more amenities than the one in Tangier. He scanned the newspapers in the gift shop but couldn't find one in English. A French paper proclaimed that war between Britain and Spain was imminent. There was a photo of Domingo Espada, surrounded by bodyguards, giving a speech at a bullring. Several matadors were standing beside him.

Bond recognized one of them. Javier Rojo was a young bullfighter whom Bond got to know by accident just a few years ago at an art gallery in Lisbon. Bond's date had been a friend of the artist. Apparently Javier's date was, too. They had met at the bar, where Bond was busy with a vodka martini in an effort to avoid the small talk of the art crowd. Rojo was having a soft drink, and he turned to Bond and said, in English, "The only alcohol I drink is wine at dinner."

"Why?" Bond had asked.

"You have to be sober to do what I do."

He was a handsome, fiery young man in his mid-twenties, and he had come from a long line of bullfighters. His grandfather had been one of the most famous matadors in Spain until he was killed in the ring. Rojo's father was also a very successful bullfighter who had passed the torch on to his two sons when he retired. Javier Rojo was wealthy, popular, and as much a celebrity as one could be in Spain.

Bond blinked when he saw the headline of a related story on the inside of the paper. "ROBERTO ROJO MURDERED."

That was Javier's younger brother!

Bond read with incredulity how the young matador and the body of an unidentified young girl had been found slain in his hotel room in Ronda. According to the police, the bullfighter's "throat had been cut."

It was the Union way. Could it be a coincidence? Bond wondered.

He thought back to the beginning of his friendship with Javier Rojo.

That night in Lisbon, Bond and the young bullfighter had struck up a conversation and found that they got along well. Bond had always held the art of bullfighting at arm's length until Rojo had enlightened him. Like most non-Spaniards, Bond was of the opinion that bullfighting was both cruel and archaic. This notion changed after Rojo convinced Bond to come to a *corrida* and watch him fight. Rojo had taken the time to teach Bond the history of bullfighting and its traditions, and why the Spanish were so passionate about it. After a week as Javier's guest, Bond began to see why men like Ernest Hemingway and Orson Welles had become fascinated by bullfighting. Bond grew to appreciate the art and drama behind the spectacle, and he admired the courage of the matadors who risked their lives to face a charging bull.

Bond studied the newspaper carefully. So Javier Rojo was in with Domingo Espada now. Bond wished that he didn't have the Union to deal with. Otherwise, he could be in Spain, seeking out Espada and stopping him from instigating this idiotic conflict between their two countries. Perhaps Rojo could be of help.

Bond sighed. He couldn't think about that now. He had other, more important things to worry about. Britain would deal with Spain. If war broke out, it would be over quickly. NATO or the U.N. would negotiate a settlement. Bond didn't have to worry.

Or did he? The terrorists aboard the ferry in Tangier—they had claimed that they were working for Domingo Espada.

The police sketch of the suspect was also on the front page. The caption said that the "British terrorist was still at large." Although he hadn't been identified yet, there was some speculation that he was with British secret intelligence.

Wonderful, Bond thought. He wagered that the press would know his name within a day.

He rejoined the train after eating a dry roast beef sandwich and drinking a Spéciale Flag beer. His compartment now had three new people in it—a man, his veiled wife, and a small boy, who was already fussing over a toy that his father had taken from him. Bond wasn't about to stand for that, so he excused himself and went back out to the corridor as the train pulled away from the station.

He went to the rear of the train to smoke another cigarette and watch the remnants of Rabat disappear. Trains were Bond's favorite means of traveling if he couldn't drive a fast car. There was something old-fashioned and romantic about train travel. Airplanes simply dropped a person in the middle of a location. With trains, one was injected into the bloodstream of a country, and enabled to see the people and places and cultures. It took more time to get around, but it was far more gratifying.

The door to the corridor opened behind him and Heidi Taunt came out to join him.

"Hi there," she said, brightly. She was smiling broadly, as if the earlier encounter in the train compartment had never happened. "We've got to stop meeting like this."

Bond didn't say anything, wondering what her game was. He did offer her a cigarette, which she took.

"Thanks," she said. "Hey, what time do you want to meet for dinner?"

Even more confused, Bond said, "Eight o'clock?"

"Fine," she said. "The Moroccan restaurant. I can't wait to see the King Hassan II mosque. I hear it's one of the wonders of the world. Have you seen it?"

"Yes, it's lovely," Bond said. "But I must say that Casablanca is not my favorite city in Morocco."

"I hear it's not so great," she concurred. "Marrakesh is supposed to be *the* place to go. I hear Fes is nice, too."

"You're right on both counts." Bond finished his cigarette. Why was she so friendly now, when just a little while ago she had treated him with disdain?

Without warning, she said, "Excuse me," and reached up to remove Bond's sunglasses. She peered at his face, studying it. "I just wanted to see your eyes. They're very sexy." She handed back the sunglasses. "Here you go."

She stubbed out her cigarette and tossed the butt into the air. She squeezed his arm lightly and said, "See you tonight, handsome." She reentered the train, leaving Bond dumbfounded.

Bond took the time to smoke another cigarette, then went back inside. He didn't feel like sitting in his compartment, so he walked through the first-class car and entered the adjoining second class. It was very crowded. He moved through the people standing in the corridor and went on into the next car.

He saw Heidi coming toward him, holding a soft drink she must have purchased from the food and drink cart.

"We're going to be in the gossip magazines if we keep bumping into each other like this," Bond said with a smile.

Heidi looked at him as if he were the rudest man alive. "Stop following me or I'll call the conductor," she said much too loudly. She pushed past him, opened a compartment door, and went inside.

Bond squinted and rubbed his brow. What the hell was going on here? Why the hot and cold treatment? Was she some kind of nut?

His old friend, the headache, was returning. He rubbed his temples, turned around, and went back to the first-class car. He rejoined the family in his compartment and sat in his seat, glumly looking out the window.

After six hours, not including the stop in Rabat, the train pulled in to Casablanca Voyageurs station, located four kilometers east of the city centre. It was midafternoon, and the place was buzzing with activity—commuters were trying to get home, tourists were catching the next express to another destination in Morocco, porters and guides were attempting to hustle business. . . .

Bond got off the train and looked around for Heidi. He didn't see her in the mass of people. The train had filled up at Rabat, and now there was a rush of passengers trying to get on for the next leg of the journey.

He went outside into the warm air and hailed a taxi. The driver took him to Le Royal Mansour Meridien on Avenue des FAR, easily one of the most exclusive five-star hotels in the city. Ten stories high, it lay in the heart of the city's business center and bore the name of Ahmed Mansour Addabhi, the most glorious line of Saadi monarchs.

Bond registered as John Cork in the circular reception space. The lobby was a large open hall, much like a cloister, with blue square divan pieces surrounding a thick marble column. The lobby was very bright, accentuated by the mirror panels set in a geometric pattern around the room. An indoor waterfall at the back and numerous potted plants created a garden atmosphere.

There was a message for him at the concierge desk. It was hastily scribbled on hotel stationery and read, "Dinner at 8:30 instead of 8:00. OK? Heidi."

Fickle woman, Bond thought. He had a good mind to stand her up.

He took the lift to the third floor, where his suite was located. Bond was impressed with the size and tastefully decorated room. The suite contained a functional office, sitting room, bedroom with twin beds, and a bathroom tiled in white marble.

This would do nicely, Bond thought, but he needed a drink. His head was still pounding and he needed to unwind.

Rather than use the minibar, Bond took the lift to the ninth floor. La Terrasse, a bar overlooking the city, offered a superb view of the vast flat rooftops with antennas and satellite dishes, the splendid Hassan II Mosque, and Casablanca harbor. Bond ordered vodka with ice and sat at one of the tables to gaze upon the metropolis.

Bond didn't like the city, but he appreciated its history. Originally called the port of Anfa, Casablanca had been created by Berbers. From the mid-nineteenth century onward, Casablanca became one of the most important ports in Africa, and once the French Protectorate took over in 1912, it had the biggest harbor in Morocco. Casablanca is now the fifth largest city on the continent.

Bond whiled away the remaining hours watching CNN in his room. The news was full of the British/Spanish conflict. Spanish tourists had been mobbed in London. The border between Spain and Gibraltar had been declared a no-man's zone. All traffic across the border had been stopped. The Royal Navy patrolled the waters of the Mediterranean. The U.S. president had offered to broker a settlement. At the center of it all was the man who had sparked the trouble—Domingo Espada. He was seen in parades, marching with his supporters, calling for the return of a Franco-inspired government. The administration in Madrid had finally spoken out against Espada, claiming that he was a "rebel." They were sitting on their hands, though, choosing to wait and see what was going to happen.

Plans for the summit meeting in Gibraltar had gone awry when the Spanish Prime Minister refused to sit at the same table with Espada. The king of Spain was intervening, and it looked as if the meeting would finally take place in four days, on Monday. Attendees would include Espada, the Spanish PM, the British PM, and several United Nations representatives from interested countries in the area.

It all seemed so far away and unimportant to Bond. At the forefront of his mind was the Union, the score he needed to settle, and the nagging fear that he was going mad.

Never mind, he thought. His rendezvous with Walter van Breeschooten was tomorrow morning.

At 8:30 sharp, Bond went down to the restaurant, Le Douira, which was designed as two distinct representations of Moroccan culture. One side was in a genuine caïdal tent, and the other was decorated in intricate blue and white tile work, like the inside of a traditional Moroccan palace.

Bond had decided he would confront Heidi about her erratic behavior on the train. He wasn't about to put up with games, no matter how attractive a girl might be.

He waited for ten minutes and finally heard Heidi's voice behind him.

"Here we are, sorry we're late."

Bond turned and blinked. He thought he was seeing double.

"John," Heidi said. "I'd like you to meet my sister, Hedy."

Now everything was clear. Hedy was Heidi's identical twin.

FIFTEEN

"AS TIME GOES BY"

The two girls had identical faces, but Hedy had short red hair, which Bond quickly decided was really a wig.

"*This* is the guy?" Hedy asked her sister.

"Hedy, this is John Cork," Heidi said, beaming. "It's okay that my sister came along, isn't it?" she asked Bond.

Bond couldn't help but laugh. "I believe we've already met but didn't realize it. You weren't wearing the wig on the train, were you?"

"No," Hedy said. She folded her arms and looked at Heidi with a frown.

Heidi said, "Oh *no,* not again! This happens all the *time!* Damn it, Hedy, that's why we never have any boyfriends."

"You'll pick up *anyone,* Heidi! He made a pass at *me* out of nowhere. I thought he was a pervert," Hedy said, glaring at Bond.

"I'm sorry, John," Heidi said. "It really *does* happen a lot. Men have a problem telling us apart. It's a sore subject with us both. That's why we sometimes take turns wearing the wig. It's not that we compete with each other, it's just that whoever we happen to be dating always ends up hitting on the other one, usually by accident."

"Sometimes *not* by accident," Hedy added.

Heidi agreed and nodded. "It can be a problem. I guess we should have used the wig on the train."

She was right. Hedy was an exact copy of Heidi in every respect. They were both wearing full-length, relaxed fit-and-flare sundresses made of ribbed cotton, buttoned in front down to their knees. The only difference was that Heidi was in gray and Hedy was in black.

"Well, the wig helps, but have you considered dressing differently?" Bond suggested wryly.

Hedy looked at Heidi and said, "He's a wise guy, too, Heidi." She turned back to Bond and asked, "How do we know you're not a serial killer?"

"Ladies, please," Bond said. "My apologies, Hedy, if I offended you earlier today. It was not intentional. As you say, you do look uncannily like your sister. Now, if you're saying that your dilemma is that the same man falls in love with both of you, I can understand why. Might I suggest a reasonable solution to your problem? That would be to agree to share the man, and I'm afraid that's just what you'll have to do this evening. Let's have dinner, shall we? I'm starving."

Heidi laughed, but Hedy remained unreceptive. She followed along grudgingly when the maître d' asked them to first wash their hands, the Moroccan way, with a pitcher and basin. They were then shown to the tented side of the restaurant, where they sat on cushioned seats at low tables. Heidi commented on the beautiful décor and Hedy said, "Let's hope the food warrants it."

As it turned out, the food was excellent. For starters, they shared *panaché de briouates aux crevettes,* a variety of puff pastries stuffed with shrimp, chicken, and minced meat. Bond had *tagine de kebab maghdour aux oeufs,* a traditional Moroccan dish of meat kebab in a spicy paprika sauce with a fried egg on top. It was served in a *tagine,* the Moroccan pot shaped like an inverted top. Heidi had roasted rack of lamb, and Hedy opted for chicken with couscous. The girls insisted on drinking cold beer, so it was Spéciale Flag all around.

"So does this meet your expectations?" Heidi asked her sister.

"It's pretty good," Hedy admitted, finally cracking a smile.

They exchanged the usual sort of small talk that occurs when people are meeting one another for the first time. The girls talked about growing up in California, as Bond suspected, on the beach. They had been models when they were children, doing print and television ads for a variety of products.

"We were cute kids," Heidi said.

"You still are," Bond added.

"But we decided to join the real world when we became teenagers," Hedy explained. "We both liked the traveling part of the modeling jobs, so that's what we decided to do. We're pretty good travel writers, if I say so myself."

"I do most of the PR because Hedy says I'm more bubbly than she is," Heidi said. "Hedy does the lion's share of the writing. We both do the research. We make a good team."

"We've always been inseparable," Heidi explained. "We do everything together."

"Everything?" Bond asked.

"Not everything," Hedy quickly answered.

"If we ever disagree on something, we flip a coin. Heads I win, tails she loses."

"Very funny," Hedy said.

There was a moment's silence before Heidi said, "Mr. Cork says he's an importer and exporter."

"Oh?" Hedy asked. "And what exactly does that mean?"

Bond shrugged. "I make sure things go in and out. Smoothly." Heidi grinned at Bond. Hedy caught the exchange and frowned.

"Seriously," he continued, "I work for a firm in London that deals with arts and crafts. Carpets, mostly. There's a man in Tangier we buy from. I need to see someone in the medina tomorrow. I arrange the deals and let others deliver."

"You were in Tangier last night?" Hedy asked.

Bond nodded.

"Did you hear about what happened on that ferry?"

Bond felt a sudden stab of paranoia. Had she been reading the papers? Had she recognized him?

"Yes, I heard about it this morning."

Heidi shook her head. "It was terrible. . . ."

Looking at Bond, Hedy said, "I hope they catch the guy who did it."

"Me, too," Bond said, meeting her gaze. She was studying him intently. Had she seen the drawing in the newspaper? Was it safe to be in their company?

The girls shared a piece of chocolate cake for dessert and they all had coffee. A live band had begun playing traditional Moroccan folk music. Finger cymbals rung throughout the restaurant, casting a mesmerizing and exotic charm over the diners.

"Do you go back to London after you're through here, John?" Hedy asked.

"I think so," Bond said. "I may . . . I may be sent somewhere else. I'm not sure yet."

"What should we do now?" Heidi asked cheerfully. "The night is young, as they say." She winked at Bond.

"The night is quickly fading," Hedy said. "Come on, Heidi, I want to hit the sack."

"Hedy! It's so early!"

"We have to get *up* early, remember? We have that guided tour of the city. . . ."

"Big deal. I'd rather stay up and hang out with Mr. Cork." Heidi was a little tipsy from the beer.

"I don't think so, sis. I'm sure Mr. Cork needs to go to bed early, too," Hedy said.

"Hedy, don't be rude," Heidi said. "I know, let's flip for it."

"Please, Heidi."

Heidi looked at Bond, shrugged, and shook her head, as if she were asking, "What am I going to do with her?"

"As a matter of fact," Bond said, "I am a bit tired. Bit of a headache, too. I think Hedy has the right idea. I'm sorry, Heidi, but I'm afraid I will be retiring after dinner, too."

"Well, shoot," Heidi said. "Here I am in the city where 'As Time Goes By' came from, and I have to go to bed early."

"Heidi, *Casablanca* was made in Hollywood," Hedy said, rolling her eyes.

Bond insisted on putting their meals on his bill, for which Heidi was overly grateful and Hedy seemed resentful. He bid good-bye to the girls as they walked to the lift.

"We're in room 415, if you can't sleep," Heidi said with a giggle.

"Heidi . . ." her sister groaned.

Bond got off at the third floor and went to his suite. He had enjoyed the girls' company, but there was something odd about them that he couldn't quite place his finger on. The wig business was a bit strange. He didn't completely buy their explanation for their taking turns wearing it. Hedy could be a problem, but he wasn't going to worry about her. He didn't think she would try to turn him in to the authorities, even if she did suspect him of the terrorist attack. It was too bad he couldn't have found a way to be alone with Heidi. She seemed rather spirited . . . but after further thought he knew that he needed to rest. She probably would have kept him up all night. . . .

Bond undressed, took a warm bath, took four of Dr. Feare's tablets, and got into bed naked, his Walther PPK safely underneath his pillow. He fell into a deep, troubled sleep and dreamed fitfully about his double. The other Bond was pointing a gun at him and smiling malevolently. Heidi and Hedy were on either side of him, laughing. The gun went off and Bond thought he was falling into a dark, bottomless pit.

That's where he stayed until the alarm clock woke him at six o'clock.

At 7:45, Bond stood on the street called Ville de Casablanca inside the medina, watching the exterior of the address on Clayton's piece of paper. The door was part of a large building with several shop fronts. *Berrakas* had been built in around several of them, including number 14. Various wares were displayed for sale, but number 14 was curiously empty. The door itself was cloaked in shadow and couldn't be seen.

A beggar sat cross-legged just on the outside of the *berraka,* a tin plate with a few coins in front of him. He didn't look particularly homeless; on the contrary, he was dressed in a clean *jellaba* and appeared healthy. A watchman, perhaps?

Bond had arrived at the scene fifteen minutes earlier. The night had not given him the rest he had hoped for, so he had begun the day with the persistent headache and a nervous energy that bordered on anxiety. He had eaten a light breakfast of eggs and toast in the hotel (and hadn't seen the twins, thank God), then walked the quarter mile to the medina. Now, though, as he watched the old quarter of town come alive with the noise and smells of the day's bartering, Bond felt a little better. The anticipation of something happening, of some possible revelation, brought back the welcome rush of excitement and interest.

A man in a business suit stepped up to the *berraka,* tossed a coin into the beggar's plate, then went under the covering. He disappeared into the shadows, and ultimately into the building. In fact, it appeared that the man had gone into the *berraka* and walked straight into the brick wall. Bond was pretty sure that he didn't see a door open.

Now more curious than ever, Bond thought he should get a closer look at the inside of the *berraka.* Playing the tourist, he wandered over to the beggar. Instead of holding out his hand and pleading for a handout, the beggar sat still, staring straight ahead. Was he waiting for some kind of signal?

Bond reached into his pocket, grabbed a couple of ten-dirham coins, and dropped them into the plate. The beggar nodded and muttered something in Arabic. Bond went under the *berraka,* and, as he suspected, found himself facing a brick wall. The number 14, which was displayed outside on the *berraka,* was also painted on the bricks. But there was no door.

He reached out and ran his fingers along the edges of the bricks, searching for a trapdoor catch. He knew it had to be there somewhere.

Bond looked at his watch. It was now nearly 8:00. He backed out of the *berraka* and walked across the street. The beggar looked up once at him, then continued his stare into space. Bond resumed his station, where he was partially hidden by a fruit cart.

Right on time, Walter van Breeschooten came walking down the narrow street. Bond drew the PPK, put it in his jacket pocket, and then smoothly joined the Dutchman in his stride. He leaned in close, nudging the barrel into van Breeschooten's side.

"Keep walking, up this way," Bond said, gesturing past number 14 to another narrow street full of vendors.

"You!" van Breeschooten said. He was clearly shocked.

"Shut up and walk," Bond said.

They maneuvered in and out of the crowd of people, turning several corners and up a small flight of steps. Bond escorted him to an out-of-the-way passage where no one was about. He then frisked the man roughly and found a Smith & Wesson Model 60 .38 Special. Bond threw it on the ground away from them.

"I don't know anything!" van Breeschooten pleaded, falling to his knees.

"I don't want to know anything," Bond said with murder in his heart. "I already know that you slit Helena Marksbury's throat." He pulled out the gun and aimed it at the Dutchman's head. "Empty your pockets. Slowly."

Van Breeschooten took a stuffed envelope out of his jacket and dropped it.

"You're making a big mistake," he said.

"How is that?" Bond asked menacingly.

"The Union are after you in a big way."

"What else is new?"

James Bond exercised his licence to kill and pulled the trigger. He felt no remorse, but it didn't give him any satisfaction either. He felt absolutely nothing. Bond had once again transformed himself into the blunt instrument of death, something which he had been able to do at will ever since he began his career in government service. When he did it, Bond shut himself off from every possible emotion and performed the task coldly and objectively.

As for van Breeschooten, his last, terrifying thought was that he now realized that the Union had set him up to die this way. He had been a piece of Yassasin's plan all along. This was his punishment for the failure of the Skin 17 project.

Looking down at the corpse's face, Bond used his foot to roll the dead man facedown.

The stuffed envelope was still on the ground. Bond picked it up and opened it. Inside was a map of the Málaga province of Spain, which included the Costa del Sol cities of Málaga, Marbella, and Torremolinos. There was an "X" marked slightly north of Marbella.

Also in the envelope was a ticket to a bullfight in Málaga, scheduled in two days. It was paper-clipped to a flyer announcing a "public rally" by Domingo Espada to take place before the *corrida*. Bond noted that the headlining matador was Javier Rojo.

Bond holstered his gun, put the envelope in his pocket, and slowly walked away from the bloody scene. He considered what had just happened and the implications of the envelope's contents.

They meant that the Union were involved with Domingo Espada in this conflict with Britain. Otherwise, what would van Breeschooten have been doing with a ticket to Espada's rally?

Bond's thoughts were rocked by the deafening sound of an explosion. It wasn't far away, just a few streets over. He looked up and saw a billowing black cloud above the rooftops. Bond ran out of the deserted street and retraced his steps back toward Ville de Casablanca. People were running and screaming in sheer panic.

He got to the site of chaos and saw that it was the Union's building that had been bombed! The *berraka* was completely gone, replaced by burning rubbish. He could hear sirens approaching, but as the streets were so narrow, the authorities would be running in on foot. A small police cart, however, quickly appeared on the scene. Two officers got off it and immediately began to set up barriers to keep people away.

Bond took refuge behind the fruit barrow he had used earlier and watched the unfolding drama with confusion and wonder. What the hell had happened here?

What was particularly strange, Bond suddenly realized, was that no one was coming out of the burning building. In fact, it appeared to be completely empty.

More officers arrived on the scene and were talking to a few witnesses. Bond recognized the beggar in the crowd of onlookers. The beggar wasn't watching the building; he was looking right at Bond.

The man then approached one of the officers and said something, pointing at Bond. The policeman spotted Bond and shouted. The other officers looked up and in his direction. All of them drew their weapons and aimed them at him.

Faced with no other choice, Bond slowly put up his hands.

SIXTEEN

CHANGE OF PLANS

Bond pushed up on the end of the fruit cart, causing the entire contents to topple to the ground. Oranges, apples, grapefruit, and assorted vegetables spilled across the street. He then shoved the entire cart forward on its wheels, toward the police, blocking their sight lines and giving Bond just the right amount of confusion he needed to make a run for it. A policeman fired his gun, but the bullet zinged off one of the walls. People screamed and parted the way for Bond as he rushed through the crowded bazaar.

Two teenage boys, trying to help the police, attempted to grab him as he ran by. One of them caught Bond's legs, tackling him; the other one jumped on his back to pin him to the ground. Bond didn't want to hurt them, but he didn't want to be captured either. He rolled hard, knocking the boy off his back. He then kicked his legs wildly, preventing the other boy from holding on. Once he had freed himself, Bond got to his feet and continued to run. By now, though, the police had nearly caught up with him.

Bond took a sharp turn through a group of Berber women selling live chickens. The chickens squawked and fluttered, which prompted the women to shout at him and point the way for the police. The Berber men joined the chase, ready to make the rude foreigner pay for what he had done.

Bond ducked into a doorway and found himself in a shoemaker's shop. The place was covered with all manner of footwear, from Moroccan *cherbil* slippers to the latest American athletic varieties. Bond looked around quickly and noted a large rack of shoes next to the front door and another door at the back of the shop. The policemen's shouts were coming closer.

The shoemaker, who was sitting and working on the floor, looked at Bond with bewilderment. Bond said, "Forgive me," then pulled down the rack of shoes, blocking the front door. He then leaped over the shoemaker and ran to the back door.

It emptied into another part of the twisting medina. Bond ran outside and turned a corner as quickly as he could. Now he was truly lost in the maze, so he simply kept running, turning this way and that, hoping that he could lose the police. Up ahead was a small mosque with scaffolding on one side. Bond tried to go inside the building, but a man standing in front blocked his entrance. Only Muslims were allowed in the mosque.

Bond didn't have time to argue. He heard the police running at the end of the street, so he leaped onto the scaffolding and began to climb. Another shot rang out, barely missing him, as the police arrived at the foot of the scaffolding. Bond got to the roof and ran across, jumping over a large hole where repairs were being made. At the edge of the building, he found that he could make another leap to the top of the adjoining building.

The horrible smell there was overpowering. It reminded Bond of manure and vomit mixed with chemicals . . . turpentine or something. A stone staircase led down into a courtyard that was revealed to be part of a small tannery. The pungent odors were coming from the vats where men were up to their knees in red and orange liquids, scrubbing hides. The exotic ingredients used in the process included pigeon dung, cow urine, fish oils, animal fats and brains, chromium salts, and sulphuric acid.

Bond held his breath and leaped over the vats, one by one, causing the men to shout at him in anger. He ran past a wall of hides that had been hung up to dry after they had been scraped of the hair and extraneous flesh and soaked in the putrid dyes. Not seeing a convenient way out, Bond took a running jump and gained a handhold in the cracks in the wall. He swung one leg up and over, but unfortunately wiped the front of his body over one of the wet hides. He dropped down the other side of the wall and was in another street full of people and mule carts.

Bond pushed his way through, slowing his pace so as not to attract too much attention. He could see a horseshoe-shaped arch at the end of the street, one of the medina's exits. He made his way toward it, but three policemen suddenly appeared there. They were looking intently at the crowd. Bond turned around abruptly and merged with a group of men in *jellabas* marching in the opposite direction. As soon as he could, Bond rounded a corner and got off the street. Unluckily, it was a dead end, with a wall much too high to climb.

He looked back around the corner and saw that the three policemen were headed his way. Surely they would notice a Westerner emerge from the passageway if he attempted to do so.

A rope suddenly dropped and dangled beside him.

"Up here!" whispered a female voice. Bond looked up. It was one of the Taunt twins! She was standing on the roof of the building and was holding the rope.

"Don't just stand there. Climb!" she ordered.

Bond did as he was told. He climbed the wall and bolted onto the roof just as the policemen reached the street and inspected it. All they saw was a rope being pulled up the building.

"Am I glad to see you," he said. She was wearing the same tight blue jeans, but was now dressed in a red silk blouse with the sleeves rolled up.

"Hush up and follow me," the girl commanded. She ran across the roof to the other side. Bond accompanied her, dazed by this sudden turn of events.

"Which one are you?" he asked.

"I'm Hedy." She took a sniff and grimaced at the stains on his clothing. "Lovely smell. Come this way." She took a running start and leaped across the eight-foot gap between buildings, then turned and shouted, "Don't just stand there. Come on!"

Bond mimicked her action, then they both ran across the second rooftop.

"Where are we going?" he asked.

"Just shut up and don't stop. We're trying to save your ass."

She led him across two more rooftops until she pointed to a fire escape. "Down, mister. Go in the open window, first floor down."

Bond climbed down the stairs and slipped into the window. He was in a bedroom with Western furnishings. Hedy slithered inside behind him. She led him out of the bedroom, down a hallway, and into what was some kind of office. Heidi was dressed identically and sitting at a desk, looking at a computer monitor. Neither of them wore the red wig. Filing cabinets, a fax machine, a copier, telephones, and other pieces of high-tech equipment dominated the room.

"What the hell is going on?" Bond asked.

"Welcome to the Casablanca headquarters of the CIA, Mr. Bond," Hedy said.

Bond's jaw dropped.

Heidi pointed to the monitor, where a satellite image of the medina was magnified hundreds of times. "We thought they had you there for a second. It's a good thing you found us."

"I found *you?*"

Bond dropped into a chair. He was trying to project some semblance of composure, but he was, nonetheless, dumbfounded.

Heidi laughed when saw the expression on his face. "We got you good, didn't we?" Then she noticed the stains. "Pee-uuu . . . ! What did you get on you?"

"Someone better start explaining. I'm in no mood for jokes," Bond said.

"We *are* travel writers," Heidi said. "But that's just a cover. Hedy's a senior agent with the CIA. I'm a junior agent. We don't live in Japan. We live right here, in this building."

Hedy added, "I'm the one who went into the CIA first. When they found out I had an identical twin, they came up with an unorthodox plan and made us a proposal."

"As far as official records go, I don't exist," Heidi said.

"And neither do I," Hedy continued. "But there does exist a *Hillary* Taunt, CIA agent, who works in the North African sector. Either one of us can pose as Hillary during the course of our work. The boys in Virginia figured that Heidi could be used as a decoy in special cases. We rarely travel together, which is why you never saw us at the same time on the train. We rode in separate cars on purpose. We confuse a lot of people, especially conductors and flight attendants."

"If we have to be seen in public together, one of us wears the wig," Heidi said. "The only people that know that *we* aren't Hillary Taunt are our bosses at the Company. If, say, your own organization at SIS wanted to find out information about CIA agent Hillary Taunt there would be nothing in her file to indicate she might be an identical twin. This can be very advantageous in the field."

"I can see that," Bond said. "So you've known who I am all along."

"Sure," Heidi said. "We were sent to track you down. We got lucky and made contact with you on the train. If you hadn't found us this morning, we would have had to come after you. You're in a lot of hot water, mister."

"Tell me about it," Bond said. "I'm not sure what happened back there. The Union headquarters was blown up. Someone made it look like I was responsible."

"To hell with Union headquarters," Hedy said. "What about that doctor in London and the ferry in Tangier? What do you have to say about those things? You're a wanted man. Your chief has put out an all-points alert for your arrest."

Bond winced. "I didn't do any of those things."

"Tell it to the judge," Hedy said. "Our orders are to escort you to London. We've already checked you out of the hotel and we have your things." She pointed to his holdall on the floor in the corner. "Now, you have to hand over your weapons. All of them." She held out her hand.

Bond was aghast. "You're not serious."

"Please don't make me use force," Hedy said. "I'm pretty good at what I do."

"I believe you," Bond said. He reached into his jacket.

"Carefully," Hedy commanded.

Bond froze, then continued in slow motion. He brought out the PPK and tossed it on the desk.

"The knife?" she asked.

"Oh, right," Bond muttered, and took the sheath off the back of his belt. "This really isn't necessary, you know. I'd much rather be arrested by you two than the Moroccan police. I'll be a good boy."

"We're just playing it safe," Hedy said. She was definitely the "bad cop" of the two.

"I seem to have lost a Walther P99 in Tangier," he said.

"Yeah, you left it on that ferry after killing those civilians," Hedy said.

"No, I didn't. I wasn't there."

"Sure," Hedy said with a sneer.

"I'm sorry, James," Heidi said with sincerity. "We might have had some fun together."

"We still can," Bond said. "It's a long way to London."

"Hush," Hedy snapped. "We've got a car outside. We're going to take a drive to the airport. There's a plane that leaves in three hours. But first you're going to shower and change out of those stinky clothes."

"I must know what you think is going on," Bond said.

"We don't know what's going on," Hedy said. "All we know is that we have to escort you to London and hand you over to your chief."

"You *do* know that was the Union headquarters that blew up this morning?" Bond asked.

"We had come to that conclusion but didn't have proof," Hedy replied. "Actually, our suspicions were focused on another part of town, the Central Market, southeast from here. Maybe what you found this morning could have been another entrance. Anyway, we were already in the process of coordinating a raid on the Central Market entrance with

Interpol and the Moroccan police when all this business with you and the ferry happened. I guess that sorta screwed up our plans."

"Sorry."

"We were told that you had gone renegade, had joined the Union," she added.

"That's why you were in Casablanca, we thought," Heidi said.

"Well, it looks like the Union might have suspected something and got the hell out of Dodge," Hedy continued. "That building was completely empty. The police reports are still coming in. They've begun to explore it and apparently there's some kind of underground complex. If I didn't have to deal with you, I'd be one of the first officials in there to find out if it really was Union headquarters." Hedy looked at him out the corner of her eye. "You *sure* you're not Union?"

"I'm not a member of the bloody Union," Bond said.

"I'd like to believe you," Hedy said.

"I believe you," Heidi added.

Hedy rolled her eyes. "My sister has a one-track mind."

"Look," Bond said. "There's something . . . there's something going on. Some kind of plot that the Union have cooked up. I'm a part of it. I can't explain it, though. Not yet. If you take me to London, something terrible will happen. My hunches are usually pretty good."

"We don't know what you're talking about," Hedy said. "Better hit the shower so we can get going."

"Wait a minute," Bond insisted. "Listen to me. For the past few days, I've felt as if I've been knocked here and there like a pinball. Whoever committed those crimes in London and Tangier—he's some kind of double. I think I've seen him. Once, in London. He looks just like me and he's certainly Union. I'm also pretty damned sure that I'm being manipulated by them; to what end, I don't know, but I would bet my life that there's something monstrous behind everything that's happened. The murder of Dr. Feare . . . the shootings on the ferry . . . the explosion in the medina today . . . They're all connected somehow, and I think that this Spaniard, Domingo Espada, is involved."

Heidi and Hedy looked at each other. "What do you mean?"

Bond reached into his pocket and pulled out the envelope he had taken from van Breeschooten. "I got this from one of the Union's top men. He was responsible for recruiting—and killing—someone close to me at SIS. I tracked him from London to the very location where that explosion occurred this morning. As you can see, he had something to do with Espada."

The girls looked at the bullfight ticket and the map. "What's this 'X'?" Hedy asked.

"I don't know yet."

"It's not far from Marbella," Heidi observed. "Domingo Espada's home is just north of there. I think that 'X' marks the spot."

"Hey, I think you're right, Heidi," Hedy said. They gave the material back to Bond. "The U.S. government is very concerned about Espada. We've been on alert ever since he started all the ruckus in Spain over Gibraltar. We're afraid your people might get into a nasty scuffle with Spain over it."

"We're all afraid of that," Bond said. "You've got to give me the benefit of the doubt. If I'm taken out of the picture, we'll never know what's going on. I'm a part of it, don't you see? The Union *needs* me for something. If I don't follow this scheme through to the end, then we'll never know what it is."

The girls were silent. Finally, Hedy said, "I want to talk to Heidi in the other room. Don't try anything."

"I wouldn't dare leave," Bond said. "Being with you two is the safest I've felt in days."

When the girls went into the bedroom, Bond shut his eyes and tried to relax. They returned, and Hedy sat down in front of him. Heidi draped herself on the desk, one long leg bent like an inverted V.

"All right, James," Heidi said. "We're going to play it your way. But we're going to have to clear it first."

"You have to call your boss," Hedy said. "You have to convince her. If she gives us the okay, then we'll trust you on this one."

"Give me the phone," Bond said. He fought a wave of panic. Could he convince M that he was sane and not guilty of the crimes he was accused of? Would she allow him to continue this possibly aimless wild goose chase?

Hedy handed him a white phone. "It's a secure line."

Bond dialed the number and was put through to Bill Tanner.

"My God, James, are you all right?" The Chief-of-Staff sounded very alarmed.

"Yes, Bill."

"I'm glad to hear that. We were very relieved a few minutes ago when we got the message that the CIA had found you. You have to come back, James. You know you do."

"Bill, I didn't do those things, and you know it."

"I believe you. But . . ."

"No 'buts,'" Bond said angrily. "You have to trust me. I'm on to something and must speak with M."

"Certainly," Tanner said. "I'm sure she'll want a word."

Bond waited a moment. He looked at the twins, who suddenly felt uncomfortable and exchanged glances, but didn't bother to get up and give him some privacy.

"Double-O Seven." The voice was hard.

"Ma'am."

"Well? Are you on your way back to London with Agent Taunt?"

"Agent Taunt?" Bond asked.

"That's what it says here, Double-O Seven, agent Hillary Taunt."

"Are you listening, Bill?" Bond asked. He knew that Tanner monitored some of M's phone calls when she gave him the order, and he was sure that this would be one of them.

"Yes," came the voice, after a beat.

"I'm with . . . er, Miss Taunt, now," Bond said. "If you insist on it, ma'am, yes, I will come back to London. However, I must ask that you hear me out first."

"Very well."

"I may have evidence that Domingo Espada is linked to the Union."

That got her attention. "Go on."

"I disobeyed your orders, ma'am; I freely admit that," he said. It was one of the most difficult things he had ever confessed in his life. "But I had to go after the Union. If not for Britain, then I had to do it for myself. I swear to you that I'm not responsible for Dr. Feare's murder, or the terrorist attack on the ferry. I identified and traced Helena Marksbury's recruiter and killer to Casablanca and almost got into the Union's main headquarters. The CIA here was on to them, too. The Union must have suspected discovery, so they left. Vanished."

"What's this about Espada?"

"The man I followed here had a map on his person with the location of Espada's home marked on it. He also had a ticket to a political rally and bullfight at which Espada is speaking."

"When is that?"

"The day after tomorrow."

"Interesting," M said. "The summit meeting in Gibraltar has been scheduled for the day after that."

"Who's going to this summit meeting?" Bond asked.

"The PM. Spain's PM. Espada . . ." Tanner answered.

"Ma'am, all this is connected somehow," Bond said. "I'm sure of it."

"But you have nothing, Double-O Seven. What does a ticket tell you? Perhaps this man simply likes bullfighting."

"*Liked,* ma'am," Bond said. "He's, uhm, no longer with us."

"I see."

"Why would he have a road map to Espada's house? This man was *Union!* It either means that the Union is involved somehow with Espada, or that they are interested in him for some reason. Maybe someone has paid the Union to kill him! I think I should try to meet Domingo Espada before the summit meeting and see what I can determine." He then presented M the same argument that he had given the twins—that he believed he was a cog in the Union's plan. If he were taken out of it, something awful might happen.

"Agent Taunt . . . and I . . . would like your permission to pursue this," he said.

M was silent. After a moment, she said, "Hold the line, Double-O Seven."

Bond heard a click. She was conferring with Tanner, and probably the Minister of Defence.

She was back in three minutes. "Double-O Seven."

"Yes, ma'am."

"I've just spoken to my opposite number in the CIA. I should probably have cleared this with the PM, but I'm not going to. You are to stay in Agent Taunt's company at all times. You are under house arrest, although you'll be mobile. You are not to attempt to escape, do I make myself clear?"

"Yes, ma'am."

"You can go to Spain. I realize that you're interested in this because you think it will bring you closer to the Union. Be that as it may, I think you might be on to something with regard to Espada. Providing you can get close to the man, you are to gather any information that you can that might link him to something as reprehensible as the Union. He's already a controversial figure in Spain, but I think that would all but destroy the people's confidence in him. It would give us more bargaining power. At the same time, we wouldn't want any harm to come to him before the meeting in Gibraltar. It's the most important thing on the government's plate right now. We can't have it jeopardized, but we can certainly have it slanted in our favor. Do we understand each other, Double-O Seven?"

"Clearly, ma'am."

"Very well."

"One more thing. One of the Union recruiters I tracked to Morocco—Michael Clayton—has a cousin in London who is connected to the Union. You might want to investigate that."

"Noted. Now let me talk with Agent Taunt. Good luck."

Bond thanked her and held the phone up for one of the twins to take. Hedy grabbed it and listened, occasionally replying, "Yes, ma'am." Then she said, "I'll call him right now. Thank you."

She rang off and said, "I have to call my chief in the States." She received the same instructions, and then she hung up and looked at Bond.

"Well. Looks like we'll be spending more time together after all. Heidi, I think we should use the yacht to get up to Spain, what do you think?"

Heidi nodded. "That's the safest. We can't risk bringing him through Immigration anywhere."

Hedy explained. "The Company has a boat in a hidden marina on the coast not far from Tangier. We can use it, but we'll have to drive to Tangier."

"Let's go, then," Bond said, standing.

"Oh boy!" Heidi cried, jumping up. "This is going to be fun!"

"Just watch it, pal," Hedy told Bond. She patted the Browning 9mm at her side. "I'm pretty good with this. And we also carry extra-strength, high-powered OC pepper spray that will stun an elephant. So don't try anything that would be considered conduct unbecoming of a gentleman."

"I wouldn't dream of it," Bond replied.

"Now go shower and get dressed," Hedy ordered.

"Wow," Heidi said. "I just thought of something."

"What?" Hedy asked.

"That for the next couple of days we get to baby-sit a British Double-O agent who's suspected of being a terrorist!"

"So?"

"It doesn't get much cooler than that!"

SEVENTEEN

MOUNTING EVIDENCE

Margareta Piel took a sip of white wine, and then stretched lazily, providing the men on the dock a spectacular view of a superbly built, beautiful woman in a skimpy bikini.

"You have an audience," Espada said, lighting a Havana cigar. He, too, was wearing swimming attire. Agustin was asleep on a recliner behind them, dressed in bathing shorts and a T-shirt.

"I always have an audience." Margareta sighed. "They just won't leave me alone."

They were on the deck of Espada's yacht at Puerto Banús, the chic Marbella harbor where the rich and famous liked to be seen. He owned an American-made 70-foot Cheoy Lee MY, a high-tech luxury boat with extensive extras. Like many of the other boats in the harbor, it was registered in the tax-free paradise of the Cayman Islands. Espada had rarely used the yacht for sailing. Mostly, he simply liked to lounge about on the deck half-naked with half-naked females waiting on him. It was the one public place where he didn't mind being a bit of an exhibitionist, and that was simply because he liked to show the other millionaires that docked at Puerto Banús who was on top. The area had become quite fashionable with Marbella's rise in tourism. Consisting of long stretches of beach clubs, shops, restaurants, and bars, the harbor was always alive with people. Even now, at noon, a group of male tourists were standing at a bar on the other side of the dock, gawking at Margareta. By nightfall, Puerto Banús would be packed.

"Roberto Rojo's death is causing quite a stir," Margareta said casually. "Have you seen this morning's paper?"

"No."

"At least three prominent matadors have announced defection, claiming that you are mad."

"Who are they?" Espada demanded.

She told him. Espada threw his drink at the edge of the dock, shattering the glass.

"They will turn public opinion against you," she said. "You can't afford that right now."

"Would you shut up?" he snarled. "Who made you my spiritual adviser?"

Margareta laughed. "Oh relax, Domingo. I'm teasing you. We all know you're unstoppable."

"I will have those three taken care of," he said. "Tomorrow night's *corrida* in Málaga will solidify my position with the matadors. When the people see me in the ring with men like Javier Rojo, they will follow me to Gibraltar."

"Don't you think the king will have you stopped?"

"He hasn't made a sound yet," Espada noted. "They're all afraid of me in Madrid. They're scared that I might actually run for office and win."

"We have company," she interrupted, gesturing to the dock. Espada squinted and saw his prize matador, standing near the boat.

Javier Rojo was tanned, muscular, and nearly six feet tall. His long black hair was combed back behind his ears and flowed down around the back of his neck. Margareta, like most warm-blooded women in Spain, found him very attractive. At twenty-six, the older of the two Rojo brothers, Javier was easily the most dynamic and charismatic in the bullring. Now, however, he was staring at Espada with hatred in his eyes.

"*Hola,* Javier," Espada called. "Come aboard and join us!"

Rojo hesitated, but then stepped over the railing and jumped onto the deck. He strode over to Espada and stood before him.

"How are you, Javier? You know Margareta, don't you?" Espada asked. "Have a drink."

"I didn't come to drink with you, Domingo," Rojo said. "I have come to ask you something."

"What is it, *mi amigo?*"

"My brother. Did you have him killed?"

Espada made a show of pain. "Mother of God, Javier, you can't possibly ask *me* that. Do you really believe I would do such a thing? I loved Roberto as much as I love you. He was such a promising young matador. Did your mother receive the flowers and the money I sent?"

"Yes, she did, and she thanks you. But Domingo . . ." Javier said, narrowing his eyes. "The talk is that Roberto did something to displease you. What was it? The police are baffled by the murder. Who was that girl he was with? I think you know something and are not telling me."

Espada looked at Margareta and shook his head. She continued to look at the young man, admiring his build.

"Can you hear this, Margareta?" Espada asked. "He is accusing his manager of murder. I am like an uncle to him."

"He's upset, Domingo," Margareta said, stone-faced. "Surely you understand that."

Espada acknowledged this with a nod of his head. He turned back to Rojo and said, "Please, Javier, sit and have a drink. I share your sorrow, believe me. I promise you on the soul of Pedro Romero that I had nothing to do with your brother's death."

Javier blushed and relaxed a little at the mention of the famous bullfighter. "I'm . . . I'm sorry, Domingo," he said, now feeling foolish. "You're right, I *am* upset. It's just that no one seems to know what really happened."

"Sit down, have a drink, Javier," Margareta repeated.

"No, thank you," the matador answered. "I must go and rest. I am fighting tomorrow, remember?"

"Of course I know that," Espada said. "And that is precisely the thing to get your mind off of this terrible tragedy."

Javier turned to leave, but stopped and looked back. "If I ever find out who was responsible for this," he said, "I will kill him with my bare hands."

With that, he jumped off the boat, walked down the wharf, and disappeared.

Espada looked at Margareta and rolled his eyes. Agustin had woken during the exchange and was applying suntan lotion on his shoulders.

"We'll have to be careful about him," Espada said. "I don't want him flying off the handle."

"I thought you came out here to get away from business, Domingo," Margareta said a half-hour later. "Look who's here now."

Espada looked up and saw Nadir Yassasin standing on the dock.

"Permission to come aboard, sir?" Yassasin asked.

Espada waved him on, and the man climbed over the rail and took a seat on the deck. Agustin sat up in his chair, alert and ready to serve his master.

"Get yourself a drink," Espada said, gesturing to the bar.

Yassasin poured a glass of sparkling water from a bottle that was sitting in a bucket of ice.

"Everything will fall into place tomorrow night after your rally and bullfight, Domingo. The plan has succeeded beyond my wildest dreams. Each step has proceeded exactly as I predicted. Tomorrow night at dinner you will meet the assassin we have chosen."

"How do I know he's any good?"

Yassasin smiled. "Because he's an ex-British SIS agent. He's now a member of the Union."

"Who is it?"

Yassasin pulled a photograph out of his jacket pocket, and handed it to Espada.

"His name is James Bond," Yassasin said. "He's a very formidable killer. He will be one of your bodyguards at the summit meeting on Monday. That's how we get him inside the Convent."

"He'll do this for me? Betray his country?"

"It is inevitable, *señor,*" Yassasin said, slightly bowing. "Jimmy Powers has been on his tail for the past several days, reporting his movements to me. He should be arriving in Marbella later today."

"If this guy is as good as you say, he'll spot the tail," Espada said.

"No one spots Jimmy Powers," Yassasin said. "You know that."

Espada shrugged, unconvinced. "What else?"

"The Union has put together a force of new recruits—a thousand men from North Africa. They will unite with your men at La Linea as of tomorrow morning. We're counting on you to recruit at least one thousand men tomorrow at the rally. If that happens, combined with the number you already have, you will be four thousand men strong."

"That's incredible!"

"Now. The meeting. The British Prime Minister is coming, as well as several United Nations delegates. Of course you are allowed to bring as many people with you to Gibraltar as you wish, but only three bodyguards or assistants may accompany you into the banqueting hall of the Convent, where the talks will take place. One of those will be Mr. Bond, who will use an alias, of course."

"Agustin will be my lieutenant," Espada said. "Margareta will also accompany us." He turned to Agustin. "Make the necessary arrangements when we get back to the ranch."

Agustin nodded in compliance.

"That's what we thought you would say. Mr. Powers and myself—we have secured false documentation as U.S. State Department officials. I am a Moroccan citizen working in America. We will be there to make sure everything goes smoothly. In essence, Jimmy Powers will be there to protect you if things get out of hand."

"What about weapons?"

"Powers will be going to Gibraltar tomorrow to make those arrangements. Everything will be in place before Monday."

Espada was impressed. "It sounds as if you have everything under control. I feel so helpless. It's a disconcerting feeling, but I suppose I must commend you."

Yassasin produced a rare smile and lifted his glass. "Well then. Here's to our continued success. I have no doubt that when you take over as the new Governor of Gibraltar, the government of Spain will have no choice but to acknowledge your power as a political leader."

"Detective Inspector Howard is here, ma'am," Moneypenny said into the intercom. The green light above the door illuminated. "You can go on through, inspector," she told him.

Detective Inspector Howard found M with Bill Tanner. She was sitting behind her desk, and he stood alongside her like a sentinel.

"Sit down, Inspector," M said. "Can we get anything for you?"

"No, thank you, ma'am," Howard said. "I'm sorry to disturb you on a Saturday."

"That's all right, we were here anyway."

"Yes. Well, I'm afraid I have some rather serious news."

"I gathered that from your telephone call. What do you have to tell us?"

"It's your man, Bond. He killed Dr. Feare. The forensic evidence is irrefutable. We found his blood at the scene, buttons from his shirt, hair. . . . I'm afraid we have to find him, and find him quickly. He's going to be charged."

"What if I don't believe you, Inspector?" M asked.

"Ma'am?"

"I cannot believe that Double-O Seven would do something like that unless he had a damned good reason. It's not his style."

"Ma'am," Howard said. "We've obtained information that he was seeing Dr. Feare as a patient. He had an evaluation and tests performed two months ago. For psychiatric evaluation and other complaints. You were aware of that?"

"Of course I was," M answered.

"We'd like to know the results of those tests. I was hoping you might have copies."

"We have a summary report that the doctor sent to me after seeing

Double-O Seven," M said flatly. "I can let you have a copy of that. But let me ask you this, Inspector. Do you really think Double-O Seven would commit this crime and flee?"

"All of the evidence leads us to believe that Mr. Bond is very unstable," Howard said. "Look what he did on that ferry, for God's sake!"

"There is no proof that the man responsible for that horrible act was Double-O Seven!" M said sternly. "That is still under investigation."

"Well." Howard sighed, realizing he was fighting a losing battle. "I'm here to deliver this arrest warrant for James Bond. He's officially wanted by the police for murder."

Tanner took the documents.

"Thank you, Inspector," M said. "If we find Double-O Seven, we'll make sure he gets them."

"We'll let you know as soon as we hear anything," Tanner said.

Howard nodded, stood and walked toward the door. He turned and faced M again. "Ma'am."

"Yes, Inspector?"

"You wouldn't be protecting Double-O Seven, would you? For some . . . reason?"

"He's a Double-O, Inspector," M answered. "He doesn't need me to protect him."

The Inspector smiled grimly and walked out.

M and Tanner exchanged glances.

"Bill, could it possibly be true?" she asked him.

"No, ma'am," Tanner said, shaking his head. "It's not James. It can't be."

M gripped the pen in her hand and stared straight ahead. "He sounded quite lucid when we spoke, I'll give him that. God, I hope I've made the right decision. I could lose my job over this."

"We have to let James work it out," Tanner assured her. "He always does. When he's on to something, he's usually right."

M repeated her Chief-of-Staff's words in her head a few times, then said, "Right. Let's move on. Double-O Seven and the CIA agent will arrive in Spain at what time?"

"Certainly by this evening," Tanner said. "They're traveling to Marbella by boat."

Moneypenny buzzed again.

"What is it?" M asked, punching the button.

"It's Captain Hodge. He's here and says it's urgent."

M winced. "Send him in," she said, simultaneously pressing the button that lit the green bulb outside her office.

Hodge came in stiffly and approached the desk.

"Yes, Captain?"

"Ma'am, we've just received the guest list for the summit meeting in Gibraltar. As you know, everyone entering the Governor's Residence is screened in advance. This information is made available to all of the countries involved."

"Yes?"

"Domingo Espada's entourage will consist of two assistants and a bodyguard. They're all Spanish except for the bodyguard. According to the documents, he is a British exile now residing in Spain. His name is Peter Woodward. Have a look at his photograph."

He handed her a file with a black-and-white head shot attached to it. She inhaled deeply when she saw who it was.

"It's Double-O Seven," she said.

"Yes, ma'am."

Tanner leaned in closer to get a better look. He furrowed his brow. "It certainly looks like him," he concurred.

"We're going to have to arrest him as soon as he shows his face in Gibraltar," Hodge said.

"You can't," Tanner said.

"Why not?"

M answered for him. "Because he'll have diplomatic immunity. With Spain."

Hodge was horrified. "My God, I hadn't thought of that. What are we going to do?"

M said, "Captain, would you allow me to confer with my Chief-of-Staff privately? For a few minutes?"

"Of course, ma'am," Hodge said, standing. "I'll be outside."

After he had left, M looked at Tanner and said, "This changes things, doesn't it?"

Tanner looked unsure.

M asked, "What about Double-O One?"

Tanner nodded. "He's been briefed and is all set to accompany the PM to Gibraltar. They leave early Monday morning."

"Then you had better give him additional orders."

"And they are?"

"If Double-O Seven really accompanies Espada to this meeting, then Double-O One should be prepared for anything. He is to keep close watch on Double-O Seven. If Double-O One determines that Bond is dangerous, he should respond appropriately."

"Do you mean . . . ?"

"Yes, I mean," M said. "If the need arises, Double-O Seven must be eliminated."

ACT THREE

TERCIO DE LA MUERTE

EIGHTEEN

THE YOUNG MATADOR

"Look at that mountain!" Heidi exclaimed as Hedy drove the 1998 BMW 320i onto the so-called Golden Mile of five-star hotels and resorts in Marbella. Conch Mountain hovered over the city, a magnificent backdrop for the seaside resort.

"It's a great town if you like golf," Hedy commented. Among Marbella's numerous golfing establishments was Europe's only night course; it was floodlit so that golfers could play after dark.

Hedy pointed to a huge estate on their left and said, "The king of Saudi Arabia built all that." Beyond expansive gardens was a sparkling white mosque and a mansion that was an exact replica of the White House in Washington, D.C. A large outline of a scimitar made of white stone was embedded in the grass.

"Wow," Heidi said. "Pretty cool, huh, James?"

Bond was in the backseat, where he was happy to be. It was a pleasure not having to drive or constantly look over his shoulder for a change. It was nice not having to *think* for a few hours. They had picked up the BMW, apparently a CIA company car, in a discreet garage not far from Tarifa, at the most southern point of Spain. They had stored the boat and had driven up the coast, past Gibraltar, and on to Marbella. Bond couldn't sleep because of the persistent throbbing in his head, but he was thankful for the rest, even though the twins talked about the scenery along the way. He took four of Dr. Feare's pills in the hopes that the headache wouldn't grow worse.

They drove past the restaurant owned by the famous Italian singer Tony Dalli, and Marbella's hot discotheque, Olivia Valere, and soon pulled in to the entrance of the Marbella Club Hotel on Bulevar Principe Alfonso von Hohenlohe. One of the finest resort hotels on the beach, the Marbella Club offered everything from bungalows to simple rooms.

"Are you sure this guy is here?" Heidi asked Bond.

"When I phoned, he said to look for him on the beach," Bond answered. "He likes to relax the day before a bullfight."

"Yuck," Hedy said. "I can't imagine why anyone would want to *watch* a bullfight, much less participate in one."

"Don't be so quick to condemn it," Bond said as they parked and got out of the car. "It's an integral part of Spanish tradition and culture. It's not a sport. It's an art."

"Yeah, right," Hedy said. "Tell that to the bull."

Bond decided not to argue. They checked in to the hotel, where the girls had reserved an exclusive bungalow with two bedrooms, two bathrooms, a shared living room, and an enclosed patio. They walked through the grounds, which were surrounded by lush foliage and palm trees. When they entered the bungalow, Heidi was ecstatic.

"Now *this* is the life!" she purred. "We need to get the company to send us on business trips more often."

"We'll take this one," Hedy said, gesturing to the bedroom with twin beds. "You're in the other one, Mr. Bond. Don't try any funny stuff. We're going to guard you in shifts tonight."

Bond shook his head. "I keep telling you that you don't need to guard me at all," he said. "I'm not going anywhere."

"Whatever. Let's go find your matador."

"Since we're going to the beach, can I put on my swimsuit?" Heidi asked.

"Jeez, Heidi," Hedy said, rolling her eyes.

Ten minutes later, all three of them were dressed in beachwear.

Bond was wearing a pair of navy shorts, a white polo shirt, sunglasses, and flip-flops. He had asked the girls for his gun, but Hedy refused to give it to him.

Heidi was wearing a yellow and white bikini that revealed just how shapely and athletic she really was. Her muscle tone was perfect and she had an hourglass figure. Hedy chose to wear a red and black bikini, and for the first time, Bond was able to tell them apart. Hedy had a small, sexy mole on her left breast, whereas Heidi had one to the right of her navel. Otherwise, their figures were exactly alike.

"Wait a second," Hedy announced as they were ready to leave. "One of us should stay here. We have phone calls to make. And we probably shouldn't be seen together if you're meeting someone who's close to Espada."

Bond saw the logic in that. "So . . . who's coming with me?"

"Do we have to flip for it?" Heidi asked her sister.

Hedy waved her hand. "You two go on. I'll be the responsible one. I'll get some sun on the patio while I make calls."

So Bond and Heidi left her, strolled across the hotel grounds, through the beach club and shops, and onto the warm, soft sand. The Mediterranean was calm, creating a flat, blue horizon of serenity. The beach was populated with hotel guests lounging on recliners while staff fetched towels or drinks from the bar.

"Do you see him?" Heidi asked.

Bond peered up and down the beach, and finally spotted a tanned young man lying alone on a lounger some fifty yards away from the rest of the crowd. He was wearing swimming trunks and sunglasses.

"*Hola,*" Bond said as they approached. Javier Rojo turned his head and smiled. He immediately jumped off the lounger and removed his sunglasses.

"James Bond!" he said enthusiastically. "How are you, my friend?"

They shook hands and embraced.

"I'm fine, Javier, it's good to see you," Bond said. "I'm very sorry to hear about your brother."

Javier lowered his head. "Thank you. I am trying to come to terms with it."

"Any ideas on how it happened?"

The matador shook his head. "The police are clueless."

Noting Javier's unease, Bond quickly changed the subject. "Allow me to introduce you to . . . Hillary."

Javier smiled warmly at the beautiful woman. "I should have known that you would be in such company! I'm very pleased to meet you, *señorita.*"

Heidi was speechless. Javier was a superb specimen of a Latin male. He had large, round brown eyes and a wicked smile that could melt any woman's reserve.

Javier held out his hand to Heidi and she took it gingerly, as if she were in a trance.

"Hi . . ." she muttered.

"Sit down," Javier said, gesturing to some empty loungers nearby. "Pull them over here. I was trying to stay away from the crowd so no one would recognize me."

Bond dragged the lounger next to Javier's and they sat, facing the sea.

"Where have you traveled from?" Javier asked.

"We came from North Africa," Bond said.

"Ah, that's a different world over there," Javier commented. "Nice place to visit, but I wouldn't live there."

"I do," Heidi said.

"Oh? Do you enjoy it?"

"Sometimes," she answered.

"So, James, how long has it been? Three years?" Javier asked.

"Something like that. Four perhaps?"

"I don't know. The time, it is flying. Ever since I got my *alternativa,* the world has been spinning," the handsome young man said.

"What is that?" Heidi asked.

Bond explained. "It's like a graduation, when a *novillero,* or novice, bullfighter becomes a full-fledged matador. It occurs at a special *corrida,* and the novice is proposed and seconded by senior matadors. It's almost like a christening."

"Very good, James," Javier said. "You remember!"

Bond shrugged. "Javier, I asked to see you because we need some information about Domingo Espada."

Javier nodded. "I thought so. What do you want to know?"

"Tell us your impressions of him. How close are you to him?"

"Domingo is my manager," Javier said. "He manages several matadors. In the beginning, he was like an uncle. He was a friend. He looked out for his matadors, and I was no exception. He took on my brother when he was a novice. He has a lot of power in the world of bullfighting. Alas, sometimes he misuses that power. I think he bribes bullring owners. I know he bribes the regulators and the presidents at bullfights. He can make sure that the bulls he breeds are sold for *corridas.* At the same time, as a manager, he can dictate which bulls his matadors will fight. He is a good manager, but I sometimes question his ethics. Lately, he has started demanding that his matadors publicly support his political causes. I don't particularly like that."

"Why can't you just leave?" Bond asked.

"It's dangerous to leave Domingo Espada. They call him *El Padrino* down here. I don't mind telling you; he's a crook. He has been linked with organized crime for many years. I never used to pay any attention to it. But now . . . I have reason to believe he's a murderer. I think he may be responsible for Roberto's death."

"Why?" Heidi asked.

"Because Roberto crossed him. I'm still trying to piece together what happened. You see, I know that Domingo Espada also deals in prostitution. He finds young girls from poor families and literally buys them and trains them to be high-class whores. Sometimes special guests are allowed to 'try them out' before they go out to work for real. Espada keeps this all very quiet, of course, and he's got judges and policemen on his payroll. Anyway, I think Roberto—he was, you know, a ladies' man, as you say—I think he fell for one of Espada's girls and helped her to escape from the ranch where they are kept as prisoners. They went to Ronda, where Roberto was supposed to fight in a *corrida.* Espada was there, doing one of his rallies to recruit volunteers for his army."

"Excuse me," Heidi said. "How come he's allowed to do that?"

Javier shrugged. "Because he's Espada. He *runs* the *corridas.* He can do what he pleases."

"Go ahead," Bond urged. "What happened to your brother?"

"He and the girl were found dead in his hotel, minutes before the *corrida* was supposed to have begun. His throat had been cut. No one knows how the killer got away. The hotel had only one entrance—the front."

"When you say his throat was cut, do you mean ear to ear?" Bond asked.

Javier nodded, swallowing. "I swear, if I find out that Espada was responsible, I will kill him. I'm thinking of killing him tonight."

"Javier, don't do anything rash. Have you ever heard of the Union?" Bond asked.

"Which union?"

"Not a bullfighting union, but a criminal organization called 'the Union'?"

"I don't think so."

"They're like a mafia, only they operate worldwide. We think Domingo Espada may be associated with them. As you know, he's stirring up trouble between my country and Spain over Gibraltar. If we can prove that the Union is backing Espada before Monday's summit conference in Gibraltar, we may have a chance of bringing him down."

"Being Spanish, I have mixed feelings about that situation," Javier admitted. "Gibraltar is a part of Spain and always has been."

"Not according to treaty, Javier," Bond said. "Gibraltar rightfully belongs to Great Britain until we decide otherwise. You wouldn't want a war to break out over it, would you?"

"Of course not."

Heidi interrupted. "We think Espada and the Union might be planning something catastrophic for Monday. It could affect everyone in this region . . . Spain, Gibraltar, Britain, North Africa . . . the whole Mediterranean."

"What's he going to do?" Javier asked.

"We don't know. We'd like you to find out, if you can."

"Me? What can I do? I'm not *that* close to Domingo. I'm beginning to hate him. I can't believe that I've treated him like family for years. I feel betrayed. The more I think about it, the more certain I am that he killed Roberto."

A sharp pain shot though Bond's chest. The look on his face must have given it away, for Heidi asked, "James? What's wrong?"

It was the suffocating anxiety again. He suddenly felt disoriented and nauseated. He shut his eyes, willing away the uncomfortable, dreadful feeling.

"I'm all right," he whispered. He rubbed his brow and lay back on the lounger.

"You don't look so good," Heidi said. "Maybe we ought to go back to the room?"

Bond shook his head. "It will pass. Keep talking, Javier. How about it? Will you help us?"

"James, I'm twenty-six years old. My entire career is ahead of me. I can't afford to cross a man like Espada. I have a fiancée. We plan to get married next year. If Espada doesn't kill me, he could make things very difficult for me. I might not get to fight at all, and that's my livelihood. But . . . Domingo has given the art of bullfighting a bad name lately."

"All we need is some kind of evidence that Espada is with the Union," Heidi said. "We need it before Monday. Can you get to his ranch and snoop around?"

"Somehow that seems more risky than killing him," Javier said. He was obviously frightened, but he took a deep breath and then said with resolve, "It was Pedro Romero, the father of modern bullfighting, who said, '*El cobarde no es hombre y para el toreo se necesitan hombres.*' 'A coward is not a man, and for bullfighting you need men.' I'm certainly not a coward in the bullring, and I'll be damned if I will be with this. He deserves to die!"

"We have to keep him alive for the time being, Javier," Bond said, sitting up again and looking at him. "He's part of some Union plot and

I'm sure that it has to do with the summit meeting on Monday. Please . . . wait. Don't do anything yet. If not for the sake of Spain, then for the sake of the future of bullfighting."

Javier looked out to sea. He knew that his British friend was right and nodded. "I'll see what I can do. Maybe I can go to the ranch tonight. I can't promise anything, James. If I find out that he did kill my brother, I cannot say what I will do or not do."

"I understand. Can we meet before the bullfight tomorrow?" Bond asked.

Javier shook his head. "Not before. After. There's a café across the street from the bullring in Málaga. It's called Bar Flor. I'll try to sneak away from the crowds and meet you there immediately after the *corrida.* Again, I can't promise anything."

"That's all right, Javier," Bond said. "I have a ticket to the bullfight, by the way. Only twenty-six, and you're already the senior bullfighter on the roster. Congratulations."

"I still don't see what the big deal is with this bullfighting," Heidi said. "It's not really fair to the bull, is it?"

Bond shot her a look, but Javier was used to such comments. "That is a common misconception among non-Spaniards. You see, the fighting bull is specially bred *just* to fight in the ring. It is a species that would otherwise be extinct if not for bullfighting. You must understand that the bulls live a glorious life on the ranches before their day of destiny in the bullring. They are treated as gods. The bull is a very special animal in Spain. We respect them because of their courage and their will to fight."

Javier became even more introspective as he gazed out over the Mediterranean. "There is a kind of duality that occurs between the matador and the bull. The entire *lidia* is a dance in which both the matador and the bull size up each other. They look into each other's eyes. The matador must know what the bull is thinking at all times, and this he must detect simply by watching the bull from the moment when he first enters the ring. The matador must *become* the bull, and in many ways, the bull does the same thing—he attempts to outthink the matador as the *lidia* progresses. With every pass of the *capote,* with every charge, the bull learns from his mistakes. If he misses the matador by two inches because the man performed a flawless verónica, the bull will remember it and charge a little closer next time. It is up to the matador to predict what the bull is going to do and then meet the mighty beast at the halfway mark. It is a dance. In the ring, the bull becomes the matador's mirror image."

Javier glanced at the wristwatch lying on the little table next to his lounger. "I must go now," he said. "I will see you tomorrow."

"Good luck," Bond said, shaking his hand again. "It was great to see you."

"You, too, James." He stood up and shook hands with Heidi. "And, *señorita,* you are as beautiful as any woman on earth." With that, he walked away toward the hotel grounds.

"Is it a requirement for all bullfighters to be gorgeous hunks, or is it just him?" Heidi asked.

Bond laughed. "Come on, let's go back to the hotel."

As they walked away from the beach, Jimmy Powers made a call on his mobile. He had been lying on a lounger some fifty feet away, his nose buried in a magazine. He was sure that Bond had not noticed him at any point over the last few days. Jimmy Powers learned his special ability while growing up first in the swamp country of Louisiana and later in the forests in Oregon. He wasn't known as the Union's best tracker and expert in shadowing a target for nothing.

When Nadir Yassasin heard what Powers had to say, the Moroccan made a quick decision. "Bond's contact with the bullfighter is dangerous. It was unforeseen that he would be a friend of the young matador. I think we need to take care of this situation before something unexpected happens. We're too close now, I don't want anything to derail the plan. Do you know who the girl is yet?"

Powers answered, "Preliminary search reveals that she is a CIA agent. Name of Hillary Taunt."

Yassasin smiled. "Good. She will have reported Bond's whereabouts to SIS in London. They know he's in Spain now. Things couldn't be better. You ought to return to the ranch, Jimmy. I am confident that Bond will appear at the bullfight tomorrow, right on schedule. We need to talk about what we're going to do about the matador, and then get you on your way to Gibraltar. I think there's a way we can use Bond's friendship with the matador to our advantage."

NINETEEN

DEATH IN THE AFTERNOON

Javier Rojo arrived at the Espada estate at 7:00 on Sunday morning. He told the guard at the gate that he had been invited to breakfast on the morning of the *corrida.* Since Javier was a familiar face at the ranch, the guard let him in without verifying the appointment.

He drove the Porsche around the annex and parked at the back. He quietly entered the house from the back door, which he knew would be unlocked. Javier thought that if Espada were really involved in criminal activities, then he should have better security!

He heard people talking in a room beyond the kitchen. They were indeed having breakfast on the patio, located off the immense living room. If he could creep into the living room and hide behind some furniture, perhaps he could hear their conversation.

Javier started to sneak into the room, but the sound of footsteps in the corridor to his right stopped him. He quickly moved back and stood behind a tall cactus in a painted clay pot.

He couldn't believe what he saw.

A man came out of the corridor and went into the living room, obviously headed for the patio.

It was James Bond! What the hell was *he* doing here?

In confusion, Javier stepped out from behind the cactus, hoping to get another look before the man disappeared outside.

"May I help you?"

It was the woman. Margareta Piel. She must have been just behind Bond.

"*Hola,*" Javier said. "I thought I saw someone I knew. . . ."

"Were you invited here this morning, Javier?" she asked.

"Well, no, but I thought that . . . considering that today . . . tonight . . ."

"Domingo isn't here," she said. "As much as I'd like to say I would love to have breakfast with you, Javier, it's just not convenient this morning. I'm sorry. You'll have to leave. Besides, Javier, you need to be ready for tonight! Go on! You know Domingo wouldn't like it if he saw you here, anyway. You're supposed to be preparing for the *corrida!*"

"Fine," Javier said. Now he wasn't so sure that he had seen what he had thought. Perhaps his eyes had been playing tricks on him. "I'm sorry to disturb you, *Señorita Piel.*" He said it as if he were spitting on her.

She flared her eyes at him as he left the way he had come in.

Jimmy Powers stepped out of the corridor. He had been listening just a few feet away the entire time.

"I hate to say I told you so," he said to Margareta. "He came looking for something, all right. What did he see?"

"I'm not sure, but I think he saw Peredur," she replied.

"Well," Powers said. "Please tell Nadir. Someone needs to keep an eye on the kid and make sure he doesn't go near our friend in Marbella before tonight. I'm off to Gibraltar."

Powers left the room. Margareta turned and went outside to the patio to find Yassasin.

"Nadir, I need to speak with you," she said. She led him to a corner of the patio and whispered softly. Peredur Glyn watched her, totally absorbed by the gorgeous woman he had spent the night with. When they came back to the table, Margareta sat in the chair next to him and squeezed his thigh.

Margareta told the servant what she wanted, then turned to Peredur. He was one of the most handsome men she had ever met. Dark. Cold. She liked that.

When Peredur Glyn had arrived at the ranch yesterday, she knew she had to sleep with him. He was terribly good-looking. The fact that she knew he was going to die tomorrow excited her even more.

They killed time in Bar Flor, the sidewalk café directly across the street from Málaga's *Plaza de Toros La Malagueta.* Bond sat with Heidi at one of the sidewalk tables, while Hedy, wearing the red wig, a scarf and sunglasses, sat inside the cafeteria, apart from them. She could hear their conversation by means of an earpiece and a small microphone attached to a button on Heidi's blouse.

It was a busy little place, crowded with anxious spectators waiting for the doors of the bullring to open. The two slot machines made a tremendous racket, and the air was buzzing with patrons' exuberance. These were people who loved bullfighting, and bullfighting is as widely discussed there as football is debated in Britain.

The throngs of people outside the bullring fascinated Bond and Heidi. They were all dressed in traditional garb for *corridas*—the women wore large, colorful dresses and headpieces, and carried fans. Every man was equipped with a cigar, and groups carried *botas,* pouches full of wine. While the atmosphere was not as festive as during the annual August *feria,* which had occurred a week earlier, there was still enough excitement to generate anticipation in even the most jaded person.

Bond wanted to catch Domingo Espada's speech before the bullfight, so he finished the sherry and took one last bite of pork.

"Hedy doesn't like the idea of you going in there alone," Heidi said.

"Hedy, don't worry," Bond said, directing his voice at the button on Heidi's blouse. "Something is destined to happen here. I just wonder if the Union are expecting me. And . . . thanks for giving me back my gun."

Hedy had handed it over before they reached Málaga. "I'm giving this back to you on one condition," she had said. "That you promise not to run away from us, do anything rash, shoot us, or kill more tourists."

She had gradually warmed to Bond over the last twenty-four hours. While Heidi was the consummate flirt and continued to show the most obvious interest, Bond was beginning to find Hedy the more attractive of the twins. He liked her style.

"I suggest you follow me at a very safe distance," Bond said to Heidi. "No doubt I'm being watched. You know whom to call if something goes wrong. I'm going to do my best to obtain a face-to-face meeting with Espada. Hopefully this ticket will be for a seat somewhere near him."

He stood and left some *pesetas* on the table. He leaned over and kissed Heidi on the cheek. "That was for you, too, Hedy," Bond said to the button.

"Good luck," Heidi said.

Bond crossed the street and joined the masses of people entering the beige bullring. While not as old as the one in Ronda, it is a beautiful, historic landmark. It is the site of not only bullfights, but also rock concerts, motorbike shows, operas, elections, and political rallies. The city had grown around it; tall apartment buildings stood on all sides of the ring, offering spectacular views for tenants owning binoculars.

The energy around him was palpable as Bond entered the *pasillo* and walked past the refreshment stands. Much like at an American sporting event, hawkers sold sweets, sunflower seeds, beer, and soft drinks during the *corrida.* Bond stopped and bought a beer, and then swallowed four of Dr. Feare's tablets, noticing that he was running low. What would he do when he needed to refill the prescription?

The place was filling up quickly, so Bond made his way to the *tendidos.* His seat was in one of the best sections, the *tendido sombra,* where patrons are able to sit in the shade. Next to it was the *apoderados* section, where managers and other bullfighting regulators sat. Some prime seats there had obviously been draped and reserved for VIPs, presumably Espada and his team. The president of the *corrida* and his aides sat in a section a few rows higher than Bond. Directly across the ring was the orchestra, the members of which were settling down, ready to begin the music. The fight was completely sold out; the roar of the spectators grew louder as the seats filled, section by section. The seat next to Bond's, however, remained empty.

Bond looked around the place with interest. Ever since he had met Javier and learned a thing or two about bullfighting, he genuinely enjoyed the spectacle. It was already an assault of colors, noise, and expectation—and the bullfight had yet to begin! He noted that the flags of Spain, Andalucía, and Málaga's local provincial government hung over the *puerta de cuadrillas,* where the procession of matadors and their teams would enter. Banners or advertisements, prominently displayed during concerts and other events, were prohibited at bullfights.

He didn't notice Hedy Taunt taking a seat in one of the sections above him. She could get a good view of Bond with a pair of opera glasses she had brought.

"I see him, Heidi," she said into her microphone. "So far, nothing unusual."

Bullfights, miraculously, always began on time. At exactly 6:25, Domingo Espada walked out to the center of the ring, carrying a microphone, ready to make the most of his five minutes. The crowd immediately gave him an ovation. Espada smiled broadly and waved, then raised the microphone to his mouth and began to speak.

"My friends, ladies and gentlemen, welcome to Málaga's *Plaza de Toros.* I will not take up too much of your time, for we have an exciting *corrida* today. You probably know that I am scheduled to go to Gibraltar tomorrow morning to meet the Prime Ministers of Spain and Great Britain, and the Governor of Gibraltar. I have pledged the remainder of my life to raising public consciousness regarding the Gibraltar issue. I have no idea what tomorrow will bring, but I am asking any able-bodied men to come with me and join my security force. The pay is very good. We have nearly two thousand men already. My goal is to increase the size of the force to twenty-five hundred. I need to show the other side that Domingo Espada's party is powerful and has the will of the people behind it. You will find recruitment centers located at the exits. If you are over eighteen years of age, please, I would love to have you work for me. If you want to see Spain become a major force in the politics of the world again, you will support my cause. I need you. The people need you. Spain needs you.

"And now, I salute the brave men facing the bulls tonight!"

This brought a loud cheer from the stands. Espada waved again and began walking toward the fence. Bond noted the man's natural charisma that carried even at this distance. If he was as articulate and intelligent as he was supposed to be, Bond could see why so many people wanted to follow him.

At that point, a strikingly attractive woman with long black hair moved into the aisle and sat down in the seat next to Bond's. She was dressed in a green traditional *flamenco* dress with a yellow and orange flower pattern.

"Hello," Bond said.

"*Hola,*" she said, not smiling. She settled into the chair, then looked out over the heads as if she were looking for someone. Bond glanced at her every few seconds, but she seemed to be ignoring him.

"You're not Spanish," she said, finally, still not looking at him.

"No, I'm not," Bond answered. At last. He was getting somewhere.

"Where are you from?"

"Britain."

He saw the hint of a smile at the corner of her mouth. Bond was fascinated with her face. She had classic Spanish features, but there was something very cold in her dark eyes. The woman exuded a worldliness that was immediately attractive. She had exquisite poise, as if she had stepped out of a painting.

"My name is Margareta Piel," she said. "What is your name?"

"John Cork."

"Pleased to meet you, Mr. Cork. Do you enjoy bullfighting?"

"Yes, I do. I find it fascinating."

"I'm surprised," she said. "Most people who are not Spanish do not like it."

"It's because they don't understand it."

"Quite so," she agreed.

The band suddenly struck up the *pasodoble* and the bullring gate swung open, right on time.

A *corrida* always begins with a *paseo,* or procession, of the three matadors who are fighting, followed by their *cuadrillas,* the teams made up of *banderilleros,* picadors, and *mulilleros.*

Javier Rojo, as the senior matador, was walking in the middle. He would fight the first and fourth bulls of the *corrida.* All of the men, grouped together in their colorful costumes, made a spectacular vignette on the field.

After the procession, the field was rapidly brushed by men wielding *rastrillos,* the wooden brooms used to smooth the dirt.

Bond felt a twinge of anxiety as he watched Javier prepare for the entrance of the first bull. One never knew if a matador would live or die in the ring. It is a far more dangerous "sport" than most people realize, although it is no sport to the Spanish. Javier assumed his position near one of the shields in front of the fence. The music ceased and the crowd grew quiet. The moment at which the bull entered the ring was among the most dramatic in a bullfight. It was then that a matador could see exactly how brave and strong the bull was.

The gate swung open and a huge, black beast thundered into the ring. The first act, the *tercio de varas,* had begun. With the help of his *banderilleros,* the bullfighter would now test the bull by having him charge at the capes. One of the *banderilleros* called to him, waving a cape. The bull immediately charged the target, but the man stepped inside a shield in the nick of time. The bull's horns slammed into the wood. The crowd cried, "Olé!"

Another *banderillero* called to the bull and waved the bright red cape. The bull turned, snorted, and rushed toward him. Again, the man stepped inside a shield, barely escaping injury.

At last, it was Javier's turn. He stepped out into the ring and called to the bull. Much of the appeal of a bullfighter was the way he carried himself. The more arrogant and egotistical he was, the more popular he would be. There was a great deal of posing and grimacing involved in being a matador, but even that required skill. Javier did it well, simultaneously displaying pride, honor, and a demand for respect.

Somehow, the bull knew that this was the man who was his true enemy. The bull pawed the dirt in front of him, then charged. Javier performed a neat *verónica* and sidestepped the bull. The crowd went wild.

"This matador is one of the best," Margareta said. "Have you seen him before?"

"As a matter of fact, I have," Bond said.

The picadors entered the ring on horseback. It was their job to wound the bull with lances called *varas* without causing injury to the horses, even though coverings made of cotton and steel mesh protected the animals to some extent.

At this point, Domingo Espada and two men entered the stands and sat down in their seats not far away from Bond and the girl.

"He's also quite an orator," Bond said.

"And very popular with the people," Margareta agreed. "At one time he was a great matador. Now he is a great politician."

"It sounds as if you admire him," Bond said.

"I have to. I work for him."

"Do you? Why, I'd really like to meet him. As an interested expat, of course."

"Of course," she said. "I can arrange that. After the bullfight."

"I'm beginning to believe that our rendezvous was no coincidence," Bond said.

"You might be right," she said seductively, as she rubbed her leg against his.

Out in the ring, the bull had been stabbed twice with lances. A good deal of blood was streaming down the animal's side.

Before the third lance, Javier spent several minutes in the middle of the ring, taunting the bull. The bull would rush him, but the matador deftly countered with the cape in a series of maneuvers. His movements were pure and smooth as he stood, feet together and back arched. Bond could appreciate that a matador's dance with the bull was very sexual; it was no wonder that bullfighters were considered sex symbols. It was almost as if the matador was seducing the bull. As Javier had said, the two living things—man and beast—had become one in the ring. With the cape, the matador had molded the animal's wild charges into something of beauty.

Javier gave way so that the picador could gallop his horse around the ring, leading the bull into a charge. The horse turned sharply, heading off the bull so that the picador could thrust the lance into the bull's withers, the hump on its back that was the gateway to its vital organs.

The signal was given for the change in acts, to the *tercio de banderillas.* The *banderilleros* were older men, usually matadors who never made it to the top. They strutted out into the field, each holding a pair of the colorful spikes called *banderillas.* Again, each man had to taunt the bull to charge and, as it came within inches of his body, accurately thrust both spikes into the bull's withers. It was one of the most dangerous parts of the bullfight, since the bull, at this point, was in pain, angry, and ready to gore anything that moved.

The bull charged Javier's first *banderillero,* who was standing alone and unprotected near the center of the ring, the sticks held high above his head, back arched, and raised on tiptoes. He neatly sidestepped the animal and stabbed it with the spikes. The crowd cried out in approval. After the second pair of spikes was delivered, Javier motioned to the *corrida* president that he would opt to administer the third pair.

Javier moved to the center of the ring and beckoned to the bull. The animal was now wary of the men in the colorful costumes. He was learning and adapting his strategy for attack. Without warning, the bull charged and brushed against Javier, knocking him to the ground. Javier dropped the spikes and rolled to avoid being gored. The spectators gasped loudly. Javier jumped to his feet before the bull could turn and charge again. Forced to retreat to the fence, Javier brushed off the accident and picked up two more spikes.

This time, Javier boldly moved to the center of the ring and called to the bull. He arched his back and held the sticks high. It charged and the matador perfectly administered the spikes. The spectators roared.

It was time for the third and final act, the *tercio de la muerte.* The president gave his permission for the bull to be killed, something that was always traditionally asked for by the matador. Javier then looked around the bullring for someone to dedicate the bull to. Matadors would often pay tribute to a woman, a visiting dignitary, a friend or relative, by offering his hat to that person. If he wished to dedicate the fight to the entire crowd, he would throw the hat into the ring.

Javier strode toward the section where Bond was sitting. Their eyes met, and Javier flung the hat up and over the heads of the people in the first rows. Bond reached and caught the hat as the audience applauded. Javier smiled at Bond, then took his cape and sword from his assistant.

The matador has a time limit in which to kill the bull in the third act. It has to be done with precision, for no one likes to see the bull suffer. Aimed correctly, the *estoque* would sever the bull's spinal cord and other vital organs, killing it quickly. If it were still alive after falling to the ground, a member of the team would stab it in the back of the head with a short knife. Death was then instantaneous.

Javier stood in the middle of the ring, daring the bull to come closer and closer with each charge. He expertly twirled the cape, holding back the sword so that the bull would not expect it. This is the point at which a matador indulges in his most risky maneuvers, allowing the bull to get as near to his body as possible. With each pass, the crowd cried, "Olé!" and cheered. The music started up again and the first bullfight was quickly approaching its climax.

The dance of the matador and the bull became a ballet as Javier created beautiful flourishes with the cape, sometimes dropping to one knee to accept the animal's charge. He enthralled the crowd by performing a kneeling pinwheel maneuver. In this vulnerable position the matador moved the cape to one side, crossing his body with his arm. Then, once the horns passed, he spun in the opposite direction to the bull's charge, wrapping the cape around his hips. It was a decorative pass, but it was necessary with a quick-turning bull such as this one.

Finally, Javier faced the bull and dropped to his knees again. He called to the bull, daring it to charge a defenseless man on his knees.

"He is brave, that young man," Margareta said.

At that moment, one of the *banderilleros,* the only one dressed in red, stepped out of the shield directly behind the bull, in Javier's view. He stood there a moment, as if waiting for some kind of reaction from Javier.

Bond could see that something was wrong. Javier stood and, for a moment, he looked at the *banderillero.* He rubbed his eyes and appeared disoriented. The bull sensed the man's hesitation and charged.

The crowd screamed as Javier was picked up by the bull's horns and thrown over the animal's back. Javier landed with a thud on the ground. The rest of the team ran toward him, shouting, attempting to attract the bull's attention, but the animal wasn't to be distracted. It turned and plunged its horns into the matador's body. There were more screams from the spectators. Bond stood in alarm, clutching Javier's hat.

The *banderillero* in red had disappeared.

The men brought out a stretcher and rolled Javier's body onto it. The blood on his side was quite evident. In the meantime, one of the other matadors came out to finish the job. Taking a cape and sword, the new man stood in front of the bull and held the sword out in front, taking careful aim. Then, just as the bull charged, the matador lunged forward and thrust the sword into the bull's back. It was a perfect kill. The crowd cheered wildly as the bull collapsed, the blood pouring out if its wound.

Bond began to move out of the stand. "I have to see about Javier," he muttered to the woman.

She followed him down the stairs into the *pasillo,* where a number of people had already gathered to see about Javier Rojo's condition.

Hedy stood and spoke into her mike. "He's on the move, and that woman who was sitting with him is right behind him. Damn, he's getting lost in the crowd." She shoved her way out of the row and attempted to keep sight of Bond, but the swarm of spectators blocked her view.

Bond pushed through the crowd, running toward the *enfermería,* a fully equipped emergency room.

What the hell happened out there? Had he imagined it?

He got caught up in the mass of people, and suddenly Bond's head started to spin and he felt pressure in his chest.

"Let me through!" he tried to shout, but no one could hear him.

Someone cried, "Javier Rojo is dead!" There were screams of despair from the crowd.

Bond's vision blurred and he stumbled, but he felt a soft hand take his.

"Come with me," Margareta said.

Bond let her lead him out of the crowd and into the chapel, often called the "place of fright," because that's where the matadors left their fear before entering the bullring.

Bond collapsed to his knees.

"You don't look well, Mr. Bond," Margareta said.

"Who . . . are . . . you?" Bond asked, but the words came out as gibberish.

Margareta walked around him and opened a side door. The *banderillero* in red entered the chapel and began to remove his costume.

Bond looked up through the hazy film in his eyes and attempted to focus on the man who had killed his friend.

"Murderer . . ." Bond gasped.

The vision became a little clearer.

The *banderillero* was the double—the man who looked like Bond! Javier had become fatally distracted when he saw his "friend" in the bullring!

Margareta slammed the butt of a pistol down on the back of Bond's head.

Hedy made her way into the *pasillo* and frantically searched the faces of the crowd for James Bond. It was pandemonium, as the media had already descended into the area to find out more about Javier's condition.

"Heidi, I've lost the bastard," she said.

"Keep looking," Heidi instructed. "I'm watching the street."

Hedy was near the chapel when the door opened and the woman with the dark hair emerged. Hedy spotted her and watched as the woman directed a couple of men to follow her. They were carrying a stretcher, upon which lay a body covered by a sheet. Hedy moved forward, but then she saw James Bond come out of the chapel and bring up the rear of the little group.

Hedy followed them out of the *pasillo* toward the VIP parking area. There, the men loaded the stretcher into a red minivan. The woman got in the back with the stretcher, and James Bond took the passenger seat. In a moment, the van backed out of the parking space and was on its way.

"Damn!" Hedy said. "Heidi, get the car, quick!"

James Bond became aware of a low rumbling sound as he opened his eyes. He was on a stretcher in the back of a vehicle—a van perhaps? His wrists were bound behind him and his head felt as if it were on fire. Then he noticed that his clothes had been removed and exchanged for a white cotton shirt and dark trousers. Margareta Piel sat across from him with a Glock in her hand.

"Just stay calm, Mr. Bond," she said. "We're going to your meeting with Domingo Espada."

Bond squinted and saw that another man was riding in the front with the driver. It might have been the *banderillero,* but a shaded barrier made it impossible to tell.

"Women who point guns at me usually regret it in the end," Bond said.

"Is that a threat, Mr. Bond?" she asked.

"Just a warning."

"You're awfully handsome, Mr. Bond. I like dark men like you. You don't have any Spanish blood, do you?"

"Not that I know of."

"Pity." She crossed her legs, inviting him to gaze at her.

Instead, Bond looked out the window and saw that the minivan had entered the motorway, heading west toward Marbella and the home of Domingo Espada.

TWENTY

THE MAN WHO CAME TO DINNER

They were sitting in the BMW, which they had parked not far from the bullring. Hedy was driving and the car screeched out of the parking space onto the main avenue.

"How far are they ahead?" Hedy asked.

"They're pulling onto the expressway," Heidi replied.

Hedy accelerated, shooting past the slower-moving vehicles. "I sure as hell hope he didn't skip out on us."

"I don't think he would do that," Heidi said.

"How do you know?"

"I think he likes us."

Hedy snorted. "Then he'd better be hot on Espada's tail."

"It looks like they're heading for Torremolinos . . . and Marbella is just beyond that. How much do you want to bet he's headed for Espada's ranch? You know, the 'X' on that map he had . . ."

"If we lose him, we'll have hell to pay."

They drove silently for a few minutes, and then Hedy asked, "You really think he likes us?"

Heidi turned to her sister and smiled. "Sure. Can't you tell?"

Hedy shrugged. She had a mischievous look in her eyes. "I think he likes *you*."

"Isn't that the same thing?"

"Heidi, we're not going to get into another situation like that, are we?" Hedy asked.

"Don't you like him, too?" Heidi asked. "I think he's a hunk and a half."

Hedy acknowledged her sister's remark with an approving grin. "All right, I admit it. He's not bad."

"Not bad, are you kidding? The guy oozes sex." Heidi squinted at her sister. "You *do* like him, don't you?"

Hedy refused to answer, but instead observed, "You saw him first."

Heidi shrugged. "Well, you're the one who's undersexed. We can work that out later. . . ."

The tension in the air over Gibraltar Town's Main Street was palpable late on Sunday afternoon. Nevertheless, the shops had remained open, their proprietors hoping that at least one tourist would venture in and spend some money. But it was not to be. Gibraltar's ports were closed, and the airport open only for official governmental business. It would seem that the inhabitants should panic and flee in fear of a Spanish takeover. Instead, the stalwart Gibraltarians chose to put their faith in the existing government. After all, the Rock had been threatened many times in the past, and it had a long history of surviving.

With or without tourists, the King's Chapel was always open to the public at the weekend. Officially a part of the Convent, the Governor's private residence, it dated back to 1533. The original Franciscan Chapel had been built in the shape of a cross, although a portion was later appropriated for the Governor's residence. The shape is more or less retained and today is used by both the Church of England and by Roman Catholics.

Jimmy Wayne Powers sighed, finishing a pint at one of the Angry Friar pub's sidewalk tables, perfectly situated across the street from the Convent and the chapel. He noted the heightened security around the front of the Governor's residence. On a "black" security code day, there would be at least one guard from the Gibraltar Regiment standing outside, whereas, on an "amber" code day, there might be four. Today was a "red" code day, and Powers counted eight men outside the Convent. There was no telling how many more were inside.

Powers thought this whole thing was crazy, but he didn't attempt to question it. If Nadir Yassasin claimed it would succeed, then he had to believe him.

Time to get to work.

He left some money, picked up his brown briefcase, and crossed the street. The soldiers eyed him suspiciously, but they treated everyone that way. He went straight into the King's Chapel and found himself in a surprisingly quiet and peaceful room furnished in exquisite elegance. The front of the chapel was on the east end of the "cross." A locked white door led to the Convent at the south end. The congregation sat in the western portion, and the entrance and memorial hall lay in the north section.

He was alone.

Powers was good at this kind of work. He excelled in stealth skills and was an expert in sabotage. Why, he had tailed the great James Bond for over a month and the fool never knew it! Powers was pleased that he could supply such reliable information about the Union's target.

Now he had something different to do.

He quickly opened the briefcase, working silently at high speed. He removed six white silk bags and a roll of tape. Each bag contained a firearm: three of them Spanish 9mm Super Star automatics, two Brownings, and one Walther PPK.

Powers spent the next five minutes taping the bags under various pews in the chapel. When he was done, he put the tape back in the briefcase, closed it, and made his way past the memorials to the entrance. He paused long enough to sign the guest book.

In it, he wrote the date and "Richard Bunyon—Washington, D.C."

He glanced at his watch. By now, Union killers would have pulled off a relatively simple job in the United States capital. The limousine driver for two State Department officials, the real Richard Bunyon and an Arab named Said Arif, would inadvertently get lost on his way to Dulles Airport.

The two men would never check in for their flight to Gibraltar. By the time their superiors discovered they were missing, it would be too late.

Powers walked out of the chapel onto Main Street, ignored the guards as he strolled past the front of the Convent, then climbed the hill to the Rock Hotel, where he would spend the rest of the evening enjoying dinner and a good book.

The minivan zipped through Torremolinos and made it to Marbella in an hour. The sun was setting as the van turned north to drive into the hills. Margareta had stayed silent during the trip, but the way she stared at Bond unnerved him. She had a glint behind her eyes that he recognized all too well. He had seen it many times before, and it meant bad news. This woman was a killer. His experience had taught him how to identify that particular trait in a person. She might be beautiful and refined, but Margareta Piel was probably as dangerous as they come.

When the minivan pulled into the drive in front of the ranch, two guards peered inside. They saw Margareta and waved the van through as they opened the gate. Bond was impressed with the spread. It was a beautiful location here, up in the hills overlooking the Mediterranean. They drove past enclosed fields full of bulls, and a large barnlike structure that looked as if it was some kind of slaughterhouse. Bond noted the circular annex to the building, and guessed that it was probably a practice bullring of some kind.

The dirt road curved up and around a small hill, and the main estate loomed ahead of them. It was a splendid mansion built in a Roman tradition with Arab influence and Mudéjar decoration. It was a flat-roofed structure common in *cortijos,* built of earth, mud, and lime. Wood was only used as a framework for the walls, for the roof, and as beams. The windows and doors were framed. The overall impression was that it was a modern version of an eighteenth-century neoclassical palace.

The minivan turned and drove on a side road around behind the barn. Eventually the driver stopped at the back of the building, out of sight from the main road.

Margareta leveled her gun at Bond and said, "Get out. No funny stuff." The driver opened the door for him. The other passenger had already got out and walked into the building before Bond could get a good look at him. He could have sworn that the man had been wearing Bond's clothes. Was he really a double, or had Bond's eyes been playing tricks on him again?

The woman marched him inside, through a passageway, and into a small room furnished with a table, chairs, and a television. The walls were covered with old bullfight posters.

"Sit there," Margareta said, pointing to the largest chair in the room, facing the television.

"You're not so cruel that you're going to make me watch Spanish television, are you?" he quipped.

"Shut up." The driver shoved Bond into the chair and then secured him to it with leather straps.

"So, *señorita*, how long have you been with the Union?" he asked.

Margareta expected that he would know and would have been disappointed if he had not figured it out. "Not long. In fact, I won't officially be a member until after tomorrow. That's when I get my tattoo."

"Your tattoo?" Bond asked.

Margareta drew a sharp intake of air. She suddenly wasn't sure how much Bond knew about the Union. The laser-implanted tattoo on a new member's right retina was a part of the initiation. How secret was it?

"I thought I told you to shut up," she said.

"What happened to our bullfighting friend?" he asked. "I'm afraid I didn't catch his name. . . ."

"You'll meet him formally in a while. First, though, you've been invited to have dinner with Señor Espada. Unfortunately, you won't get to taste the wonderful food his chef prepared for tonight's feast. However, you *do* get to watch it on TV."

Margareta turned on the television. It was a closed-circuit picture of a dining table. A servant girl was placing silverware and glasses at the settings.

"Virtual dinners, I love them," Bond said. "Low on calories."

Margareta stepped closer to him and took his chin in her hands. "You won't be making jokes too much longer, Mr. Bond. This is the end of the line. I'm sure you've been traced here, which is exactly what we want. You've walked right into the trap. It won't be long before your people in London know that you're at Domingo Espada's home."

"So?"

Margareta smiled. "In time you will know all. . . ." With that, she leaned over and kissed him hard on the mouth. He let her do it, but he didn't reciprocate at all. When she was done, she licked her lips and said, "Mmm, not bad, Mr. Bond. You taste . . . like fresh meat."

She turned to go. The driver held open the door for her.

"Don't try to escape. You're heavily guarded. I'll be back after dinner," she said. "Enjoy the show."

With that, she left. The driver slammed the door shut and Bond heard the locks turn.

Heidi and Hedy pulled over about a mile away from Espada's ranch.

"He's there, no doubt about that," Heidi said. "What do we do now?"

"I wish we knew if he went willingly or not." Hedy thought for a moment. "Should we call for backup?"

"Who's gonna come?" Heidi asked. "Our operatives are in Madrid, Barcelona, and Seville. By the time anyone gets here, the show, whatever it is, will be over."

"You're right." Hedy opened the glove compartment and removed a pair of binoculars. She got out of the car, adjusted the glasses for infrared vision, and put them to her eyes. She had a fairly good view of the entire estate, save for a portion of the main house that was blocked by the large annex.

"I see some men at the gate," she said. "I don't see the minivan. It might be behind that barn." She scanned the buildings and then said, "Oh no."

"What?"

"I see him," Hedy said. "It's James. He's walking from that other building to the main house. Look." She handed the glasses to Heidi. Sure enough, James Bond was entering the front door, accompanied by other men and the Spanish woman.

"Goddamn him!" Heidi said. "Do you think he really *is* in cahoots with Espada? He walked in there like he owned the place! And that woman! Who the hell is she?"

"Heidi, I think he fooled us."

Heidi looked as if she might cry.

Hedy took back the binoculars. "I wonder if there's another way around. You know, an approach from the back."

Heidi peered at the road ahead and pointed. "Look," she said. "There's some kind of trail there. See? It leads down to that valley. You think maybe there's another trail that leads up and around?"

"I don't think the car will make it. I'll have to go on foot. Let's split up."

"Why you? I should go."

"No, I'll go."

"Let's flip for it."

"Forget it, Heidi, I'm going!"

"Well, what's our plan?" Heidi asked. "We gotta have a plan."

"I'm making it up as we go along," Hedy said. "You stay here. Is your communicator still working?"

"Of course."

"If you see anyone come out of the house, let me know." She handed the binoculars to her. "If you get into trouble, just press the panic button. I'll do the same thing. Either way, we come running, all right?"

"How the hell will I know where you are?"

"I'll scream," Hedy said, shrugging. "If nothing happens, let's meet back here at midnight. If he's not out by then, we'll call London."

"Okay," Heidi said hesitantly.

Hedy checked her weapon and ammunition, and gave her sister a peck on the cheek. "Don't worry. I'll be fine." Before Heidi could respond, Hedy had set off down the road toward the trail.

The pain in James Bond's head had increased tenfold since he had been tied to the chair, exacerbated by the recent blow. He had to force himself to concentrate on his surroundings and search for a way out of his predicament. The bindings were terribly tight, but he could scoot the chair across the floor if he wanted to. That wouldn't do much good, unfortunately. Perhaps it was best to let them play out the game. They had some kind of a plan in mind, and he was part of it. He couldn't intelligently plot a course of action without knowing what it was.

Something started happening on the TV monitor. Margareta Piel entered the picture, accompanied by a tall, black man in a fez. They sat at the table as Espada's voice boomed out of the speakers.

"Sit, sit," he said. "We have some wonderful *paella* tonight."

Espada and another man, a bit older, entered the frame and sat at the head of the table. "Wonderful *corrida* in Málaga, although it was unfortunate about Javier." He shook his head and made a "tsk tsk" sound. "I am sorry to lose him."

Bond couldn't help but catch the glance that Margareta gave the Moroccan.

"So, Nadir, are we on schedule?" Espada asked him.

"Yes, Domingo, everything is prepared. Jimmy Powers is in Gibraltar and was successful in planting the weapons in the chapel. We will leave here tonight after dinner. I suggest that you leave only a skeleton force here, for we will need every competent man with us," the man called Nadir said.

"I was planning on it. Now, what about the assassin?"

Margareta spoke up. "He should be here any minute. He had to change clothes and wash. Oh . . . here he is now."

Espada stood and looked toward the camera. A man entered the frame, his back to Bond.

"Domingo Espada, I'd like you to meet James Bond, formerly with Her Majesty's Secret Service in Great Britain."

Bond's jaw dropped when the man turned to reveal his profile and shake hands with Espada.

"Welcome, Mr. Bond," Espada said. "I have heard great things about you. Despite my hatred for your homeland, I welcome you here." He gestured to the other man at the table. "This is Agustin, my *mozo de espadas.*"

"Thank you, sir, I've already met Agustin," the imposter said. "It's a pleasure to be here."

My God! The man *was* an exact replica of him! He hadn't been imagining a double at all . . . there really was one! How had they done this? The man didn't completely *sound* like him, Bond thought. The speech was a little off . . . in fact, the accent was Welsh. People close to Bond might detect the slight differences in inflection, but for all intents and purposes, the man on the television was James Bond.

Beads of sweat began to form on Bond's forehead. He knew that the science of plastic surgery had advanced by leaps and bounds in the last few years. The best in the field could literally do anything short of cloning a person. That was what they must have done. But . . . why? Just to frame him? To set him up as a criminal? Surely London would see through such a ploy. . . .

A servant girl poured wine, and then the *paella* was served. As a first course they had *tortilla de patatas*, an omelette made from potatoes. Bond felt his stomach rumble as he watched them eat.

"So, Mr. Bond, what are your feelings about what we are about to do tomorrow?" Espada asked, picking up a crawfish with his hands and biting into it with a crunch.

The look-alike made an offhand gesture that Bond instantly recognized as his own way of dismissing an idea. The man, whoever he was, had done his homework.

"I have felt for years that my country has been extremely selfish with Gibraltar," the pseudo-Bond said. "I am half Scottish, so I can sympathize with anyone who takes issue with who runs their government, who owns their land, and what constitutes a fair treaty."

"Why did you leave your country? Why do you want to help me?" Espada asked.

"British intelligence is no longer interesting," the man said. "In the past decade, SIS came out of the woodwork, so to speak. We . . . er, *they* used to be a secret organization. No one knew where our headquarters were located in London. Our covers were solid, all around the world. Nowadays, SIS is in plain sight, in that ugly building on the Thames, and the newspapers print photographs of the leading personnel. Foreign intelligence networks seem to have an uncanny knack of identifying agents. The Union infiltrates them and embarrasses the company. While the work was always political in nature, the mere machinations of *playing* at secret agent have become political. It got to where I couldn't make decisions on my own. Too much red tape. Too much bureaucracy."

Bond shook his head in disbelief. The imposter had him nailed. While Bond was nowhere as cynical in his opinions, he *had* entertained similar thoughts recently.

"Mr. Bond," Espada said, "I suppose what I really want to know is if you are prepared to perform the task which Nadir Yassasin and Margareta Piel here tell me that you have been hired to do. You are about to betray your country, commit treason and murder."

The imposter Bond smiled and replied, "I have no love for Britain anymore. I have lost . . . people I have loved . . . because of my work for the British government. One was my wife. It is time for me to pay them back. What have they done for me? My salary was adequate, but compared to what a hit man in the Italian Mafia makes for an assassination, I'm a pauper. Killing people has always been a part of my job. It's time I was paid properly for doing it. That's why I joined the Union."

Espada seemed pleased with the answers. He turned to Yassasin and said, "I believe you were right, Nadir. This man will do nicely. I like him." He raised his wineglass, and the others followed suit.

"To James Bond," he said. "May you perform your deed tomorrow morning with finesse and accuracy."

So that was it, Bond thought. The Union was going to use a double to assassinate someone—someone important—and *he* would get the blame.

Hedy made her way into the dark valley, trying her best not to stumble over a rock or a fallen branch. The area was thick with oak trees, and the half-moon barely penetrated the leaves. Nevertheless, she finally made it to the path leading up the hill and soon found herself back in the pale illumination of the night sky.

She crept over a ridge overlooking the estate and crouched in the shadows. The back of the annex was visible now, and she could see the minivan parked by a few other vehicles. She wondered what the circular section of the building might be, not realizing that it was a bullring.

The main house was well lit, and she could see at least two guards pacing the grounds around it. A barbed-wire fence surrounded the entire property.

What the hell should she do now? she wondered. She spoke into her microphone.

"Anything happening over there?" she asked in a whisper.

"Nothing," Heidi answered. "What about you? Where are you?"

"I'm above the main house, on the hill looking down into their backyard. I see a swimming pool, tennis courts, a garden . . . the van's behind that barn and there are . . . two, three, four other vehicles parked there. There's another parking area at the side of the house, and I see at least a half-dozen cars over there."

"So if there's one person per vehicle, then we're outnumbered," Heidi said. "Assuming that there are at least two people per vehicle, we're *seriously* outnumbered."

"We can't just go rushing in there like the cavalry, either. We have no grounds, no warrant. Espada is expected at a major political to-do in the morning, and who are we to screw that up?"

"Maybe we should just make a report and get instructions," Heidi suggested.

"You're probably right. You do it. I'm going to stay—"

She screamed when a torch beam flooded the area around her. A voice commanded her in Spanish to stand up and raise her hands. Without thinking about the consequences, she went for her gun. A blow on the back of her head put a stop to that, and she fell over.

Espada apparently liked to talk, and he dominated the dinner conversation.

"Reclaiming Gibraltar for Spain has been an ambition of mine since my days with Franco. Bless his soul, he shared my views on the matter. I made a promise to him that one day I would do something significant to further our cause in that regard. Tomorrow, that dream will be fulfilled. It is Spain's destiny. And . . . I am willing to die for the cause, if that is the final outcome."

"Don't be ridiculous, Domingo," Margareta said. "Mr. Bond here is a professional. He will not miss his targets. And Nadir, Jimmy, and I will be there, too, just in case something goes wrong."

"And I will not let anything happen to you," Agustin said, "if I can help it."

What the hell were they planning to do? Bond wondered. Keep talking! What were the details of their terrible scheme?

But before he could learn more, a guard entered the dining room and whispered something to Espada.

"Bring her in, let's have a look," Espada said aloud. The guard went out of the room. "It seems we have another guest. An uninvited one."

After a moment, the guard brought in Hedy. The wig was gone. Her blouse was torn, revealing a white bra, and her hands were tied behind her back.

Oh no! Bond thought. Which one was she? Heidi or Hedy . . . ?

The guard held her as Espada addressed her in English. "Who are you, my dear?"

She kept silent.

"Oh, not talking are we?" The guard tossed some things onto the table. They were her identification, microphone, and earpiece. Espada picked up the ID.

"Hillary Taunt. Travel writer," he read. "What makes you want to spy on my house, eh? You're not really writing about a private property, are you?"

The girl continued to glare at him.

"She's with the CIA," Yassasin said. "We know all about her. She's based in Casablanca."

"She's beautiful," Margareta said. "So blond . . . nice figure . . ."

"Yes, indeed," Espada agreed. "CIA, eh?" He addressed the guard. "Take her to the compound. I think I might keep her a while. She's a little older than what I'm accustomed to, but she might provide some amusement for a few nights before she's discovered missing. After that . . ." He shrugged.

The guard pulled her away and out of the room. Espada turned to the imposter Bond and asked, "Perhaps you would like to try her out tonight? She will be my gift to you in appreciation for what you are going to do for me tomorrow."

The imposter Bond smiled lecherously and said, "Why, thank you, Señor Espada. I might just do that."

Nadir Yassasin cleared his throat. "Whatever happens, we must not be late for the boat. Domingo, you and Agustin and the rest of the men are expected in La Linea by midnight. We have some final preparations to do with Mr. Bond, and he and Margareta will join you in the morning for the border crossing into Gibraltar. Jimmy Powers and I will arrive separately. Remember, when we're all together at the Convent, you do not know us."

"I'm no fool," Espada said. "Very well. Shall we go?"

He stood and held out his hand to the imposter Bond. "I will see you in the morning, then."

"Thank you, sir, for this opportunity," the double said.

Espada said good-bye to Margareta and Yassasin, then started to leave the room. He turned back and addressed them all. "Mr. Bond can have his way with that girl tonight, and then we'll get rid of her. I don't need a blond American in my harem."

After Espada and Agustin left the room, Margareta looked at the camera.

"Dinner is over, Mr. Bond," she said, addressing him. "It's time for dessert."

TWENTY-ONE

DOPPELGÄNGER

The locks rattled and the door swung open. Margareta Piel and the Moroccan entered the room. She was carrying a leather briefcase, which she set on the table.

"Did you miss me, Mr. Bond?" she asked. "This is Nadir Yassasin. Say *hola.*"

The tall man bowed slightly. "It's a pleasure to meet the real James Bond after all this time. You have my respect, sir, but not my benevolence."

Bond spat an obscenity at them both.

"Tsk tsk," Margareta said, closing the door. "How was the television program? Did you get it all, or would you like someone to explain it to you?"

"Who is that imposter going to kill?" Bond growled.

It was the man who answered. "The Union have worked very hard these last three months in order to humiliate and embarrass your country and your feeble intelligence agency. The leadership decided that you, specifically, had to pay for a certain past Union failure."

"We call Nadir the 'strategist,'" Margareta said. "He came up with an absolutely brilliant scheme to lure you here so that we can pull a . . . what do the Americans call it? . . . a 'Switcheroo'?"

Yassasin began to walk around the room, his hands clasped behind his back. "Think about it, Mr. Bond. Think back to how you felt when you returned from the Himalayas. We knew that you would want to go after us just as much as we wanted our hands on you. Lucky for the Union, you had some medical difficulties. Am I right?"

Bond didn't answer.

"You see, Mr. Bond," he continued. "We knew you were on medical leave. This made you particularly vulnerable. Mr. Bond, I profiled you the way the FBI in America profiles serial killers. I got to know you *personally.* I studied your history, I had you followed, I know what you like and don't like. . . . We even knew what *medications* you were taking for your condition. Let's just say that . . . we tampered with them a bit."

Bond squinted at Yassasin. *Tampered with the medicine? How? What had they done to him?*

"You became so psychologically unstable that you were able to play right into our hands. By the power of suggestion, we provided you with hints as to how you could avenge your personal assistant's death. As a result, we were able to lay a trail for you to follow and make it appear that you were doing all the work. You sniffed out every bread crumb we dropped in front of you. It all began with the visit to your neighborhood Chinese restaurant, didn't it? Our best surveillance man, and one of the Union's founding members, had his eye on you for a month after the Himalayan business. We learned your daily habits. When you were followed to lunch that day, the fortune you got was planted by a cantankerous customer."

Bond remembered the rude man with the screaming toddler. He would never have known. . . . Now he realized that his feelings of paranoia and of being watched, which he had dismissed as part of his ailment, had been genuine.

"We sent you the book that led you to Walter van Breeschooten's shop in Soho. We let you follow him to Morocco. It was only logical that you would contact your friend in Tangier. The photos of your prey were sent to him just in time for you to see them. That, in turn, led you to the Union training camp in the Rif Mountains. We allowed you to uncover just enough information to lead you to Casablanca, where, of course, we threw Mr. van Breeschooten to you." Yassasin shrugged. "He had displeased the Union's management, so he was dispensable. But not before you received the ticket to the bullfight. I knew that you would be headstrong, stubborn, and reckless. I knew that you would show up, one way or another. I honestly didn't think you'd pick up a ride to Spain with the CIA, and I must say that was very resourceful. We had a more complicated plan to abduct you from the bullfight, but when I learned that one of the bullfighters was your friend, I thought of something better. It was . . . easy to get you out of the crowd and down below the seats where we could take care of you. Poor Javier . . . such a fine young matador. Seeing *you* standing there, dressed as a *banderillero*, distracted him so much that he became careless. The bull took advantage of that. It's a pity."

Bond seethed in anger.

"While all this was going on, a man named Peredur Glyn created the public impression that you were causing all kinds of trouble," the Muslim explained. "After it had come to my attention that a Union mercenary working in Africa was a dead ringer for you, we had extensive photos made. No, you weren't identical twins by any means, but Glyn was the same weight and height; he had the same body type, and he had similar enough features that one might mistake him to be a member of your family.

"So we turned to Dr. Iwan Morelius, a Swedish plastic surgeon who is known for his high-priced and elite clientele in Beverly Hills and Hollywood. Perhaps you have heard of him? No? Dr. Morelius arrived in Hollywood with a very unique talent. He's a true artist, this Dr. Morelius. He is a master of dermabrasion, in which outer layers of skin are removed by "sanding off" or abrading the layers with a carbon dioxide laser. Morelius is an expert with the laser—he can precisely "sculpt" a face. He has such a skilled hand that he can quite literally mold a person's face into any shape or likeness. He got into a bit of trouble with the Screen Actors Guild when he created two uncanny look-alikes of famous movie stars. The real film stars sued and Dr. Morelius was forced out of business. Luckily for him, the Union learned of his talents and employed him. Dr. Morelius performed the rhytidectomy, or face remodeling, on Glyn. It was expensive, but certainly worth it. Dr. Morelius will no doubt be useful for the Union in the future.

"Glyn needed a fairly major overhaul for the outcome to be totally believable. Besides a complete dermabrasion, he was subjected to blepharoplasty and rhinoplasty. Fat tissue was removed from his cheeks to make them less full, and from his lips to make them thinner. The remodeling did the trick. Using computer-generated three-dimensional models of your head, adapted from Union file photographs, Dr. Morelius performed a Hollywood miracle.

"After six weeks, the face had healed. Glyn went through the next three weeks learning to be you—he memorized your daily routine, based on reports provided by Jimmy Powers. It didn't matter that his voice is dissimilar to yours. It's the visual effect that counts."

"He is a murderer," Bond said.

"And you're not?" Yassasin asked. "Yes, you're right. First, he murdered poor Dr. Feare, who had the unfortunate luck of being your girlfriend for the night."

"You're all bastards," Bond muttered.

"Now, now, Mr. Bond," Yassasin said. "There's no need to insult my family. The next thing Mr. Glyn did was to shoot a few British tourists on a ferry. Again, you were blamed. By then, your people were surely convinced that you had become renegade. You had disappeared, disobeyed orders, and are now wanted for a number of crimes. Therefore, it will come as no surprise to the world when 'James Bond' commits a few more terrible crimes tomorrow morning." He nodded to Margareta. She opened the door and the man whom Bond had dreaded meeting walked in.

"Mr. Bond," she said, "meet James Bond."

The man glared at Bond, the cruel mouth turning into a snarl.

Bond stared back and examined the imposter's features up close and in bright light for the first time. The clear blue eyes, the black hair, the scar on the right cheek . . . it was all correct and flawless. Anyone who actually knew Bond would most assuredly perform a double take if they saw the imposter.

"How does it feel to meet your double, Mr. Bond?" the man asked. "Your doppelganger? And you know what they say happens to you when you meet your doppelgänger, Mr. Bond? It means you're going to die." With that, he punched Bond hard in the face. Blood spurted out of Bond's nose and ran down his mouth.

"How does it feel to be hit by *you?*" he asked, laughing.

"That's enough, Peredur," Margareta said.

"Stop it with that Peredur crap. I'm James Bond now," Glyn said roughly.

"Of course, James," Yassasin said, humoring the imposter. "That will be all. Meet us in the ring in ten minutes."

The imposter smiled coldly at Bond, then left the room.

Yassasin seemed pleased with himself. "As you can see, the results are most extraordinary. With the aid of a little brainwashing, Mr. Glyn will now do anything I command. He would perform a suicide mission, if he was told to do so."

Yassasin stared fiercely into Bond's eyes. "And he *was* told to do so."

"Who's he going to kill?" Bond asked, fighting back the horrible anxiety that was beginning to envelop him.

Yassasin nearly smiled. "The primary targets are two men. The Governor of Gibraltar and Britain's Prime Minister. And their bodyguards, of course. He will kill the Spanish Prime Minister if he has to, for he will then follow Domingo Espada's orders. Espada will make demands, such as the ceding of Gibraltar to Spain and his appointment as the new Governor. If the Spanish Prime Minister doesn't sign the pact with Espada, he will die, too. The rest of the U.N. delegates, including me, will be held 'hostage' until Espada gets what he wants. We'll make sure Miss Piel gets out alive. If the antiterrorist forces manage to free the hostages and kill Espada, so be it. The foolish man is willing to die for his cause."

"Domingo has a martyr complex, that's for certain," Margareta said. "He doesn't like becoming old. It's what he really wants."

"Domingo wants to make a political statement that will be heard the world over," Yassasin said. "That's all he cares about. That's enough for him to justify the enormous amount of money he raised to finance his coup."

"You'll never get away with it," Bond said.

"Correction, Mr. Bond," Yassasin said. "Peredur Glyn will never get away with it, but he doesn't know that. He thinks the escape plan is foolproof. Such is the power of suggestion. It is expected that he will die in that room in Gibraltar tomorrow. In fact, someone that he least expects will kill him. As for the rest of us, we will be released as soon as we provide our statements as to what happened. Diplomatic immunity is a powerful weapon. At any rate, after tomorrow 'James Bond' will be a blight on the history of British intelligence."

"They'll know he's not me," Bond said. "Anyone examining his corpse will know."

Yassasin conceded. "Oh, you're absolutely right. Fingerprints and dental records cannot be changed. But it will be at least a day or two before someone from London identifies the body, or rather, fails to identify the body. By then, though, the damage will be done."

"All we have to do now is to make sure that there is no trace of you," Margareta said.

"We thought we'd leave that unpleasant task to Mr. Glyn," Yassasin continued. "He's convinced that there can be only *one* James Bond, and you're not him. Therefore, he wanted to see you perish personally."

"Let's go, *amigo,*" Margareta said. "You have an appointment with destiny."

Heidi moved as silently as possible toward the barbed-wire fence. After she had lost communication with Hedy, she abandoned the BMW and crept in the dark toward the front gates of the estate.

She had to roll into the ditch when she heard several vehicles start their engines. Headlights shone on the road ahead, and the guards ran to open the gate. Heidi raised her head just enough to watch as two

Land Rovers, a Rolls-Royce, and the minivan drove out of the compound. It looked as if everyone in the place was leaving!

Of course, Heidi remembered. They were going to Gibraltar.

The guards were about to close the gate behind the caravan. Heidi crawled back to the road and walked calmly toward them. She drew a Heckler & Koch USP45 and held it loosely in her right hand.

The two guards looked up and were momentarily confused by the sight of a beautiful blonde walking up the road. Before they could speak, Heidi asked, "Where's my sister, creeps?" and then raised her arm and shot both men in their chests. They flew backward, landing with thuds on the ground.

Heidi walked through the open gate and went inside.

TWENTY-TWO

BULLRING

They led him through the bullring entrance and shoved him to the soft dirt in the center of the bullring. With his hands still tied behind his back, there was not much that Bond could do to fight back. Peredur Glyn, the man who looked like James Bond, stood against the fence. Three Spanish guards were at the shields, watching Bond intently.

"This is Domingo's practice bullring," Margareta said. "It's a marvelous facility. The annex is equipped with everything one needs to breed fighting bulls. Domingo also uses part of the complex as a slaughterhouse. Have you ever seen what those vats of acid do to the remains of animal parts, Mr. Bond? The acid melts the skin right off the bones, and before long, the bones disintegrate as well. You get to experience this once-in-a-lifetime sensation firsthand!"

Yassasin addressed Glyn. "After you've had your fun, make sure there is nothing left. Report to Margareta when you're finished, then you can have your blond American."

"Yes, sir," the imposter Bond said, not taking his eyes off the man he was going to kill.

Yassasin turned to Margareta and said, "I'm off to Gibraltar. Needless to say, make sure he makes it to the meeting on time." He indicated Glyn.

"Don't worry," she replied. "That American girl will keep him occupied. We'll set off bright and early."

The pair began walking back through the door. Yassasin turned and said, as an afterthought, "Good-bye, Mr. Bond." The door closed and Bond was alone with his double and the three men.

Bond struggled to his feet and looked at his captors. What now? he wondered. He prepared himself for a beating, for he was certain they would want him alive when they were ready to use the acid. Bond scanned the ring for any sign of an escape. The shields were well covered by the guards.

One of the men said something in Spanish that Bond didn't catch. Glyn nodded, then all of them moved behind a shield. One man remained in the ring, moved to the bull's gate, and opened it.

A full-grown, fighting-mad black bull charged into the ring. The guard closed the door behind the animal, then quickly ran to the safety of the shield.

Bond froze, knowing full well that if he moved, the bull would charge. The bull was agitated. It ran to and fro, looking for a way out of this strange pen. Then it saw Bond, standing in the middle of the ring. Bond held his breath, but it was no good. The bull sensed the human's fear, and it charged at full speed.

Bond broke into a run across the ring, but the bull was fast. It attempted to slam into its moving target, but Bond sidestepped the animal just in time. The bull dug its front hooves into the dirt and skidded to a stop. It turned around and charged again. This time Bond ran to a shield, but the guard there thrust a spike at him. The sharp barb jabbed Bond's shoulder, causing him to recoil in pain. He fell back against the fence, only to see the bull charging straight for him. Bond spun around and away just as the bull's horns smashed into the fence. The men laughed and taunted Bond in Spanish. Peredur Glyn shouted, "If I were you, Mr. Bond, I would let the bull kill you. That would be preferable to watching your skin fall off in a vat of acid, don't you think?"

The bull recovered from the missed attack, then charged at Bond again. Bond ran along the fence, searching for anything that might cut the binds around his wrists.

Suddenly, the bullring entrance opened, and a picador, carrying a pair of lances, entered on horseback. The bull, seeing the horse, forgot about Bond momentarily and charged at it. The picador expertly maneuvered the horse around the bull and successfully thrust a lance into the bull's withers. The bull snorted and bellowed, becoming even angrier.

Bond could feel the bull's immense power even from across the ring. There was no other beast quite like it. It was a galloping locomotive weighing over a thousand pounds. It had one intention, and that was to destroy what it perceived to be its enemy.

The picador galloped his horse around the ring, leading the bull in a chase. Bond managed to get out of the way, but the bull's concentration was on the horse at the moment. In a surprise turn, the picador doubled back and threw the second lance into the bull.

The bull, confused and angered by the pain, stopped to take stock of its situation. The gate opened again, and the picador rode out, leaving the bull alone with Bond again.

It turned to Bond, breathing heavily. A crimson stream flowed down its side.

Bond turned his back on the bull and walked slowly toward the fence. As long as he didn't make any sudden movement, perhaps he could continue to avoid the bull until it tired out.

But he had no such luck. The bull pawed the dirt, snorted, and bolted toward him. Bond ran to the shield, but he heard Glyn shout something in Spanish. The sound of machinery echoed in the ring as the shield suddenly moved back into the fence, blocking off the safety zone. In fact, all of the shields in the ring had slid back and were now flush with the fence. There was no way out.

Glyn and the others were now behind the fence, whistling and taunting Bond.

Bond ran along the fence, the bull close on his heels. Bond zigzagged, attempting to throw the bull off its concentration, but the animal stayed with him. He ran faster, but he could hear the pounding of the bull's hooves on the ground coming closer and closer behind him.

The force of the impact took Bond by surprise. He felt a hammer-like slam in the small of his back, and for a moment he was in midair. The bull had butted him and thrown his body into the air like a paper cup. Bond landed hard on the ground, knocking the wind out of him. The bull turned and charged with its head down and horns pointed forward.

Bond rolled out of the way with split-second timing, avoiding a terrible goring.

The men laughed and jeered.

Bond got to his feet and stood in front of the bull, attempting to adapt a matador's stance. He stared at the bull, daring it to make another move. The bull hesitated just a moment, then charged again. This time Bond was ready. He allowed the bull to broadside him close enough so that Bond could perhaps grab one of the lances sticking out of the bull's back. It was an awkward maneuver with his hands tied behind him, and the first time he tried it, he missed. Bond beckoned to the bull again, and this time he spun around as the bull passed him and took hold of the lance with his right hand.

The bull, confused by the additional pain of having the lance's barbs tear out of its wound, stopped. It trotted to one side of the ring, staking out what was called a *querencia,* an area of the bullring where the bull felt secure. Many times in a real bullfight, a bull might retreat to this area and refuse to leave. It was up to the matador to draw it out to fight.

Bond used the momentary lull to thrust the lance's handle into the soft dirt, with the point sticking up. Even with his hands behind him, Bond managed to angle the lance so that he could reach the barbs with his wrists. He rubbed the bindings against the barbs.

"Hey, that's against the rules!" Glyn shouted.

The other men shouted at the bull, trying to provoke it into attacking before Bond could cut the binds.

The barbs cut into his hands as he did it, but Bond was finally successful in freeing himself before the bull charged. Somehow, it had sensed that Bond was about to gain an advantage over it.

Bond pulled the lance out of the ground and pointed it at the bull. Now aware that the strange polelike object brought pain, the bull slowed its charge and moved away.

The men booed the bull. One of them climbed on top of the fence and sat on it, his feet dangling over the now-flat shield.

A gunshot rang out, reverberating in the enclosed bullring. The jeering stopped as the men looked around.

The man on the fence clutched his chest and fell over into the ring.

The others immediately jumped into action, pulling out their weapons and looking around the seating sections.

"James!" came Heidi's voice. "Here!"

An object flew down from the darker area of the upper stands and landed on the dirt near Bond. He picked it up and found that it was her high-powered OC pepper spray canister.

Peredur Glyn fired his weapon into the stands but missed the girl.

"Get her! Don't let her escape! I'll deal with the prisoner!" he shouted.

The two other men raced up the stands as another shot ricocheted around the ring. Bond could now see Heidi as she ran from the seats to the exit, into the *pasillo.*

Meanwhile, the bull, frightened and confused by the sudden loud noises, seemed to pick up a second wind. It charged full speed at Bond.

Bond opened the canister, aimed, and sprayed the bull head-on.

The bull bellowed and tripped on its own front legs. It fell over with a crash, blinded and in pain. It managed to pull itself up, shaking its head, then sauntered around the ring in a daze. The fight had gone out of it for now.

Peredur Glyn jumped into the ring from the top of the fence. He was holding the thin sword that could pierce the hide of a thousand-pound bull. Running it through a human being would be like slicing butter.

Bond readied the lance as he came face-to-face with his mirror image.

Meanwhile, Heidi had run into the *pasillo* and around to the passage she had found when she had come looking for a way in. She ran through it as bullets whizzed past her. She turned and fired her USP45, but it was too dark to see anything. She kept running and eventually found herself in the slaughterhouse.

The stench was overwhelming, and the place was a nightmare of hanging carcasses, animal body parts—bulls, cows, horses—and slimy, foul vats where the beasts were dismembered and skinned.

Heidi searched frantically for a way out, but the sound of the men behind her forced her to duck between two hanging bull carcasses.

The men entered the room, muttering to each other in Spanish. They paused a moment, then split up. One man moved to the right, the other to the left, so that they could cover the entire room in a circular sweep.

As soon as one man was in her sights, Heidi aimed and squeezed the trigger. The blast knocked the man into a table covered in offal and blood. She ducked just as the remaining guard leveled his gun and fired a succession of shots in her direction. The bullets penetrated the hanging carcass with a *thump-thump-thump.* Heidi ran, keeping low, but a burning, knifelike pain shot through her left shoulder as one of the bullets connected. She fell back into a carcass and bounced. The gun slipped from her hand and slid across the concrete floor.

Heidi was in terrible pain. The bullet had entered her body just below the collarbone. It was a perilous wound. She didn't know if her lung had been pierced or not. Using every bit of strength that she could muster, she reached down to her calf and took hold of the object that was secured to her leg. Then she lay very still.

The guard cautiously approached her, gun in hand. Was she dead? He stepped up to her body and nudged it with his foot. Blood was spreading all over the floor and her eyes were closed. She had to be dead.

He made the fatal mistake of bending down to see if she was still breathing.

The hunting knife swung up and perforated the man's heart. His gun discharged into the air as he fell over next to her.

Heidi attempted to sit up, but the room was spinning. The pain was unbearable. *God, don't let me die here,* she prayed.

She tried to stand, but couldn't. Blood was pouring out of her wound like tap water.

The last thing she was aware of before blacking out was that she had still not found her sister.

Back in the bullring, James Bond and Peredur Glyn circled each other with their respective weapons. The bull, curious but wary of the two humans, stayed at the edge of the fence to let them fight it out. It was still smarting from the pepper spray.

Bond thought it was one of the most unsettling sensations he had ever felt. Here he was, facing an enemy that was, to all outward appearances, himself. If ever he had needed a clear head, it was now. Unfortunately, the throbbing in his head had taken over and his heart was pounding from the exertion and anxiety.

Glyn charged at Bond like the bull, the sword held straight in front of him. Bond feinted, swung the lance, and caught the imposter in the stomach. Glyn doubled over and dropped the sword. Bond broke the lance over Glyn's head, but the man merely fell to his knees and shook it off. He reached out, grabbed Bond's legs, and tackled him.

They rolled together on the dirt, their hands clutching at each other's throats.

Glyn managed to get on top. Bond was exhausted from the ordeal with the bull, and his increasingly disorienting condition was not making it any easier.

The man who looked like Bond whispered through his teeth, "When you see . . . your double . . . it mean you're . . . going to die. . . ."

Both grips tightened as each man attempted to strangle the other before their strength gave out.

Then the hazy dark cloud that had been plaguing Bond for months began to descend again.

No! Not now! Bond screamed to himself. I *mustn't* black out now!

His enemy's fingers dug into his throat. The lights in the ceiling spun above the imposter's head, bringing on nausea and the inevitable feeling that death was mere seconds away.

Bond fought the blackout with every ounce of willpower he could summon from the depths of his soul . . . but it was no use.

The dark curtain fell with a crash and then there was nothing.

TWENTY-THREE

BLOOD AND LUST

Margareta peered through the peephole and saw the blond woman sitting in a corner of the room, her knees folded in her arms. With the guards accompanying Espada to Gibraltar, the compound had been left unattended for a night. Margareta wanted to make sure that everything was secure and that none of the girls could escape. Everything appeared to be all right, she thought.

The rest of them were in their rooms, quietly enduring the long hours of waiting for the times when they would be called upon to perform their duties. Some of them who were literate would read books, others might sew. Some slept, some watched television, while others simply sat and stared at the wall, wondering if they would ever see freedom again. Some of them looked forward to their new life away from poverty and hunger, but most of them knew that they had been sold to a fate worse than their most horrid nightmares.

Margareta was satisfied that the girls were safe. She closed and locked the door, then went through the corridors and out of the foyer. She relocked the front door of the compound, then crossed the yard to the house. It was hauntingly quiet with everyone gone. In just a few hours, she, too, would leave with the assassin and join the others at the border.

She went to her room and checked the bag that she had packed. Now she would take a quick shower and get ready for bed. Sleep would probably be elusive, though, for she felt tense about the upcoming events. She needed something to relax her, so she pulled a bottle of red wine off a shelf, uncorked it, and poured a glass.

Margareta undressed and went into the bathroom to start the water. She waited until it was hot, filling the room with steam, then she got in the shower stall.

Margareta had finished washing her hair when the knock startled her. Someone was in the bedroom, just outside the bathroom door.

"What is it?" she called.

"It's me," came the voice. Peredur Glyn.

"Just a second," Margareta said. She rinsed, turned off the water, and stepped out of the stall. She wrapped a towel around her body and opened the bathroom door.

The imposter was standing in the middle of her room. There was a cut above his eye, and red marks were evident around his neck.

"What happened to you?" she shouted. "You look terrible!"

He laughed. "It was the prisoner," the man said in the distinctive Welsh accent. "We had a scuffle. It's all right, though. You won't be hearing from him anymore."

"What happened?"

"The guy passed out in my hands," Glyn said. "Just fainted dead away. I said, 'To hell with this,' and let the others handle it. I left him with them, they were going to take him to the slaughterhouse. The job should be finished by now."

"You need to get cleaned up. It won't look right if your face is messed up tomorrow," she said, leading him to the bathroom. She ran water in the sink, took a washcloth, and dabbed the wound on the assassin's head.

She smiled as he winced. "That plastic surgeon did an incredible job. I have to admit that James Bond was a handsome man."

"You mean *is.* That's who I am now," Glyn said as he slipped his hand inside the towel, feeling her firm breast.

"Right," she said, ignoring the gesture. He wondered if that, in itself, was an invitation to continue.

Instead, though, he said, "Sorry, Miss Piel, but tonight I have a date with a certain American blonde, if I remember correctly." He withdrew his hand.

"Hmmm," Margareta said. "I suppose you do. Well, don't overdo it. You need your wits about you in the morning. Don't stay up all night."

"I can come back and do you again after I'm finished," he suggested.

"Last night was lovely, dear, but I do need my beauty rest," she replied. "But if I can't sleep . . ."

Glyn grinned lecherously, then left the room.

The phone woke her two hours later.

Margareta grabbed it and answered, "*Que?*"

"Something bad has happened." It was the imposter. He sounded out of breath.

"What's the matter?"

"She's dead."

"What? Who?" Margareta had to fight the clouds of drowsiness away.

"The girl. The blond American."

"Dead? How?"

"I don't know. . . ." he stammered. He sounded upset. "I didn't mean to hurt her. . . . It was an accident. . . ."

"I'll be right there." Margareta slammed down the phone and put on a silk robe over her naked body. She removed the Glock from her bedside table and stormed out of the bedroom.

By the time she got to the compound, she could hear the cries of the girls. They were bemoaning their predicament in Spanish. One was demanding to know what had happened to the "new girl."

Margareta told them to shut up, then went straight to the American's cell. She gasped when she opened the door and saw the bloody mess that was inside.

The imposter Bond was sitting on the bed with an odd expression on his face. He looked like the naughty boy who had just been caught with his fingers in the cookie jar, and his hands and chest were covered in blood.

The blond girl was lying on the floor. She was wrapped in a red-soaked bedsheet.

"Peredur, what happened?"

"My name is James Bond," the man said, choking back a sob.

"Fine, James, tell me what happened."

"She wouldn't cooperate," he said. He held up a bloody knife. "I only wanted to scare her with it. She fought me. When I forced her to . . . you know . . . she pushed herself against the blade. She stabbed herself. It made me very angry. So I . . . stabbed her some more. . . ."

"You damned fool," Margareta said. "What's the matter with you?"

"I'm sorry," he said.

"Domingo won't like this. You have to get rid of her. Clean up this place. Take her body to the slaughterhouse and get rid of it. Throw her into the vats. Do you hear me?"

The imposter nodded.

"Get one of the others to help you. Where are they?"

Glyn shrugged. "I suppose they're still in the annex. Don't worry, I'll take care of it. I'm sorry I disturbed you."

"Never mind that. Just get her out of here. Then get cleaned up. I think I had better keep my eye on you for the rest of the night. We have to leave very early tomorrow. Come to my room when you're finished."

The man stared at the body on the floor.

"Do you hear me?" she demanded.

"Yes," he muttered.

She walked out and slammed the door closed.

It was after midnight when the knock came.

"It's open," Margareta said.

Glyn walked in. He had showered and was dressed in a terry-cloth robe. The earlier persona of little-boy helplessness had disappeared. Now he was all man, handsome, virile, dangerous. . . .

"Well?" she asked.

"It's done," he said, sitting on the sofa. "The place is clean. There is no trace of her."

"There had better not be. What made you do that? You really are one sick *hombre.*"

He shrugged. "I kill. It's what I do."

Despite the savagery of his act, Margareta couldn't help but feel a twinge of excitement as she gazed upon his magnificent body. His animalistic nature appealed to her and she felt the stirrings of desire. The compulsions that had given rise to her nickname of *Mantis Religiosa* were not about to dissipate anytime soon.

He was a lot like her, this Union assassin. Sex and murder were intrinsically linked in their psychological makeup. Margareta knew full well that she and Peredur Glyn weren't . . . normal.

Margareta loosened the sash around her robe and let it fall open. She stood in front of him, then ran her fingers through his hair.

"That's not all you do well, Peredur," she said.

Glyn looked up at her and replied, "My name is James Bond now."

"Yes, that's right," she said. "Mr. Bond."

A smile played around his lips. He slipped his hands inside of her robe and felt the soft warm flesh. His right hand snaked around her waist and rested on her buttocks. He squeezed a cheek, then pulled her closer to him. He nuzzled his face between her breasts, kissing them, licking them. . . .

Margareta sighed as she straddled his lap. Men who had the capacity to kill had always excited her. Her first lover had been a Spanish bandit who was notorious for robbing grocery stores and murdering the staff. She had accompanied him on a few of his sprees, but the police had never caught up with her. She had been fourteen years old at the time.

She took the assassin's chin and raised his mouth toward hers. Their lips met, then she pushed him back on the sofa.

They both needed a relief of tension to prepare for the big day. . . . She climbed on top of him and took the initiative. She found that the anticipation of the next morning's violence served to enhance her pleasure.

It was unlike anything she had felt before.

TWENTY-FOUR

BACK TO THE BEGINNING

The reception was scheduled for 10:00 A.M.

Margareta Piel and the assassin left Espada's estate at 6:30 and drove into Marbella, and then on to La Linea, where Espada and Agustin were waiting for them. Jimmy Powers was already in Gibraltar. Nadir Yassasin was making his way to the Rock by way of Tangier. They would assume the identities of the slain delegates from Washington.

During the journey, Margareta had struggled with a dilemma that had risen overnight. She wasn't quite sure how to deal with it. If her suspicions were correct, it could mean that the Union's plan might end in disaster. On the other hand, it was possible that she could be able to use her newly gained knowledge to her own personal advantage. She had been eager to break away from Espada for a long time. The opportunity to join the Union was a welcome one. This could be her chance to show them her resourcefulness. She decided to play it by ear, see how the morning progressed, and make her move when the time was right.

A Governor's aide, an attractive brunette who might have been a Miss Gibraltar at one time, met them at the airport. The four Spaniards and the man from Britain piled into a limo and then went to the Convent. Main Street had been closed, blocked off to all traffic, both pedestrian and otherwise. It was 9:45 by the time they stepped through the impressive brick façade that framed the main entrance to what was at one time an old Franciscan convent. The name had stuck.

Security was extremely tight. Officers from the Gibraltar Regiment were everywhere. The four of them were directed to produce their papers, walk through a metal detector, and submit their bags to be searched. The assassin's passport and documents bore the name "Peter Woodward." One of the security officers spent a long time examining at the passport. There was a moment when Margareta doubted if any part of the Union's plan could be pulled off. Finally, the imposter Bond was allowed to go through.

After signing the guest register, they were led up the red-carpeted wooden stairs to the first floor and upper Cloister. Margareta noticed a copy of the original Grant of Arms to Gibraltar by Queen Isabella of Castille in 1502. The first British Governor of Gibraltar later used these arms, which were eventually adopted as the castle and key symbols on the coat of arms of the City of Gibraltar. The colony's flag, of course, grew from this.

They were led into the ballroom, where a number of people had already gathered.

It was a lovely room, surrounded by a collection of royal portraits of British monarchs commencing with Queen Victoria. Sparkling chandeliers hung from the high ceiling, and large mirrors reflected the illumination. There was a stage at one end with a string quartet playing Mozart; at the other end was a table set up as a bar.

Margareta saw Nadir Yassasin near the bar, standing alone. Should she tell him about her suspicions? Their eyes met briefly, but she then made a point of ignoring him throughout the remainder of the reception.

Jimmy Powers was in an animated conversation with two other men who appeared to be American. She slowly made her way toward them so that she could overhear what they were saying.

"Mr. Bunyon, I've been with the State Department for ten years," one gray-haired man was saying, "and I simply can't recall your face.

Forgive me. I thought I knew everyone in the Bureau of Mediterranean Activity."

Powers chuckled and said, "Sir, I've been around since the Reagan administration. I'm often out of the country."

Margareta was satisfied that Powers could handle the grilling. She moved on and asked a servant behind the bar for a glass of orange juice. A couple of men smiled at her, probably hoping she would introduce herself to them. One man staring at her was the Spanish Prime Minister. She gave him her best come-hither look and watched him swallow visibly.

An Arab woman in a full-length caftan and veil was sitting alone, near the quartet. Every part of her body was hidden, except for her brown eyes. Margareta decided to approach her and say hello. The woman introduced herself as a delegate from Morocco, but she didn't offer much more information than that. Margareta made an excuse to continue mingling.

Espada, Agustin, and the assassin sat down near the bar and surveyed the room. Espada sat with his arms folded as if he were bored and annoyed with the entire proceedings.

What if she didn't report her suspicions to Yassasin? Would the Union punish her if something went wrong? The important thing, she thought, was to save her own skin if it did.

To hell with it, she thought. She had better speak to Nadir. She approached him casually and said, "Hello, I'm Margareta Piel. I'm with Domingo Espada. I saw you standing here alone and thought I would introduce myself."

He shook her hand. "Said Arif. I'm from Morocco, but I live in America."

"I think we need to talk," she said, lowering her voice.

His eyes narrowed. "Are you mad? What about?"

Before she could answer, a heated exchange in Spanish was heard in Espada's corner of the room. The Spanish Prime Minister was standing in front of him. Everyone in the room turned to look at them, especially at the man who had caused all this trouble. Espada stood and glared at the Spanish PM and for a moment there was complete silence. Finally, the Spanish PM muttered something to the effect that he hoped their differences could be resolved today, and then he walked away.

Margareta had to admit that Espada looked splendid. He was wearing a uniform of his own design that closely resembled that of a Spanish officer at the time of the Second World War. Agustin, at his right, and the imposter James Bond, at his left, were dressed in smart Brioni suits. The assassin looked comfortable and relaxed, if a bit out of place as a bodyguard to Espada.

Espada noticed that he had the room's attention. He cleared his throat and managed to say in English, "Thank you all for coming. I am happy to be here."

The room seemed to relax then, and the conversations resumed. Margareta watched the assassin as he stayed close to Espada and kept his eyes on everything.

Perhaps she was wrong? Margareta wondered.

"What was it you wanted to say?" Yassasin asked.

"Never mind," she said.

The aide-de-camp entered at 10:00 and made an announcement. "We have arranged a small tour of the Convent for you that will commence at this time. If you do not care to join the tour, you may remain here. His Excellency the Governor and the British Prime Minister are due to arrive at ten thirty, at which time we'll move into the Banqueting Room."

Margareta slid next to the Americans from the State Department and introduced herself as they walked out of the ballroom to follow the brunette who had picked her up at the airport. Yassasin, Powers, and Espada's entourage joined in as well.

The group of nearly twenty people paraded downstairs, passed the main entrance, then down another five steps to the open-air ground-floor Cloister. The square was surrounded by an arched covered way, and a well had been built in the center. A black wooden statue of General Sir George Eliott, the Governor of Gibraltar during the Great Siege, was the dominating ornament in the Cloister. All around the square were samples of different kinds of shells and shot used during Gibraltar's various skirmishes. The gardens were especially beautiful, boasting the largest "dragon tree" in all of Europe. Planted in 1484, the dragon tree has a skinlike texture and bleeds red sap when poked with a sharp stick.

The brunette lectured in English but was able to answer any questions in a variety of other languages.

The tour went through the Duke of Kent Room, back upstairs to the Drawing Room and Billiard Room, then back down to the main entrance. At this point, the group turned north, went through a small white door, and entered the King's Chapel.

The guide told the tour participants that they had ten minutes to wander freely around the chapel and examine the various memorials and artwork. She even encouraged them to use the time for silent meditation. Some of the guests remained to do so, while others chose to go back upstairs.

Jimmy Powers casually sat in a specific pew, reached down, and removed the white silk bag he had planted there the day before.

Margareta walked slowly around the back of the chapel and sat down on a pew, pretending to examine a stained-glass window. She, too, groped for and found the bag that was meant for her.

Nadir Yassasin had become engaged in a discussion with delegates from the Middle East. He tactfully led them to the pew where his weapon had been planted, and they sat there for a moment. Just as the tour guide announced that the ten minutes were up, Yassasin retrieved the silk bag and put it in his waistband.

Espada and Agustin were also successful in picking up their planted weapons. It was easier than Espada had imagined. With so many delegates in the chapel, no one was paying any attention to what the others were doing.

The man who had entered the building as "Peter Woodward," obviously an expat now working as a bodyguard for Espada, found his weapon under the designated pew. The weight was familiar—it was the Walther PPK. He placed the bag in his waistband under the jacket. As he walked back up the stairs to the first floor of the Convent, he carefully undid the string on the silk bag and removed the gun. Once he was led back into the Ballroom, the Walther was loose in his waistband with the safety off, ready to be fired.

There was still another ten minutes before the British PM and the Governor were scheduled to arrive. Nadir Yassasin found Jimmy Powers by the string quartet and spoke to him.

"They are wonderful, aren't they?"

Powers shrugged. "If you like that kind of music . . . me, I prefer good ol' American rock 'n' roll."

Yassasin lowered his voice, even though the music was loud and the acoustics of the large room assured that they would not be overheard. "So, this is the moment of truth, yes?"

Powers shrugged again, as if he were hedging on a political opinion.

Yassasin seemed to be talking to himself, as Powers certainly knew the drill. "Timing is crucial. First, the assassin takes out the PM's and Governor's bodyguards, then immediately shoots the PM and Governor. Espada and Agustin will draw their weapons and shoot any other guards in the room. They believe that they will secure the room and hold everyone else hostage until the Spanish Prime Minister signs a pact with Espada. Unfortunately, that's not going to happen."

"Has the alternative plan been approved?" Powers asked.

"Yes. *Le Gérant* has given the order. Espada is to die. The assassin will kill him as soon as the PM and Governor are dead. Then Miss Piel will kill the assassin if the remaining guards in the room don't blow him away first. The fool really thinks he's going to get away with this."

Powers shrugged again. "Such is life."

"No, my friend," Yassasin replied. "Such is death."

At 10:30, everyone moved into the exquisite Banqueting Hall. Espada, Agustin, Margareta, and the assassin sat at the east end of the table. Espada took the seat at the head of the table. Agustin was on his right, the assassin on his left. Margareta sat next to the imposter Bond. The other delegates took various seats, but left designated chairs for the PM and Governor.

Margareta eyed the man sitting next to her and struggled once again with the resolve to make herself known. The man was a killer. He was unpredictable. If she didn't defuse the situation right now, there was no telling what kind of carnage might erupt.

A minute went by, and she finally decided to confront the assassin with what she suspected.

Now.

TWENTY-FIVE

FAENA

Margareta leaned over and whispered in the assassin's ear. "All right, Mr. *Bond,* I know it's you. You think I can't tell the difference between you and Peredur Glyn in bed? You gave yourself away last night with the one area of your body that the doctor in Hollywood didn't alter."

Nadir Yassasin was looking at the two of them with a furrowed brow. Bond swallowed but remained stone-faced. He had to keep his cover or the entire operation would be blown.

"Now, here's the deal," she continued as he felt the gun barrel digging into his kidney. "You're going to do exactly what you're supposed to do. Kill the PM and the Governor, as planned. If you don't do it, I'm going to shoot you in the back, and then my cohorts will do it anyway. My job here was to kill Peredur Glyn after the assassinations. Whether it's you or him makes no difference to me. That's my ticket out of here. I'll be the hero. You will lose, no matter what, the PM will be dead, and the Union's plan will succeed. This isn't about Espada. This is between the Union and your pitiful country."

She sat back in her chair. An avalanche of doubt fell on Bond and smothered him.

She knew! Was the plan ruined?

He suddenly felt his heart accelerate as a wave of panic enveloped him. The pounding in his head was excruciating. Masses of darkness clouded his vision.

No! he willed. *I must not black out now!*

The aide-de-camp remained in place by the open door. Activity could be heard in the corridor as the PM, the Governor, and their bodyguards approached. Two Gibraltar Regiment soldiers entered the room, armed and alert.

Bond clenched his fists and shut his eyes, struggling against the attack.

The operation could still work! Concentrate, damn it!

Espada looked at Bond in anticipation, but Yassasin could see that something was terribly wrong. He glanced at Powers, who was also narrowing his eyes at Bond and Margareta. He reached for his weapon, ready to draw it at a second's notice.

Bond opened his eyes as a tall, distinguished gentleman with white hair entered the room—the Governor of Gibraltar. Right behind him was a man in a suit whom Bond recognized as 001. Their eyes found each other and they shared a quick and silent acknowledgment, even though 001 could see the pain in Bond's eyes.

The British Prime Minister stepped into the room and stood beside 001. He was a short man with a bright face and charming smile. He virtually lit up the room.

The aide-de-camp announced, "His Excellency, the Governor of Gibraltar, and the Prime Minister of Great Britain."

The door had remained open. Another figure entered the room and stood beside the Prime Minister.

She was one of the Taunt twins, dressed in a smart business suit.

Margareta, Yassasin, Espada, and Agustin gasped simultaneously.

Agent 001 shouted, "Everyone down!" and time suddenly seemed to stretch into a slow, dreamlike eternity.

In the first second, 001 pulled the Prime Minister to the floor. At the same time, the soldiers tackled the Governor. Some of the delegates began to scream. Powers drew his gun, not sure whom to shoot first.

During the next second, Bond slammed his upper body forward onto the table as he pulled the Walther from his waistband. This maneuver provided a clear view of Margareta Piel. Nadir Yassasin began to draw his weapon.

At the beginning of the third second, the veiled Arab woman sitting across the table from Bond swung her right arm out from under the caftan. She was holding a Heckler & Koch USP45. A single round caught Margareta in the chest and threw her backward.

Halfway through the same second, Bond, still leaning forward over the table, angled his body onto his right shoulder and shot Powers with one bullet through the man's right temple. Powers fell against the State Department delegate, who shrieked in horror. By the end of the third second, some of the delegates jumped out of their seats and dived for the floor. The others were frozen in fear.

The fourth second. With a bloodcurdling scream, Margareta crashed through a stained-glass window and fell to the cloister below. Espada and Agustin, momentarily frozen by the sudden turn of events, jolted into action at the sound of the shattering window. Their guns were in hand, but Bond was faster. Bond swung his arm across the tabletop and shot Agustin in the forehead at point-blank range. Yassasin, his hand shaking, aimed his Browning at Bond.

Five seconds. Espada leveled his Super Star at Bond, but the Walther exploded first. The round caught Espada in the cheek and the man fell back in his chair. Yassasin's gun erupted, but the bullet whizzed past Bond's head and into the wall. The Taunt twin was immediately behind the strategist, a Beretta M93R poking the back of his head. She ordered Yassasin not to move. "Drop your weapon on the table," she commanded.

Yassasin did so and slowly raised his hands, and time equivocally returned to its normal rate of duration. Only six seconds had elapsed since 001 had shouted the order to launch the operation.

Bond knelt beside Espada, who was choking and splattering blood all over the carpet.

"That was for the matadors," Bond said through his teeth.

Espada's eyes exhibited fear and hatred, but eventually they rolled up into his head as the choking ceased.

Bond finally stood and said, "It's all over, everyone." The waves of nausea and panic were subsiding. He had fought against them and had won.

The Taunt twin turned to the aide-de-camp and indicated Yassasin. "He's all yours, sir." The Regiment soldiers immediately handcuffed the Union strategist and frisked him. The Governor, the PM, and the other delegates were slowly rising to their feet and wiping their brows. Suddenly the room was full of chatter, tears, prayers, hugs, and relief.

Agent 001 gave Bond a thumbs-up. Bond nodded at him, then looked at the blonde.

"Nice work, Hedy," Bond said. He turned to the Arab woman in the veil and whispered, "You too, Heidi."

The debriefing took place in the Governor's Drawing Room, where the day's participants could relax in a friendly environment after the terror of the morning's events. Present were the Governor, the British PM, the Spanish PM, 001, Hedy Taunt, and James Bond.

Hedy was attempting to explain how she escaped from Espada's compound without blowing "Hillary's" cover when the Spanish PM interrupted her. "Wait a second. I'm confused. I thought Double-O Seven was a captive. What happened to the double? How did you get off the property?"

Bond spoke up. "If I may? I'm not sure what happened during the fight with Peredur Glyn, but I had another one of the blackouts I have been experiencing. I continued to function, however, even though I have no memory of it. When I came to, the imposter was lying dead on the ground, strangled. I collected myself and went back to Espada's house. I thought I might be able to fool anyone still there that I was Peredur Glyn. I succeeded, except for, er, one minor detail that eventually gave me away."

Hedy almost laughed and averted her eyes.

Bond continued. "After convincing the Piel woman that I was Glyn, I went to the place they call the compound and found H—uhm, Miss Taunt. Since Peredur Glyn was reputed to be some kind of homicidal maniac, we concocted a rather unique plan to get her out. I went to the slaughterhouse to fetch a bucket of blood—animal blood."

He neglected to say that he had also found Heidi Taunt there. She was bleeding badly from the bullet wound in her shoulder and was drifting in and out of consciousness. Bond had administered first aid as best as he could, then told her to sit tight and that he would be back with her sister.

"I took the bucket of blood back to the compound and we staged Miss Taunt's death. The Piel woman ordered me to get rid of the body, as I suspected she would, so I carried Miss Taunt out of the compound and went straight to the slaughterhouse."

Again, he left out the sequence in which he and Hedy helped Heidi out of the slaughterhouse and into one of the Land Rovers that was parked outside.

"We were lucky that almost the entire staff had gone with Espada. The guards at the front gate were dead. We quickly made a plan. Miss Taunt drove to Marbella and I went back to the house to see the Piel woman."

Hedy took over the narrative. "I got on the phone to Washington and London. It took some doing, but I finally convinced Double-O Seven's chief to allow us to go ahead with the plan." This was, of course, after Heidi's bullet had been removed and she had received a blood transfusion, but Hedy didn't mention that. Heidi had insisted on coming along to the Convent, disguised in the veil.

"I must say, it sounded terribly risky to me," the PM said.

"M wasn't happy about it," 001 concurred.

"But," the PM conceded, "it was perhaps the only way we could avoid any further bloodshed. I agreed to go along with it. So did the Governor. We got word to the aide-de-camp here just in time."

The Spanish PM asked, "What would you have done if Mr. Bond's true identity had been discovered?"

No one had an answer to that.

"I'm afraid Señor Espada might have got his way," the Governor said. "By the way, what's happened to his army?"

"When they heard that Espada was dead, they dispersed," the Spanish PM said. "Our forces arrived after the King decided that he had had enough of Domingo Espada. He wasn't about to let our country go to war with Great Britain."

"I'm glad to hear that," the British PM said.

"We have sent a special task force to Espada's estate. The girls being held captive there will be freed and given financial and housing assistance. We will do our best to find them suitable and legal employment. As for Gibraltar . . ."

The Spanish PM looked hard at the British PM and then smiled, saying, "We will discuss the matter another time."

The two Prime Ministers stood and shook hands as the Governor of Gibraltar looked on.

Bond rubbed his eyes. The bloody headache was taking control once again. It had been threatening to do so all morning. Agent 001 looked at him and said, "Come on, Bond. We have to go to hospital. Someone is waiting for you there."

"What's going to happen to that Arab guy?" Hedy asked. "Yassasin."

"We're going to interrogate the bloody hell out of him," 001 answered. "We want to find out as much as we can about the Union. They've gone too far this time. SIS have declared an all-out war against them."

"Well, when you're done, just make sure you lock him up and throw away the key," Hedy said.

"You can be sure of that," 001 replied.

The two PMs and the Governor turned to Bond as he stood. "Thank you," the Governor said. "For everything."

Bond smiled, nodded, and shook their hands without saying a word. He felt curiously numb now that the crisis was over. He quietly allowed his colleague to lead him out of the room as Hedy followed close behind.

TWENTY-SIX

AFTERMATH

"Sir James Molony is here," Miss Moneypenny announced on the intercom.

M pushed the button for the green light as Bill Tanner continued his report.

"The FBI in America picked up the plastic surgeon, Dr. Morelius, in California. Unfortunately, he never actually broke the law. He was paid by the Union to perform a legitimate service. The FBI had to let him go."

"But he's insignificant in the grand scheme of things," M replied.

Tanner nodded. "The director of the FBI assured me that the doctor had the living daylights scared out of him. He's being placed in their Witness Protection Program. Hopefully he will identify his employers, and if he's lucky he can have a legitimate practice in another state."

Sir James Molony opened the door and entered. M remained seated and said, "Good morning, Sir James. Please sit down. How was your flight from Gibraltar?"

"Fine, thank you," Molony replied, sitting across from her. Tanner pulled up a chair after offering the staff neurologist a coffee.

"I appreciate you cutting short your lecture tour to attend to Double-O Seven," M said.

"Believe me, madam, it was a blessing in disguise," the doctor answered. "I can't tell you how bored I was after two months of talking to young people all over the world who had no interest at all in what I was saying. I was quite ready for something to interrupt it."

"How's James doing?" Tanner asked.

"He's doing quite well. The operation was a complete success. He should be feeling himself by now. We discharged him from hospital yesterday and he's recuperating at the hotel there. I expect that he'll fly back home in a day or two."

"Tell us exactly what was wrong with him," M prodded.

Molony sipped his coffee and placed it on the edge of the large glass-topped desk.

"As you know, Double-O Seven had a lesion on his temporal lobe. This was probably caused by the injury he sustained in the Himalayas three months ago. It was the source of his headaches, as well as what I would clinically diagnose as panic attacks. Dr. Feare, may her soul rest in peace, had originally detected the lesion with an EEG and prescribed a medication, carbamazepine, which might have cured him without the need for surgery. However, when I examined the pills he had been taking, I discovered that he had the wrong pills. They had been disguised as the correct ones. He was taking haloperidol, which is often used as a treatment for a number of psychoses. But if used improperly, it can make some conditions worse. As a result, Bond suffered from post-traumatic epilepsy. He would hallucinate, have delusions of paranoia, and even experience poriomania, or blackouts. This sometimes happens with hard-case alcoholics. They'll pass out somewhere and wake up in a completely different location. How they get from one place to the next is a mystery to them. The same thing happened to Double-O Seven. More than once. I'm still trying to determine how he got the wrong medication in the first place. Dr. Feare's prescription was correct."

"I think Mr. Tanner can answer that one," M said.

Tanner cleared his throat and said, "Sir James, I'm afraid I have to inform you that one of your employees is a traitor. Double-O Seven alerted us to the fact that Michael Clayton, one of the Union members he first encountered in London, had a cousin who was also well connected with the organization. After we further investigated the man's background, we determined that he did indeed have a cousin—Deborah Reilly."

Molony's eyes bulged. "Good Lord, that's my nurse!"

"I'm afraid so," Tanner said. "MI5 arrested her yesterday. She was pretty tight-lipped until we confronted her with all manner of evidence. She confessed to switching Bond's medication, even disguising it as the proper pills. We believe she was instrumental in setting up Double-O Seven for Dr. Feare's murder."

Molony shook his head. "It's extraordinary. She's been with me for several years. How could this have happened?"

"She was obviously promised money. She was apparently terribly devoted to her cousin. He probably got her involved. When she learned that he was dead, she broke down and told all," Tanner explained.

"So, you see, the Union was on to Bond all the time," M said. "Your nurse provided them with the information that he was not well. When we told Double-O Seven that we had found her, he remembered that he had seen her in Soho the day before he left for Africa. She had paid a visit to one of her cousin's adult bookshops, apparently to deliver information or something to Clayton. Bond couldn't place her at the time."

"She wasn't a terribly pleasant person, I must say," Molony admitted. "She was an excellent nurse, though. She correctly prescribed what kind of medication would, at the very least, have some kind of psychological effect on the patient."

Tanner continued. "From what we've gathered from preliminary interrogation of this fellow Yassasin, one of the Union's founding members, an American, James Powers, was also responsible. Apparently he was a brilliant surveillance expert. He had been watching Double-O Seven from the moment he had returned from the Himalayas. Powers even followed Bond to Jamaica and back. He got to know Double-O Seven's daily routine. Quite frightening, really."

"How effective will the surgery be?" M asked, veering the conversation back to 007's health.

"One hundred percent, we hope," Molony replied. "James has been through a lot, but he has a strong reserve. I believe he'll pull through with no lasting side effects. He just needs some time."

"Thank you, Sir James," M said.

She glanced at Bond's medical records on the table in front of her. She found a photograph of him and picked it up. "The Union really came up with something extraordinary, didn't they?" M asked rhetorically, shaking her head.

Tanner nodded. "They led Bond by the nose and made him think that he was the one making discoveries and finding clues. They even had *us* for a while—we really thought he had gone off his rocker and joined the Union."

"It was what they wanted us to think," M said. "But the Union underestimated one thing," M said, running her index finger along the edge of Bond's photograph.

"What was that, ma'am?" Molony asked.

"My belief in him."

Further south, on the continent of Africa, another man was touching a photograph of James Bond, but he couldn't see it. Somehow, though, he was able to absorb the subject's essence simply by holding the object in his hands. He could sense that this man was a far more complex and resilient human being than any of the Union's analysts could have guessed.

Le Gérant sat in his new quarters in Marrakesh, a plain, sun-baked stone building not far from the *Djemaa el-Fna.* When he had received the news that the Gibraltar operation had failed dismally and that his chief strategist was in captivity, he had dismissed the *cercle fermé* and retreated to his study. He had asked not to be disturbed and had remained in his private quarters for twenty-four hours.

Le Gérant usually had a finely tuned sense of humor. His father had taught him that, along with keen business acumen, a ruthless efficiency in dealing with obstacles, and organizational skills that commanded respect and discipline from every division of his domain. *Le Gérant* was very good at what he did. Still, he could remember his father repeatedly driving the point home: a businessman should never lose his sense of humor, no matter what happened.

At this point, however, *Le Gérant* knew that he had lost it and wondered if he would ever get it back.

Twice now this Double-O agent had made the Union look foolish. *Le Gérant* was not going to let it happen again. If it was a war that MI6 wanted, then it was a war they would get.

Le Gérant angrily crumpled the photograph with one hand and tossed it across the room, where he knew it would drop neatly into a dustbin.

As others spoke about him, James Bond didn't feel his ears burning as he lay in bed in the sea-view room in the Rock Hotel in Gibraltar. He wouldn't have been able to scratch them anyway—the bandage on his head covered them completely.

CNN was reporting that the Spanish/British crisis was over. The two governments had put aside their differences and had held a conference in Brussels to quash any further misunderstandings. The Spanish Prime Minister had, for the first time, publicly denounced Domingo Espada and his tenets. Espada's followers had staged a protest march in Madrid, but they quickly realized that it was a lost cause. The majority of the population quickly came to the opinion that Espada was a madman. When many prominent *matadors* saw fit to denigrate Espada's actions and speak out against him, the people completely turned against him. When it was reported that he had been linked to the deaths of the Rojo brothers and had kept kidnapped sex slaves on his estate, Espada was forever cast as one of the country's most notorious villains.

There was a knock on the door. Bond switched off the television with the remote but didn't get up. He called, "If you have a key, come in."

The only people who had a key to his room were a nurse . . . and the Taunt twins.

"We're the candy stripe girls and it's time to party!" Heidi sang cheerfully as they entered his bedroom. Hedy was carrying a bottle of Taittinger. They were both dressed identically again, in white blouses and tight-fitting designer jeans. Heidi's arm was in a sling.

"We're here to make you well," Hedy said.

Bond indicated the champagne. "I'm not supposed to drink, you know."

"We know that," she answered. "This is for *us!*"

"Remember that first night at dinner in Tangier? You made a suggestion about sharing," Heidi said with a smile.

Hedy began working on the bottle. The girls laughed at Bond's suspicious glare, poured glasses of champagne, and then sat on either side of him.

"Who's first, Hedy?" Heidi asked. "Or do we have to flip for it?"

ABOUT THE AUTHOR

Raymond Benson is the author of *High Time to Kill, The Facts of Death, Zero Minus Ten,* and the novelizations of the films *The World Is Not Enough* and *Tomorrow Never Dies.* His Bond short stories have been published in *Playboy* and *TV Guide* magazines. His first book, *The James Bond Bedside Companion,* was nominated for an Edgar Allan Poe Award for Best Biographical/Critical work and is considered by 007 fans to be a definitive work on the world of James Bond. A director of The Ian Fleming Foundation, he is married and has one son, and is based in the Chicago area.